the rebound

LAKE BITTERSWEET
BOOK 5

JENNIFER BERNARD

one

Even though it was five o'clock on a rainy June morning, Jason Mosedale whistled as he strode into the apparatus bay of the Lake Bittersweet firehouse. He considered himself lucky to live in the most beautiful town in Minnesota, no matter the rain, lucky to work as a firefighter, lucky in most ways —with some giant glaring exceptions. He preferred to whistle through those.

The other crew members, volunteer and staff alike, groaned at the sound.

"You got laid, didn't you?" grumbled Brent, a longtime member of the crew, the best driver they had.

"Isn't that every day for him?" Colleen Hopper, one of the three women volunteers, nursed a steaming thermos of one of her herbal concoctions. She kept trying to coax the others into trying her mixes, but got no takers. "There's hardly a woman in Minnesota who would kick him out of bed."

"Sorry, aren't you...?" Brent squinted at her from under his deer hunter's cap.

"Don't ask, don't tell," she said sternly. "But the answer is yes."

"Uh, what's the question?"

"Wouldn't you like to know?"

Jason figured they were skating awfully close to some kind of human resources rule. He'd better put a stop to it, especially if he was going to apply for fire chief.

Big "if." Would he be able to joke around like an ordinary crew member if he was the fire chief? Joking around was one of his favorite things in life. Was moving up in the world worth it? He still wasn't sure, but he'd better figure it out soon because the board of aldermen wanted someone in place before the summer season really got going.

"Can't a guy whistle just because he's in a good mood?" He dumped his duffel bag next to his locker and pulled open the door. A blowup doll burst out of it, making him jump back in surprise.

The other firefighters howled in laughter. Good one, he had to admit. Nothing like a firehouse prank to kick off an early morning training exercise.

"If he didn't get any last night, he can now," called one of the volunteers.

"I heard he goes for the airhead type," said someone else, triggering more laughter.

Jason composed his face into a serious expression, which was a big lift for him. His usual mode was fun-loving and easygoing. He loved life and saw no reason to hide that. He took hold of the doll and slowly, menacingly turned to face the ring of firefighters.

"What. The. Fuck...?" He spat the words out. Everyone's smiles dropped away. Brick, the rookie, turned white and looked like he might throw up. Jason continued after a perfectly timed pause. "...are you still doing here? Can't a guy get a little privacy?" He wrapped his arm around the doll's plastic waist.

It took a moment, but then everyone howled with a new wave of laughter. Relieved laughter. The poor crew had no idea what to make of a seriously angry Jason Mosedale. Who would? It would be as if one of the local moose wandered out of the woods and ordered a cappuccino.

Someone at the edge of the crowd, back by the entry door, cleared their throat. "Should I come back another time? Looks like y'all are busy."

Jason startled at the sight of Kendra Carter halfway in the door, her hand still on the doorknob. As always, even at this early hour, she looked stunning. Her hair was held back with a vivid red silk bandanna and she wore a tight-fitting white shirt.

He'd known Kendra forever; they'd even been friends in high school, sort of. Their lockers had been close together, and they'd exchanged friendly jabs nearly every day. She'd even tutored him in public speaking and American history.

But she'd jetted off early to an accelerated college slash business school program while he'd slogged through the rest of high school and then studied for the firefighter exam. Recently, she'd come back to town, and things had been...interesting between them. A little banter, some casual conversation, maybe even some flirting.

She had his attention, for sure. But as far as he could tell, she didn't take him at all seriously.

Then again, she might have good reason for that. He remembered that he was holding a blowup doll and thrust it behind him.

"We're about to start a training exercise, but if this is an emergency..."

"It is," she said gravely, coming forward. "Why else would I be here before sunrise?"

The plastic arm of the doll popped out from behind his back. He shoved it down. Smothered laughter came from the crew.

"What's the nature of your emergency?" He said it with hopefully enough sternness to make up for the absurdity of the blowup doll trying to sabotage Kendra's impression of him.

Not that there was much to sabotage. In high school she'd thought of him as unambitious. She'd even lectured him about it.

"How should I know? Isn't that your job?"

"Huh?" A whistling sound came from behind him. Crap—the blowup doll was losing air. It made a quiet wailing sound punctuated by odd squeals.

"Damn, Jason. You sure know how to make a woman moan," said crusty old Sven Lundgren, who should have retired years ago, if you asked Jason.

"Is this the emergency?" Kendra asked, gesturing at the doll. "Am I supposed to do something? Remedial foreplay instructions?"

Howls of laughter came from his cursed crew. Great. He felt his face turn a slow-baked red. Normally, he didn't mind playing the fool for laughs, but with Kendra around, it bothered him, just a little bit.

But at least he'd finally figured out what was going on. "You're filling in for Patty?"

"Yeah, she called me this morning. Very, very early this morning. Her bursitis is flaring up and she asked me if I could play your victim." She spread her arms open. "So here I am. Your designated damsel in distress."

Jason couldn't imagine anyone less suited for the role of damsel in distress. Kendra Carter was smart as a whip, good at everything she tried, independent, outspoken. On top of that, she had a longtime crew of friends and a retired blues legend for a father—Alvin "Redfish" Carter, with whom she ran the restaurant at the Blue Drake Club.

4

Kendra Carter was used to taking care of herself. Except that...he still didn't know why she'd left Minneapolis and come back to Lake Bittersweet. At first he'd assumed it was because of her father, but something told him it was more than that. Since she'd come back, she'd seemed more subdued than he remembered. Something had happened in Minneapolis, but she wasn't talking about it. At least, not to him.

He dragged himself back to the task at hand. Training exercise. Victim. She stood a few feet from him now, her arms folded across her chest. She wore a thin gold necklace that glinted against her radiant brown skin. "We're doing a swatting drill."

"I know how to swat mosquitoes. Those little mother-effers know they can't mess with me."

"I bet."

"What's that supposed to mean?"

And there was the feisty Kendra he remembered from high school. "Hey, you said it. I'm just agreeing."

"No, there was subtext. I heard it."

He grabbed the hand of the blowup doll and slapped his own cheek with it. "That'll teach me to keep the damn subtext out of my mouth." He slapped himself again with the plastic hand. "And not to say 'damn.'"

Her lips quirked. "Jason Mosedale, I did not drag myself out of bed at four in the morning to watch you play the fool."

"It's worth it, though, ain't it?" called Brent.

"Definitely not."

Jason decided he'd had enough of the peanut gallery. "You guys get yourselves some coffee while I bring Kendra up to speed on victim protocol. Back in ten."

The other firefighters chaotically headed out of the garage, toward the common room where they usually hung out on a slow day. Lake Bittersweet had more than its share of slow days. Hence the nonstop pranks and jokes.

Kendra tapped a foot on the ground. Busy woman, places to go, things to do, said her body language. Except that Jason detected something else, a shadow behind her brightness. He wanted to ask her if everything was okay. But they weren't exactly the confiding sort of friends, and her manner screamed "let's get on with this," so he didn't.

"So what do I do in this swatting scenario?" she asked.

"Do you know what swatting is? Not the mosquito kind?"

"Nope."

Weirdly, it felt good to know something that Kendra wasn't already proficient at. All through high school, she'd been either at the top of every class or close to it. He'd always muddled around in the middle somewhere. It wasn't until he'd dated an occupational therapist that he'd learned he probably had an undiagnosed learning disorder. The fact that he'd done as well as he had in school was probably a minor miracle. Nancy had insisted that he was highly intelligent, and that was what had saved his ass from complete failure.

"Swatting is when some nefarious person calls 9-1-1 to report a nonexistent crime happening somewhere. Law enforcement responds, full-force, and an innocent person finds themselves at the business end of a bunch of hyped-up first responders. Usually it's police, but here in Lake Bittersweet, us studly firefighters respond to 9-1-1 calls, so we need to know what to do in a situation like that."

"That really happens?" She looked appalled. "That doesn't sound like something my people would do."

Come to think of it, she probably wasn't wrong. "I don't have a demographic breakdown like that, so I can neither confirm nor deny."

Her eyebrow lifted. "Practicing for the fire chief position when you have to face the media?"

He grinned at her. "How'd you know?"

"I didn't! I was...mostly joking. Are you really going for it?"

Was that respect in her eyes? She probably thought of him as so easygoing that he'd never push for a promotion like that. And she might be right.

But man, how would it feel to see that look in her eyes more often?

"I haven't decided yet."

"So what's stopping you?"

"Who needs the stress? It's a lot of responsibility. I'm all about the simple life. Fishing, firefighting, good f...un." He deliberately let that last "f" linger before completing the word.

She rolled her eyes at his dumb stab at a joke, but then turned serious.

"Don't sell yourself short, Jason. You'd be a good fire chief."

A compliment from Kendra? Now *that* surprised him, so much so that he loosened his grip on the blowup doll and it bounced to the ground. He grabbed at it. Plastic squeaked and then a pop let out all the remaining air in one big whoosh. He dropped the limp deflated plastic to the concrete floor. "Oh yeah? Tell me more."

She burst out laughing. "Never mind. So tell me what I'm doing here, Jaybone?"

He winced at the sound of that old nickname, inspired by the fact that he played the trombone in high school. He still played, but only as part of an informal jam session organized by Redfish Carter. "I haven't heard that one since high school, and I can't say that I've missed it."

"Really? I always thought it was cute. It suited you."

Was she saying he was cute? He wanted to pursue that possibility, but they were running out of time.

"Here's the drill. You're going to play the victim of a swatting attack. All you have to do is act like you're an ordinary person sitting at home watching TV. We're going to swarm you as if we're going to arrest you. You have to act like a normal innocent person. Can you do that?"

"There won't be guns, will there? I'm not trying to get a bunch of guns pointed at me."

"Of course not. We're firefighters. We don't carry guns."

"Are you going to push me around? I don't want that either."

Trust Kendra Carter to set her boundaries so clearly ahead of time. He admired that about her. Along with so many other things.

"No physical contact. No one will touch you."

She thought it over, then nodded her consent. "I got it. Patty owes me for this one."

"Yeah, sorry. She's our usual victim. She's done it so many times that she critiques us afterwards. Catches all kinds of stuff."

Kendra's face lit up. "Ooh, now you're talking my love language. Can I do that too? You know there's nothing I love more than giving my opinion."

"Sure. We'll give you a feedback card that you can drop in the suggestion box." He gestured at the burn barrel in the corner of the garage.

"Cute, Jaybone. Supercute."

They grinned at each other. A moment. *We're having a moment. Me and Kendra. Or should it be Kendra and I?*

Because one thing he knew for sure, Kendra would correct his grammar if he got it wrong. He knew because sometimes back in high school, he deliberately got it wrong just so she'd give him that look. The one that said, "I'm smart and hot and dream on, bud."

"Okay then." Just like that, Kendra shattered the moment. "I'm ready to scream my ass off because some idiot firefighters can't tell the difference between a real call and swatter."

Ha. Yup. *Dream on.*

"Get out of my house, you're trespassing and trampling all over my civil rights and I will sue your asses!" Kendra shouted at the firefighters stampeding toward her.

"Cut!" Jason gestured at the crew. "Let's try it again." He strode over to Kendra, who'd taken a seat on a folding chair he'd set up between the paramedic van and the fire truck.

"Cut? Are we making a movie?"

"Yeah. It's called 'Why Can't Kendra Act Like an Ordinary Person?'"

"Well, that's going to look ridiculous on a movie poster."

Jason looked so frustrated—in an undeniably hot way—that she couldn't help smiling at him. He'd really, really grown up fine, and she'd been aware of that fact for a while. Quite the glow-up. It wasn't just the muscles he'd developed since he'd become a fireman. It was the gleam in his eyes, the smile always hovering in the corner of his mouth, even that damn groove in his cheek. Jason was the kind of guy people wanted to be around.

That is, other people did. Not her. That fun-loving vibe was appealing, sure, but it didn't bode well for a future. Besides, she had enough to juggle. If it wasn't the new restaurant, it was worries about her father. If it wasn't all of her friends getting engaged or married, it was the fact that she was still recovering from getting callously and shockingly dumped.

Dominic Robb, her boyfriend and business partner, had broken up with her on his way to London, where she'd assumed she'd be joining him. He'd used the business venture they'd developed together and parlayed it into a new position at a top investment firm in England.

Without her.

Now she had no boyfriend and no business.

How had it come to this? She was the naturally suspicious

one who always told her friends not to trust a man, especially a smooth-talker like Dominic. How had she been so blind? They had the same dreams. He wanted to succeed, to be the best. They were perfect for each other, or so she'd thought.

How wrong she'd been. She didn't usually make catastrophic mistakes like that, and it had shaken her to the core. Over a year later, she still hadn't so much as gone on a date with a man.

She glared at Jason. Her crushed dreams weren't his fault, but this silly victim scenario was. "You said to act ordinary. That's what I'd do if you guys charged into my house like that."

"Well, apparently you're not ordinary."

"Is that a compliment?"

"More of a compli-sult."

She remembered that long-running joke from their locker-buddy days in high school. "The dreaded compliment with an insult hidden inside? How dare you."

He raked his fingers through his hair. "How long do Patty's bursitis episodes usually last?"

"It varies. Sometimes I think they last as long as it suits her." She put a hand over her mouth in exaggerated apology. "Oops, I didn't just say that. Don't tell Patty."

"You're afraid of Patty?" His face brightened. "Good. I'm going to tell her what a godawful victim you are if you don't shape up."

She was starting to feel sorry for him. "You're sounding desperate. Okay, fine, I'll be good."

"Okay. Thank you." He gestured to the crew. "Places, please."

Now it really was starting to sound like a movie. Kendra sat in the folding chair again. She checked her watch. Almost seven. Pretty soon she had to wrap this up and get her ass over to the Blue Drake. But for now, she was enjoying the spotlight, she had to admit.

As the firefighters charged toward her for the fifth time, she let out a bloodcurdling shriek, and convulsed onto the floor, where she twitched and moaned dramatically.

All the firefighters stopped in their tracks.

"She's having a medical event!" Jason shouted. "What do you do in case of a heart attack or a stroke?"

When no one moved right away, he ran to her himself. He crouched down next to her and put his hand near her neck. Not quite touching her skin, but nevertheless, she could feel the warmth of his hand.

"You check her pulse. Make sure she's breathing. Do your ABCs. What are the ABCs?" he continued.

Colleen piped up. "Airway, breathing, circulation."

"That's right. You check all of the above. Sure, she's a potential suspect, but her medical situation comes first." Jason's hands were moving around her body, indicating her throat, her mouth, her chest. Clearly he knew what he was doing. His skill shone in every movement, even though he didn't actually complete any of the actions he was describing.

She felt herself relaxing on the uncomfortable concrete floor of the garage. It was very uncharacteristic of her to do something so dramatic. She'd done it to throw them off and annoy Jason some more. But it hadn't exactly worked out that way. It was soothing to watch him do his thing. *If I ever had a real medical event, I'd want Jason to be my paramedic,* she thought dreamily.

"Okay, you're fine," he said brusquely. She glanced up at him. They'd never been this close before, not even when they used to sling friendly insults at each other from locker to locker. His eyes were such an intensely dark blue, as if an artist had wanted black, but pulled back and gone for blue instead.

Her gaze dropped to his upper lip, searching for...there it was. That scar. She'd never forget the night he got that scar.

After all, he'd been defending her.

two

"Do you guys remember when I nearly started a brawl at the Cue Ball pool hall?" At the end of the long day, Kendra sat with her besties Carly and Gina at the bar at the Blue Drake Club and Resort. A jazz combo played on the iconic stage with its enormous statue of a blue duck.

Recently, her father had taken over the restaurant portion of the club and renamed it Alvin's Burgers and Blues. After they stopped serving, the bar stayed open until midnight. That was when she could finally relax and enjoy the acts that came through town. Thanks to Steven Gault, Carly's father and Alvin's close friend, this tiny spot on the map was a top destination for some of the best musical talent in the world.

"I heard something about it, but it was just you and Brooke, right?" Carly sipped from a bottle of nonalcoholic beer. She'd just gotten married this past New Year's Eve and was due to give birth any day—or minute—now. She sat astride the bar stool, the heels of her boots hooked on the rungs. Her dark hair was pulled into a low ponytail and she looked tired. Kendra kept trying to get her to slow down, but she was a constant ball of energy.

"Yes, and really it was all *Brooke's* fault," Kendra said. "She was the instigator."

"Well, of course. You were such a good girl." Gina pulled a sassy face, her dark curls dancing as she bopped to the music. "By which I mean you were more careful not to get caught."

Kendra laughed and clicked her vodka tonic with lime against Gina's wine glass. Gina had recently fallen in love, too. So had the fifth member of their friend group, Trixie, back in Lost Harbor, Alaska. Only Kendra was currently single. Well, and Brooke.

It's me and you, Brooke. She toasted her friend's spirit. *Me and a ghost, we're the only ones still single.*

Gina ran a finger around the rim of her wine glass. "Do you know how many times I think, WWBD?"

Kendra cocked her head. "What would Brooke do?"

"Yes. And the answer is always the opposite of what most people would do."

They all laughed. Brooke the Rebel. "Do you think if she'd lived, she would have stopped being such a revolutionary?" Kendra asked her friends.

"No. Not Brooke," Gina said instantly.

"I'm not so sure," Carly mused. "If she'd lived, she would have been a mother to Danny. She might have toned it down for him."

Kendra took a sip of her ice-cold vodka. "She probably would have dragged him to protest marches."

They all laughed, knowing it was the truth.

"I still miss her," Kendra said softly.

"I do too," said Carly. "Especially being back in Lake Bitter-sweet. It's like she's just around the corner, and if I move fast enough, I'll catch her. I love hearing stories about her, especially if I can tell them to Danny."

When Carly had married Thomas, she'd become stepmother to Danny, who was now a teenager. Danny was the result of one experimental night between Thomas and Brooke, seventeen years ago. Tragically, Brooke had died while giving birth to him, and Thomas had raised him alone. Kendra couldn't imagine anything more perfect than Carly stepping into Danny's life at this point.

"This might not be the best story to tell him."

Carly chuckled. "Let me guess. Brooke tackled some idiot and made him eat pool chalk?"

"No. Jason stepped in. He got a pool cue in the face."

They both looked at her blankly.

"Jason Mosedale," she prompted.

"The cute firefighter?"

Kendra felt her face warm. "Sure, I guess."

"Okay, now you have to tell the whole story." Gina bounced on her barstool in excitement. "Tell, tell! Where were we? Me and Carly?"

"You were all asleep. I think we smoked a little too much. Everyone crashed except me and Brooke."

"God, that takes me back." Carly sighed. "We were such *teenagers*. Sometimes I think it's a miracle we survived. Summer in Lake Bittersweet. The crazy shit that went down..."

That summer, Kendra and the other chambermaids—Carly Gault, Brooke Kendall, Gina Moretti and Trixie Tran—became the best of friends because there was nothing like being required to wear white while cleaning cabins and swabbing toilets to cement a bond.

Even on their off days, they spent time together. They'd go swimming in the lake, hang out on the Blue Drake dock, or roast marshmallows on the beach. They shared secret crushes and embarrassing confessions. They talked about their dreams for after high school. Of the five of them, Kendra and Brooke were the most ambitious; they both wanted to change the world. Fix it. Stop climate change. Stop racism. Stop exploitation.

One night in the Wood Duck Cabin, where the out-of-town girls lived, Brooke brought out some weed that she swore was the best she'd ever smoked. Kendra debated long and hard about whether to try some. Her father always warned her to avoid it, but since he'd smoked plenty—along with Gault and all their musician buddies—it seemed hypocritical. Shouldn't she at least try it and decide for herself?

Turned out, while the other girls got mellow and even fell asleep, she got hyped up. Around midnight, she looked around and the only other girl still awake was Brooke.

"What now? I want to go have some fun," she told Brooke. Brooke flipped back her blond hair and grinned. She was from a wealthy summer family, and usually lived back east.

"Let's play some pool."

"You don't want to play pool with me. I grew up in blues dives. I'll whip your ass."

"Ooooh, then I have an even better idea! Let's make some money."

They rode their bikes to the Cue Ball at the edge of town, ditching them in the weeds because they'd forgotten their bike locks. The midnight sky was so spectacular that Kendra suggested skipping the pool game and just lying in the weeds and staring at the stars until sunrise.

"Don't be chicken." Brooke hauled her inside to a smoky room filled with frowny-faced men. Pool was serious business, apparently. Kendra giggled, and couldn't stop until Brooke pinched her.

The smoke gave everything a hazy, dreamlike feel. She played a few games and barely knew if she won or lost. The round shine of the balls, the thunk of a shot landing in the pocket, the feel of the pool cue

16

sliding through her fingers, that was all that mattered. Win, lose, who cared?

She tried to explain it to the man she'd just beaten. He just sneered at her and challenged her to a rematch.

"Rack 'em up," the man growled. He looked really grumpy, she realized. Maybe she should let him win the next one. Older men didn't like it when younger women beat them at pool. Did it matter that she was Black? Maybe. The man was Hispanic. Either way, she was a girl and she was beating him and he clearly didn't like that.

Lose the game, she told herself. Just miss a few shots. It's not the end of the world. Win, lose, who cares?

Across the room, she saw a group of boys from her high school come in and claim a table. The ground steadied under her feet. This was her town. She could win at pool if she wanted to. No way was she going to hold herself back just to make some old out-of-town dude feel better about himself.

So she won. Then she won again. Brooke was raking in the dollars the man kept sliding across the table. He kept ordering more beers, challenging her to more matches. Time passed, but she didn't notice. Chalk, cue, ball, pocket. Dollar bills. It was almost as if every part of her brain except the part needed for pool turned off. The focus was intoxicating.

And then it all shifted. The man crushed a beer can against the edge of the pool table.

"Hey man, keep it cool," said Brooke.

"Shut your trap, rich girl. I saw you around the lodge. What are you, slumming it down here with the cleaning staff?"

Brooke and Kendra looked at each other and laughed. "We have the same job, idiot. That has nothing to do with the fact that she's kicking your ass at pool."

Even through her foggy haze, Kendra knew that Brooke was taking it too far. Winning was one thing; taunting another.

The man turned to Kendra, shutting Brooke out. "Are you cheat-

ing?" he demanded. "Is she helping you? No way you're winning fair and square."

"I'm not. Want to go again?"

"Yeah. But I want her out of here. Let's see if you can win on your own."

"I'm not leaving," Brooke began.

"It's fine." Kendra waved her away. "Just go hang out with Jason and the others over there. I'll beat him again and be right over."

The man snarled in anger. She beat him again. But this time, he lost it. He shifted the pool cue in his grip like a lance and lunged across the table at her. She stumbled backwards and would have fallen, except someone was there to catch her. Whoever it was had a wiry, strong body and smelled like he'd just been eating barbecue. He pushed her down just as the pool cue jammed through the air. She felt his body shudder and knew the cue must have hit him. A gush of blood spilled onto her sweater from above.

She crawled out from the melee and jumped to her feet. Several men were holding back her former competitor. One of them wrestled the pool cue away from him. And Jason Mosedale was surrounded by his buddies, who were doing things like stuffing paper napkins onto his face and grabbing ice cubes from random drinks. She felt someone tug her away, trying to get her out of there. Brooke.

But she resisted. She couldn't just leave Jason after he'd taken the blow meant for her. The pool cue had split his upper lip open. That was where all the blood was coming from. The whole lower part of his face was already swelling up. He caught her eye. "You okay?" he called to her.

She nodded, even though she felt very far from okay. She was smart. She knew better than to get herself into a position like this. How had she let this happen? What were her parents going to say?

"Let's get out of here," Brooke said in a low voice. "Before the police get here."

Police? Holy shit, she'd be in trouble for sure if the police got *involved. If she had to walk some kind of straight line, she might fall on her ass.*

Jason jutted his chin toward the exit. He was telling her to leave before she got in worse trouble. Everyone knew Alvin Carter and how proud he was of Kendra. She didn't know much about Jason's family. They seemed to be more the "benign neglect" type. Anyway, boys never got into as much trouble as girls did when they stepped out of line.

She and Brooke fled toward their bikes, and were furiously pedaling down the road when they saw the sheriff's car whiz past.

Over the next few days, she braced herself for the other shoe to drop. Surely someone would want to talk to the girl who had incited the brawl with her refusal to lose a game of pool. But it never happened. Maybe the guy had been too proud to admit he'd lost to a girl. Definitely Jason and his buddies had never mentioned her name.

The next time she saw Jason at his locker, his lip looked terrible. A big scab had formed on his upper lip. He was going to have quite the scar.

She closed her locker door and faced him. "Listen, Jason. Thanks for—"

He waved away her words. "It's al-wight." His swollen lip made the "r" sound fuzzy. "I already got three dates out of it."

"Like you need more reasons for girls to chase you." That was one of the things she teased him about. She knew why girls were crazy for him—he was so good-looking—but he was too laid-back for her, not driven enough.

"Good point." He winced as his lips formed the "p." "There's one lucky thing, though. I get to skip band practice. Like forever."

"No more trombone?"

"The nurse said I'll never play trombone again. Well, I begged her to say that. Sick of being teased for my nerdy choice of instrument." He grinned, then winced again as the movement tugged at his scab.

"So I rescued you from band practice? I guess you should thank me then."

"Yeah...maybe after the Tylenol kicks in."

She laughed a little. "Seriously, I can't believe you stood up for me like that. I could have kissed you."

"You still could." His eyes twinkled at her. "After I heal up."

"Dream on."

Carly snapped her fingers. "I knew there was something between you and Jason. I noticed him looking at you during last year's Sunburn Fest."

"There's nothing between us. There never has been. We're... friends, I guess. In high school, anyway. I haven't seen him much since then." For some reason, she felt self-conscious. "He's not my type."

"Well, he was definitely looking at you. That's all I know."

Gina propped her elbow on the bar and rested her curly head on her hand. "Good old Jason. Such a hottie. Who's he dating now?"

Kendra shrugged. "If he's anything like he was in high school, it's probably hard to keep track. He always had someone."

"No, I think he just broke up with someone. Ugh, my fuzzy hormone brain." Carly rapped her knuckles on her skull. "Thomas told me. Some girl he's dated on and off for years. Everyone thought they'd end up together, but she moved out of town and married someone else. Jason was crushed."

Kendra shook her head with a frown. She didn't like the idea of easygoing Jason getting his heart crushed. He didn't deserve that. He was one of the good ones. "Are you talking about Gretchen Pilsner?"

"Yes. Gretchen. But she's Gretchen Corsi now. I can't believe I know this. Firehouses are so gossipy. Thomas isn't even fire chief anymore and he still hears all the hot goss."

"Wow. So that's really over. Poor Jason." She had a vague memory of Gretchen Pilsner, sunny and freckle-faced. The two of them had seemed like a good match, except that Jason was one of those not-ready-to-commit guys. "When did that happen?"

"Hmm...why are you asking a pregnant woman the tough questions? I think it was earlier this year. Recent."

Gina pursed her lips. "Hmm. You know what that means."

"That he deserves our sympathy and support?" said Carly.

"That, and he's on the rebound."

"Ooh." Carly raised her eyebrows. "Which means don't go anywhere near him."

"What? No, it doesn't." Gina took a sip of her wine. "Rebounds are fun. The trick is to know going in that there's no chance of it working out because it's just a rebound. It's low-stakes, high-reward."

"How is it high reward?"

"Because someone on the rebound is just happy for the attention."

"That's cold, Gina." Kendra shook her head at her always-sassy friend. "Anyway, that's not Jason. He always gets attention. I don't know why. He's cute, but he's no Winston."

Everyone knew Winston Duke was her ultimate.

"But Jason has that dreamy Latin-lover look."

"Oooh, he does, doesn't he?" Carly made a show of fanning herself. "This is because I'm very pregnant, not because of Jason," she explained. "But Kendra, are you really surprised he's so popular? He's cute, he's a fireman, also he's hot and he's a fire-man. Meaning he rescues people while being cute and hot."

Kendra made a face at her. "Some of us are looking for more than cute and hot and rescue-y."

Carly pointed an accusing finger at her. "He rescued you from a pool cue!"

"That's true. And I did say that I wished I could kiss him for that. But his face was all swollen, so that never happened."

"It's never too late." Gina pushed her glass toward Kendra, who splashed more wine into it. "Rebound, rebound."

"Don't do it, don't do it," chanted Carly.

"Hmm." Kendra flashed a smile at her two friends. "WWBD?"

The two of them looked at each other, then back at Kendra. "Do it," they said together. They all laughed.

"It's been over a year since Dominic," said Gina gently. "Don't you think it's time to at least try?"

Kendra opened her mouth to explain that she was fine just as she was. But the words refused to come out. Maybe she wasn't fine.

"Rebound" meant that you were recovering, coming back from the worst of it, ready for something new.

Was she even rebound material?

If she told her friends how shaky she still felt, they'd be supportive, of course. But they were both so freaking happy right now. They wouldn't be able to relate.

She let out a sigh as she realized that there was someone who probably *could* relate. Jason. They could be the Rebound Twins. Both trying to claw their way back to a normal social life after getting punched in the mouth with the Pool Cue of Rejection.

She shook off the thought. She wasn't ready for any kind of dating, not even a rebound. This was the time for her to focus on her career—which Dominic had also ruined.

Luckily, Pop had asked her to help him out with the restaurant. Alvin's Burgers and Blues had been a great distraction. She'd come back to Lake Bittersweet to lick her wounds, but she wanted more for herself then running a restaurant.

An idea had been bouncing around in her head ever since she

saw the notice at city hall. "Can we stop talking about boys for a minute and discuss the fact that I'm considering a career change?"

"What?" Alarmed, Carly gripped the edge of the bar. "You're going to leave us to run this place without you?"

"Don't worry, it's a long process. I might not even get it. Sure, I'm ridiculously qualified and all that. But there's a lot of old people in charge around here who might not want me to get it. The dreaded board of aldermen."

Carly shuddered, since she'd had her own run-ins with the town powers-that-be. "What's the job?"

"Town manager. The job where I get to boss *everyone* around." She smiled gleefully.

"Oh my God. That would be perfect for you. As a local business owner, there's no one I'd rather get bossed around by." Carly offered her hand for a high-five. Kendra obliged, then high-fived Gina as well. For the first time in a while, she felt some hope. Maybe Dominic hadn't completely ruined her career and love life in one swoop.

"What about Alvin? Is he okay running the restaurant by himself?" Gina asked.

Kendra bit her lip. That would be the hardest part, for sure. Working with her father was great. She'd needed to come home after Dominic had shattered her dreams. But on the other hand... "Do you think he'll understand that managing Alvin's was a rebound job?"

They all laughed. "So you *are* open to rebounds!" Carly clapped her hands together.

"Rebound, rebound," Gina chanted softly.

three

Of course it was inevitable that Jason would run into Gretchen. Lake Bittersweet was small enough that it was impossible to avoid any particular person forever, even if they'd moved to the next town over.

With the weather finally warming up, he and Galen Cooper decided to take a canoe out for the summer's first fishing trip. They were carrying Galen's big double canoe down the pebbled beach when he spotted Gretchen's strawberry-blond head in a speedboat tied up at the public landing. She wore a visor to keep the sun off her face and bright pink lip gloss.

Probably watermelon flavored. That was her favorite. He didn't like the taste of watermelon—too sugary. But he'd never told her that and now it didn't matter since he'd never kiss her again.

"You okay, man?" Galen asked. For a wilderness dude, he was surprisingly sensitive. He was Jason's best fishing bud, a real character, a bristly-haired mountain man more comfortable in the wilderness than around people. He'd been growing his beard out for so long that no one remembered what his face looked like. Every time he tried to cut his hair or shave, he panicked.

Jason loved the guy because he was so much himself, and besides, Jason got a kick out of most people.

"Yeah, it's all good." He shrugged. Easygoing Jason. Easy come, easy go. That was his motto, right?

His phone rang, the ringtone telling him his sister Holly was calling. As her surrogate parent, he couldn't ignore her calls. He motioned to slow down, and dug his phone from his pocket. "Hey, we're about to go catch dinner. What's up?"

"I'm having friends over tonight."

"Okay..." Holly was seventeen—a later-in-life surprise for their parents—and had friends over all the time. Even though he'd been her main parental figure since their parents had moved to Minneapolis three years ago, they were more like roommates than anything else. Only occasionally did he have to play the authority figure.

"One of them has a crush on you. Just a warning."

He groaned. "I'll stay away." If anything would be guaranteed to make him stay out of the house, it would be one of Holly's friends with a crush.

"Thanks."

Something in her voice made him pause. "How many friends?"

"It's not like that."

He waited. The edge of the canoe bit into his other hand, and he adjusted his grip. A slick of green algae on the pebbles made his boots skid a bit.

"Chloe's going through a hard time and she started seeing this one guy who's a fucking bitch-ass loser, so we're having an intervention."

Jason let the curse words flow past without comment. Holly was fierce when it came to defending her friends, and that

26

extended to the language she used. *She's just expressing herself. And I'm not her damn parent.*

When their actual parents had broached the idea of moving their dance studio to Minneapolis, they'd assumed Holly would go with them. But she'd hated the idea of leaving her friends. Their older sister had enough on her plate with her own crew of hyperactive kids, so Holly had begged Jason to let her stay with him. She'd promised she wouldn't cause any trouble. To prove it, on her first night living with him, she'd announced that she didn't intend to have sex until she was at least eighteen.

So far, she'd stuck to her promise. Boys weren't an issue. Her problems came from her extensive network of friends who texted twenty-four-seven with all kinds of drama.

"Anything I can do to help? Chloe's a good egg."

"You can start by not calling her an egg."

Water splashed onto his boots as they reached the edge of the lake. Catching Galen's eye, he nodded and they lowered the canoe into the water together. "Listen, I gotta go. We just splashed the canoe."

"Who are you going with?"

"Galen."

"Okay, well, whatever you do, don't bring Galen over. Marissa has a crush on him."

Jason nearly laughed out loud. Galen, with his wild black hair and bristly beard, always looked like he'd spent the night curled up under a pile of leaves in the forest. Good to know that didn't make him immune to teenagers' crushes. Those hormones were really something.

"Are you really supposed to be telling me about your friends' crushes? Isn't that a HIPAA violation?"

"Ha ha. But it's a good point. I wouldn't tell anyone except for you. Because you know I can kill you in your sleep anytime I want."

"Damn, Holly. Are all teenage girls this bloodthirsty?"

"Welcome to the future. We're going to run this world. You're lucky I have your back."

Galen beckoned at him, looking impatient. Out of the corner of his eye, Jason saw the speedboat carrying Gretchen ease away from the dock. With any luck, it would be long gone before they made it onto the lake.

"I'll see you later," he told Holly.

"*Much* later."

"Right. Much later."

Crap. Maybe he should crash at Galen's. Or at the firehouse. Or at Gretch—Dammit. He wasn't ever going to sleep at Gretchen's again.

He wasn't going to be able to avoid her, either, he realized. The speedboat was lingering near the dock. After he slid his phone back into his pocket, he steadied the canoe so Galen could get in, then slid in after him. By the time they got their paddles out and their strokes synchronized, they were heading right toward the snappy red boat.

"Ahoy there, Jason," Gretchen called over the low rumble of the twin 500 horsepower engines. Who needed that much horsepower for a lake it took fifteen minutes to cross? Her new husband, Jack Corsi, was at the helm, ignoring their lowly canoe.

"Hey, Gretch. What are you doing back in town?"

"Oh, Jack bought this new boat and wanted to try it out on the nearest lake."

The nearest lake? He wasn't buying that for a second. Had they driven all the way to Lake Bittersweet to rub his face in their newfound bliss? Gretchen had warned him that she wouldn't wait forever for a proposal. He hadn't listened.

Or maybe he had, and just...didn't really want to propose to her.

"It's a beauty," he said cordially.

"Did you really call it the *Retch*?" Galen called to her. "Weird name, but okay."

"It's the *Gretch*, you idiot."

Jason bit back a smile. Gretchen never had liked Galen much. It had probably started the night he'd shown up with a deer strapped to his roof rack and a bloody field-dressing knife he wanted to wash in the sink.

Galen steered away from the boat, toward his favorite fishing hole where the walleye hung out.

Jason waved at Gretchen over his shoulder and caught a glimpse of her stepping to the wheel to wrap her arms around her new husband. Quickly, he looked away.

"You're better off," Galen growled. "I hope you're not eating your heart out over her."

"Me? Nah. I'll be okay."

Galen threw a dark glance at him over his shoulder. The deep green waters of the lake whispered past the hull of the canoe. "You sure? You're not yourself lately."

"We weren't even together when she met Jack. We've broken up about twenty times since high school. It wasn't meant to be."

He didn't want to admit to Galen that it hurt like hell to watch her nuzzling Jack in that cozy way she used to snuggle with him. He'd taken her for granted, he knew that. They'd had such an easy relationship. More like best friends than lovers. He still had the urge to call her up when he was bored. She'd always been up for something fun—*let's drive to Braddock and go bowling. Let's ice skate down Grant Creek. Let's fill the rookie's car with Cheetos.* Now she was having fun with a rich guy with a speedboat, and she deserved every bit of happiness.

They paddled a few minutes in silence. "How do you do that?" Galen asked.

"Do what?"

"Say goodbye to one woman and be so sure another one's going to show up."

"Experience?" Jason said with a smirk.

"Man, I wish I was you. No heartbreak for Jason Mosedale. One goes, here comes another. What's that song? 'Thank U, Next.'"

Did Galen really listen to Ariana Grande? The mountain man had all kinds of secrets up his sleeve. But did he really think Jason didn't feel any pain over a breakup?

Stung, Jason blurted out the truth, which he hadn't done with anyone since Gretchen got married. "That's bullshit. I cried real tears when Gretchen left."

"Tears? Like, out of your eyes?" Galen feathered the paddle to bring them skimming to a stop.

"Yes, jackass. It shook me up. I always figured we'd get married someday, it just never felt like the right day. I haven't dated anyone since Gretchen left me. I'm...grieving."

"That's good."

"Why is that good?"

"Maybe you'll start to appreciate how lucky you are when it comes to women," he said in a gloomy tone.

Poor Galen. He'd been hung up on the same woman for some time now. One of these days maybe he'd ask her out, but none of his buddies wanted to rush him.

"You know, I used to think I was lucky with women, but I was dead wrong. I'm just as single as you are. I lost my longtime girl-friend because I wouldn't get serious enough to propose. Now I'm Holly's latest project. She wants me to get the rebound rela-tionship out of the way quickly so I can find the real thing. She keeps bringing up things like family dynamics and psychological blocks. I don't know where she gets all the therapy shit, I think she sees it on TikTok."

But Galen wasn't listening. He was peering over the side of

the canoe. "Never mind that, I hope you're ready to catch your weight in walleye." He scooted the end of his fishing rod over the edge and dropped the line, and in the next moment, reeled in a squirming, shiny-scaled fish. "'Thank U, Next!'"

After they'd filled their cooler, Galen and Jason stowed the canoe and roasted two fat trout over a small campfire. They pronounced the summer season officially kicked-off. Then, needing beer, they made their way to Mariano's Pizza, which had the best price on pitchers. As always, it was crowded with locals and the first summer folk arriving in town.

Jason elbowed his way to the bar and signaled the bartender for a pitcher of beer. He spotted some buddies from the firehouse at a corner table. A friend from high school and his wife were canoodling nearby. A group of crafters held down the large table for their monthly night out on the town. Conor Gault and his new love, Emmaline Curtis, were sharing a pizza with her brother Henry and *his* new love, Jamilah.

Love was breaking out all over the place. Like chickenpox.

His old trombone teacher waved at him from the bar. With his hands full of pitchers of beer, all he could do was nod back at him. Old Herbert Simonson had been crushed when he'd had to quit the trombone. When he'd found out it was due to a pool room brawl, he'd nearly wept.

Good old Lake Bittersweet. Where everyone knew your name, your romantic history, and your high school misdeeds.

But still, it was his town and he loved every quirky inch of it.

Galen stopped to talk to one of the fish and game guys, so Jason headed for the table where his firehouse buddies were gathered. Halfway there, someone stepped in front of him, causing him to splash beer on their sweater. *Her* sweater. Kendra.

A shiver swept through him. Hadn't he just been thinking about that time at the pool hall with Kendra? Weird timing.

"Sorry, didn't mean to get beer on you." Droplets glistened on the garnet angora of her turtleneck sweater. She brushed them off briskly and thoroughly. Kendra did everything as well as it could be done. It used to be annoying, but now he simply admired it.

"It was my fault. I wanted to talk to you."

He looked up in surprise. Kendra Carter was seeking him out? "Are you signing up to play victim again?"

She shuddered. "I think we can all agree it's best if you find someone else to fake-rescue." She jerked her thumb at the table of firefighters. In a lower, almost intimate voice, she said, "They actually told me they'd take up a collection to pay me not to do it again."

He laughed out loud. "That's bullshit. They'll spend their money on beer and train with whoever I can get."

He started to move around her, but she blocked him. "Seriously. I want to talk to you. Can we sit?"

"Uh..." He looked around at the crowded restaurant. The canoodling couple was getting to their feet, still locked in a kiss. He gestured with his head. "Over there?"

Kendra shot off to claim the table. He followed with the pitchers of beer, which looked ridiculously excessive when he set them on the table.

She eyed them curiously as she pulled up a chair. "Big beer drinker? It doesn't show."

"Where does he put it?" He mimicked a fawning compliment, making her smile. "They're for the crew. But depending on what you want to talk to me about, I might need them. Am I in trouble?"

"In trouble?" She frowned. "Why would you be in trouble? And why would I have any authority over you to say you were?"

"You're Alvin Carter's daughter, and no one wants to disappoint Alvin," he explained. "Especially not me."

"Why especially not you?"

"He lets me play trombone in his jam sessions in Braddock. I'm always sure he's going to boot me out."

"Look at you, Jaybone. Still with the trombone."

"Go ahead and tease. I'm all grown up now and comfortable with my instrument."

She wrinkled her forehead at his ridiculous double-entendre. He took in her perfectly cut cheekbones and perky nose. On someone else, those features might add up to "temptress." But Kendra wasn't about collecting men's hearts. She'd always wanted to make her own mark on the world.

He pushed a pitcher of beer toward her. "Have a drink and tell me what's up."

She shifted in the chair, which drew his attention to the tight red jacket she wore. Kendra always looked put-together in her own particular hot-girl way. He took the stack of cups from his pocket and plopped one on the table before her. She splashed some beer into it, then drank it down.

"Have you decided about the fire chief position?"

Damn. And here he'd thought maybe she'd been flirting with him. Kendra Carter was all business. "I'm still thinking about it."

"Have you looked into the hiring process? I know it involves the board of aldermen, right?"

He raised an eyebrow at her. "Yeah. I have all the paperwork. I know what I have to do, if that's what you're wondering. I don't need any tutoring."

She poured herself some more beer. "I'm not offering help, I'm asking for it. This is top secret information I'm about to share. I know I can trust you because…" Her gaze dropped to the scar on his upper lip. It tingled under her gaze. "Well, you know."

"Sure, you can trust me. Does this involve pool?"

She snorted, then leaned forward on her elbows and dropped her voice. Her scent floated toward him, fresh and crisp, like apples in the snow. "I'm thinking about applying for the town manager job."

He digested that. If he got the fire chief position, they'd be working together, sort of. Or at least they'd attend the same meetings together. He wouldn't mind that. Seeing Kendra always sent a buzz through his system. "Cool," he told her. "Good luck."

"Wait. The thing is..." She hesitated. "I need to know if it's a waste of time to apply. The board of aldermen hated Gault, absolutely despised him. They did everything they could to shut down the Blue Drake. My dad was Gault's best friend. They might laugh me right out of the interview room."

"Well, if they do, that's their loss."

She shook her head. "You don't get it. I'm not going to put myself in a position where some old white men get to decide my future if they aren't even going to give me a fair shot. I don't mind taking my chances if I actually *have* a chance. But if I don't..." She shrugged. "Then screw them."

He gazed at her for a long, thoughtful moment. "You've never been turned down for anything, have you?"

"No," she said after a pause. "Not exactly."

"You can learn a lot from failure."

"I don't fail," she snapped. But then something darker shadowed her face. A painful memory? A regret? "I mean, I don't usually fail. But that's partly because I do my research. So I'm doing my research now. Thomas Cooper's on the board of aldermen now. You're firehouse friends with him. That kind of bond goes deep. Can you get the lay of the land for me?"

"Isn't your best friend Carly married to him?"

"Yes, but she just had her baby and I don't want to put her in the middle."

"I know she did, I'm the one who got her to the hospital. I

nearly delivered him in the paramedic van." He lifted his glass. "To baby Teddy."

"To Teddy." They clinked glasses and each took a sip.

"So you don't mind putting me in the middle?" he asked curiously. It was...different, Kendra asking him for help. The reverse of high school.

"No, I don't mind, because everyone likes you and they tell you stuff."

"Is that flattery?" He wrinkled his forehead. "Because I feel like it could be a little better."

"You're insulting my flattery?"

"Absolutely not. Best flattery ever. How *do* you do it?"

She laughed at him and he felt giddy for a moment. Making Kendra laugh wasn't like making other people laugh. It gave him a charge, like he could do anything in the whole goddamn world. "I'll do it. I'll be your spy."

"Thanks, Jason. I really appreciate it." She started to get up, but he touched her hand. She looked back at him curiously.

The contact—eye and hand—was like a punch to the gut, or a shot of adrenaline. Like that moment when a call came in and he ran to don his gear.

"I'm curious about something. You said you don't *usually* fail. What do you mean by that?"

four

Kendra hadn't intended to tell Jason about the fiasco with Dominic. She hadn't planned to tell anyone. It was too humiliating on every level. But there was something about Jason that, quietly and steadily, drew the story from her.

She began with the short version. "Long story short, my boyfriend of two years broke up with me. Since he was also my business partner, he left me hanging professionally too."

"Damn." He waited for her to say more. She didn't want to, but those steady eyes of his refused to turn away, and somehow the words kept coming.

"We met in Minneapolis, in business school. I've always wanted to run my own business. I don't have the personality to be an employee, I want to be the boss."

"Fair enough. Was that a problem for your ex?"

"No. Maybe." She frowned, thinking it over. "Probably," she admitted. "Remember how furious I was in our environmental sciences class when I learned that hardly any plastic actually gets recycled? I'm not a scientist, but I can help get the information out. I came up with this idea for an app that would let people know about all recycling options in their area, along with facts about what local businesses were doing in that space, simple steps to use less plastic, alternative plastic-free products, petitions to sign, just everything related to plastic recycling."

"Great idea. What's the name, I'll download it."

"It's still in beta form. We hadn't even named the app, but the company name is Explastica. Dominic—that's my ex—came up with it. He had more experience with app launches, so I met with him to pick his brain. We had dinner and by the end he wanted in. We became partners."

That night had been magical. She'd seen the rest of her life unfurl before her. Kendra and Dominic, conquering the world, together forever. She'd believed in that vision with every cell in her body.

"We were joined at the hip after that. We were the perfect business partners because we have similar work ethics. We both go hard, nonstop. And then we fell in love, and that made it even better. I assumed we'd be together forever."

She caught his expression, and knew that he got it.

"I heard about Gretchen. I'm sorry. Breakups are the worst."

He looked down at the table. "I just saw her on the lake. She's really happy now. She deserves it. I wasn't giving her what she wanted, so that's on me."

"She wanted to get married?" Kendra didn't remember much about Gretchen other than freckles and a sunny smile; they'd never been in the same friend groups.

"Sure." He shrugged. "I have nothing against marriage. I guess I just...I was waiting for something, I don't know what. Something that would tell me it's time to get married."

Men. Kendra didn't say it out loud, but good lord, did they need everything mapped out for them?

"If it was me, I would have just proposed," she told him. "Not to you, obviously. To my man."

"Did you? With Dominic?"

"No, because we were focusing on the business first. We had this unspoken agreement that once we got the app underway, we'd deal with our personal relationship."

"Unspoken agreement," he repeated, and she could hear for herself how sketchy that sounded. "I hope the business end of things was more official."

Warmth flooded her face. She'd been so freaking blind. "That's the problem. We have a contract, but the exit clause is too loose. Technically, he's still an equal partner, but he slow-rolls everything. It takes him weeks to answer a single email. He wants me to buy him out, but I don't have the money. In the meantime, anything I do for the business makes it more valuable and therefore more pricey to buy him out. He left me in limbo."

Jason shook his head, nothing but sympathy in those dark blue eyes. No judgement. Jason didn't judge, she realized. Maybe because he'd had struggles of his own.

"What's this jackass doing now?"

His phrasing filled her with delight. "Behind my back, he went to this big international firm and pitched himself as an expert in recycled plastic business opportunities. Companies always want to say they're doing something for the environment to offset their horrendous records. He got himself hired as a kind of recycled plastic czar with a huge budget including seed money for small ventures around the world. He gets to travel wherever he wants searching for new businesses to invest in. It's a dream job for him. He's in London now."

"My Irish grandmother used to say, you can't trust the Brits. Sometimes there was spitting involved. If she saw an English Breakfast tea bag, she'd literally stomp on it and grind it to dust. If she was still alive, you could sic her on Dominic."

It didn't fix anything, but it made her laugh. "Guess I should have listened to your grandma."

"To be honest, she was off her rocker. Not just about that. She also believed that fairies lived in her chimney and came out at night to make trouble. She made me set up a videocamera to catch them in the act. When there was nothing on the tape, she suddenly remembered that fairies are invisible."

It occurred to Kendra that talking to Jason was like floating down a river in an inner tube, soaking in the scenery along the way. He didn't rush to get to the end. He took in everything along the way.

Was that why she'd always seen him as unambitious? Because he wasn't going full-tilt for the end goal?

Kirk and Gina stopped by their table for a quick word. Gina had a question about the next day's staffing schedule for the restaurant, and asked if anyone could give her a hand restocking the cabin kitchens. Kendra answered automatically. She could probably manage Alvin's Burgers and Blues in her sleep. It presented no challenges. It posed no problems.

It also gave her a lot of comfort, working so close to her father. So there was that.

As they left, Gina gave her a quick wink. Not hard to interpret. *Rebound, rebound.*

When they were alone again, Jason sipped his beer and said, "So, not to be too critical of your ex, but he sounds like your basic selfish jerk. How does that count as your failure?"

"How? How much time do you have?"

He gestured at the crowd of pizza customers. "As much time as it takes. They close at eleven, but we could always go somewhere else."

Was that an invite? She looked at him closely, but didn't see any kind of come-on in those deep blue eyes of his. *Rebound, rebound.* Gina's chant kept running through her mind. She shushed it. Jason deserved better than just being someone's rebound. He was a good guy.

Back to her failures.

"Business mistake." She checked off item one on her fingers. "I trusted him too much business-wise."

"How? You had a contract."

"Yes, but it obviously had glaring loopholes. And there's nothing to stop him from using my ideas in his new position."

He shrugged. "Still doesn't seem like a failure. Sorry. You can't control everything. No one can."

Apparently not. Which sucked, because she really liked to feel in control.

"I failed to anticipate what an ass he was. I thought we were the same degree of dedicated. I didn't see that he was mostly dedicated to himself."

"Live and learn."

That comment rubbed her the wrong way. "I hate when people say that. It sounds like an excuse for screwing up."

"So you think you have to do everything perfectly the first time?" He swished the beer around in his glass. She noticed that he didn't actually drink very much. The beer seemed to be mostly a prop. She also noticed that his hands looked strong. Those weren't laptop hands. They were heavy-fire-hose hands.

"I usually do," she said simply.

He laughed, that dimple in his cheek flashing. "True. So maybe you're spoiled by your own incredible competence. Everyone screws up sometimes."

"I don't let myself screw up." Now that she'd said that out loud, she realized how exhausting it had been, upholding that standard. Maybe it would be a relief to let it go.

"You're awfully hard on yourself, especially because your screwup didn't hurt anyone. Besides yourself," he added. Then pulled an "apology" face. "Sorry. Did that sound bad?"

"No. I guess you're right. No bystanders were harmed by my bad judgement about men. But that's the thing. I'm always the one warning my friends about their bad choices. I'm the smart one. My entire reputation, down the drain, like that." She snapped her fingers, trying to come off as joking. "Dominic really fucked me over."

"My sister's like that." Jason shook his head and took a sip of beer. "She's seventeen now and therefore pretty much knows everything. If you can believe it, she's in the middle of some kind of intervention right now for one of her friends. I can't go back until she's done."

Kendra searched her memory for her name. "Holly, right?" She'd seen Holly and her friends at Alvin's Burgers a few times, now that she thought about it.

He nodded.

"So...you still live at home?"

"Where else would I live?" Then he got it, and burst out laughing. "You mean with my parents. No. They moved to Minneapolis. My sister lives with me. Her and a rotating cast of about ten of her friends."

Now that surprised her. Taking responsibility for an entire sister, that didn't fit with the carefree Jason she remembered.

"And she tells them what to do?"

"She does. For some reason they listen to her."

"Does she give good advice? Maybe she has some for me."

"Oh, no doubt. If you're really lucky, she'll do one of her interventions and really whip your life into shape."

"Hard pass."

After a laugh, he sat back in his chair and gave her a thoughtful stare. "Maybe it's just me, but you don't seem as torn up about losing your relationship as about the rest of it."

"You don't know me like that," she protested. "I don't show my business to everyone."

THE REBOUND

"Fair. Sorry."

His quick apology took the sting out of his observation. Enough so that she didn't mind sharing more. "I was crushed. I couldn't believe it. It took me days to realize it wasn't just a big prank. Then I was stuck in Minneapolis with an apartment I couldn't afford and a business I couldn't do anything with. Alone. That's why I came back here. Running home to daddy." She rolled her eyes a little.

His eyes softened with sympathy. "Who better to get you through a breakup than a blues legend? Alvin could write you a whole album about it."

"My dad is like...my security blanket. I knew I could come back and he wouldn't judge. He's happy I'm back. But..."

"But what?" he prompted. He was such a good listener, and questioner.

"I feel like I disappointed him. I was supposed to go off and set the world on fire. Instead I'm back here working for him."

He lifted an eyebrow. "Is he disappointed, or you?"

Ohh, good point. She laughed ruefully. "Me. Pop would be happy if I stayed forever."

"You wouldn't want that?"

Their eyes met, and she couldn't quite read his expression. Jason had never left Lake Bittersweet, and probably had no intention of leaving.

She let out a long sigh. "To be honest, Jason, I don't know anything anymore. I'm a damn mess, but no one seems to realize it. And you can't tell anyone," she added quickly.

"No one would believe me anyway. Kendra Carter, a mess? That's more of a Jason thing."

"Maybe we're trading places."

"You're saying that because you've always wanted to drive a fire truck, aren't you?"

She laughed, already feeling lighter. Jason always had that effect. "No thank you."

They sat in comfortable silence for a moment. "Thanks for telling me what's going on in your life," he said finally. "I felt like something was off. I wasn't sure what."

"Well, thanks for listening. My friends know about the breakup with Dom, but I haven't told them all the gory details about the business. It's humiliating. But I know you can keep things to yourself." Her gaze dropped to his upper lip, and lingered. His mouth had a nice shape to it, she noticed. The scar just enhanced his firm, full lines. No thin lips on Jason Mosedale.

"I won't say anything. It's your life."

That phrase rang a bell.

She remembered the last time they'd talked at their lockers, just before she left school early for her accelerated college program.

"You should pay more attention in class," she'd lectured him. *"Or you're going to end up running the cash register at the Quickie Mart. You're better than that."*

"What's wrong with the Quickie Mart? I like those little corn dogs they sell. The ones that rotate on little skewers, man, they're good."

"You're impossible." She'd grabbed the last emergency protein bar from her locker and tossed her lock in her backpack. *"It's your life. Good luck with your nowhere future."*

Her face heated again as she caught his eye over his glass of beer. She'd been pretty rude to Jason back then. Wrong, too. Being a firefighter wasn't a "nothing" future. He was very good at it, from everything she'd heard. Where had she gotten off telling him what his future was going to be?

"That was the last conversation we had before I left, wasn't it?"

He nodded with a wry look. "It had an impact, obviously."

She dropped her head into her hands. "I'm so sorry. I shouldn't have gone off on you the way I did."

He shrugged. "No worries."

"What do you mean, no worries? I had no right to come at you like that."

"It didn't bother me. I liked it."

"You *liked* it?"

"I figured you wouldn't bother if you didn't care. When I passed the firefighter exam, I wanted to rub your face in it. Seemed a little immature, though."

Oh, that twinkle in his eye, that dimple, that sexy quirk of his lips. No wonder he never had a problem lining up the next girl.

Rebound, rebound.

Shut up, Gina.

"Well, of course I cared. You have a scar thanks to me."

"Yeah, and thanks for that, too. Really. It's a great story. Girls love it."

Of course they did. The heroic kid diving in front of a pool cue to save someone else.

"As long as you keep my name out of it," she said lightly.

"It's permanently redacted. I'm pretty sure that mystery girl was just a summer tourist who couldn't handle her Jägermeister."

They both took a pause, and she realized that they'd been wrapped up in each other to such an extent that Mariano's was half empty now. The other firefighters had left. There was no sign of Galen. At the jukebox, someone put on an old country love ballad, which somehow made the lights seem dimmer. It all seemed calculated to create an atmosphere of intimacy, but it was probably just in her imagination. This was Mariano's, after all, not some hipster cocktail bar in Minneapolis.

And she and Jason didn't have that kind of vibe.

Except that he was looking at her as if she was a dessert he couldn't wait to savor.

"What are you doing?" she asked bluntly.

"What do you mean?"

"You're looking at me different."

"Different how?" He raised an eyebrow, but the look in his eyes didn't change.

"Sexy."

His lips curved slowly. "Are you saying I'm sexy? Or I think you're sexy?"

Oooh, that sounded like a trap. But she'd had enough beer that she stepped into it anyway. "Both?"

"Huh."

She waited, but he didn't add any details to that frustrating "huh." "That's it? That's all you have to say?"

"For now." He shrugged. "It's hardly big news that I think you're sexy."

He was wrong there. Her eyes widened. "It's not? Since when?"

"I always thought so. Ever since I knew what "sexy" meant. It's not so strange. Look at you." The warmth in his eyes embraced her, made her feel like a goddess. "I never thought it went the other way, though."

"Well..." She thought about it. Took another sip of beer. "It did. Sort of. I mean, I didn't think of you that way. But if I'd thought about it, I would have said you were sexy."

He tilted his head back and laughed. "Talk about a complisult."

She liked the way his throat muscles moved. He had a healthy layer of dark scruff covering his jaw. What would he smell like, right there, between his collarbone and his neck? Something told her that scent would please her. *He* pleased her, on a purely physical level.

But there was so much more to relationships than the physical. Your goals had to be aligned. You had to click on a mental level.

Not for a rebound.

He finished his beer, then grabbed his jacket and stood up. "Should we get out of here?"

"Wait. No. What are you saying? Don't you think that's a little presumptuous?"

He shot her an odd look. "I need to get home and make sure the intervention didn't turn into an emotional bloodbath. I can only handle so many sobbing teenage girls at a time."

Right. Of course. Her face felt warm again.

"I'll call you in a couple days. I'll pick Thomas' brain about the town manager job and let you know what he says."

She shook herself back to sanity. This rebound idea was absurd. Also, very bad. Rebounds were trouble. She didn't believe in them. Someone always got hurt. She didn't want that to be her, and she didn't want that to be Jason, either.

"Thanks, Jason. I owe you one. Stop by Alvin's any time and I'll set you up with a burger." She got to her feet as well, and edged her way past the table. They both headed for the exit.

Should they time their departures so that no one thought they were leaving together? No, there was no need for that. No one would put her and Jason together. They were two high school locker neighbors catching up, nothing more.

A tourist who'd had too much beer stumbled into her. Jason put his arm around her shoulders to pull her out of his path. A spray of heat shot through her body. It settled in her lower belly, a throbbing knot of awareness.

"I'm fine," she told him, trying to sound irritated. Did he notice the unusual shakiness of her voice? "Watch your step, mister," she told the tourist.

"*You* better watch *your*—"

"Okay, okay." Jason intervened, keeping his body between the two of them. "Lake Bittersweet Fire Department here. Keep it cool."

"Whatever." The man gestured recklessly as he turned back to the bar.

It wasn't until they got outside that Kendra realized he must have accidentally made contact with Jason's face. His lower lip was swollen.

"Jason Mosedale." She tugged him to a stop and touched his lip. "You have to stop getting injured on my behalf."

"Yes ma'am. I'll do my best. Wait. Does this mean you owe me another kiss? Because this'll be gone by tomorrow." He pointed at the bump on his lip and grinned.

"You're pushing it, Jaybone."

five

The "intervention" must have been really something. Jason surveyed the teenagers snoring away in the basement den. The six of them filled every sleep-worthy nook in the room. One girl—he couldn't tell who—was curled up in Rusty's dog bed with the old Irish Setter. Both were snoring.

The space reeked of popcorn and scented candles. He quickly located the candles and confirmed they were well away from any paper or cloth. Good thing he'd trained Holly on proper fire-prevention protocols.

Holly, who was sharing the couch, head to feet with Chloe, opened her eyes when Jason poked his head in the door.

She put a finger to her lips, lifted Chloe's draped arm off her leg, and carefully rolled off the couch.

In the dog bed, Rusty stirred, lifted his head, then dropped it back down as if the weight was just too much.

In the kitchen, Holly stretched and yawned. "What time is it?"

"Midnight. Did I stay away long enough?"

"Yes, but I thought you'd probably find someone to spend the night with," she grumbled through another yawn. "It's weird having you be so single."

"I'm sorry my love life isn't living up to expectations." He opened the fridge and poured himself a glass of ice water. "How'd the intervention go?"

"Not well, at first. Chloe accused us of being a bunch of Karens getting in her business. Some feelings were hurt on both sides. We talked through it. I mediated. Then we watched a horror movie. There was this girl playing the violin, and—"

"Hey. You know I can't handle that shit." It was a running joke with them that the big strong firefighter didn't like gory movies. The fact was, he saw enough upsetting things on the job, even in a small town like Lake Bittersweet. He didn't need them in his movies. Give him a fun action movie or a rom-com any day.

"Right. Anyway, we're all good now. We're talking about taking a camping trip next week."

"Is Chloe going to dump her boyfriend?"

"You mean her loser hookup who posts the worst memes in the multiverse? No. She had a point. It's her relationship. We all agreed to support her no matter what, but reserved the right to say 'I told you so' if they break up."

"Good negotiating."

"Right?" They exchanged a high-five.

He took a sip and let cold water slide down his throat. It felt good after all that conversation in the crowded pizza shop, trying to make himself heard over all the chatter.

Holly leaned toward him and sniffed. "You had pizza."

"No, just a beer." He gave a little laugh. "I forgot to order one, if you can believe it."

His sister eyed him suspiciously. She wore her favorite thread-worn sleep shorts and a t-shirt with a panda on it. "You must have been with someone fascinating. I know it wasn't Galen."

"If eccentric and fascinating are the same thing, it could be Galen. But it wasn't," he admitted. "I lost track of him early on."

"Then who?"

For some reason, he didn't want to tell her he'd spent the entire evening talking to Kendra. He loved his little sister, but she had opinions about everything.

He fudged. "An old high school friend."

"Girl or boy?"

"Do you have to be so binary about it?"

She laughed, since that was a conversation they had on a regular basis. In fact, her friend Kayla was a trans girl, and he'd gotten a front-row seat—or maybe front-row, off-to-the-side—to her experience.

"That means it was a girl. I approve. You've been moping around about Gretchen way too long. She was never right for you anyway."

Here we go, thought Jason with an inward sigh. How could Holly be so damn confident in her judgements? Had he been like that at her age? Maybe he had, but his opinions hadn't generally involved other people's relationships.

"I'm glad you approve. But there's nothing to approve of. It's not like that."

"Not like that..." She nibbled on a thumbnail, then balled her hand into a fist, since she was trying to break that habit. "Hm... interesting. A girl you went to high school with, so fascinating she made you forget pizza, but not someone you're hot for."

"I wouldn't say that," he murmured.

She pounced. "Then you are hot for her, but you aren't sure about her. I can't stand it. You have to tell me! Who? Who, who?"

"Why is there an owl in here?" A yawning Chloe shuffled into the kitchen in her Adidas slides and neon orange knee socks, a crocheted blanket wrapped around her. Hadn't he seen those knee socks on a different friend? They all seemed to exchange clothing all the time.

"I'm trying to get Jason to tell me who he just had dinner with," Holly explained.

"I had dinner with Galen. We fried up our trout. Fun time, and you know the best part? We stayed out of each other's business."

Holly blinked at him. The two of them didn't look much alike, other than the same dimple in their left cheek. She resembled their Irish father, while he took after their Argentinian mother. "Those words have no meaning to me."

Chloe propped her elbows on the kitchen island. "You know you're going to tell her eventually, so you might as well get it over with."

"Love it when you all gang up on me. Is that what the intervention was like?" He reached over and squeezed her shoulder. "I'm truly sorry."

"You have no idea." Her heartfelt tone made him laugh a little.

Kayla wandered into the kitchen. She wore a black hoodie that she'd unintentionally decorated with green paw prints when her cat got into an open container of body paint. "What's going on in here?"

"We're trying to pry info out of my brother, this won't take much longer. Just tell me what I want to know and we promise not to do an intervention on you."

Jason looked desperately for an exit, but they were all blocked by teenagers. Was this some version of hell? He sighed and gave up. It wasn't a secret anyway. Half of Lake Bittersweet had been at Mariano's. "I should probably get that in writing, but fine. I was talking to Kendra Carter."

Holly straightened up. So did Kayla and Chloe. They all

exchanged alarmed glances, then simultaneously shook their heads. "No. Oh no. You can't hook up with Kendra. If you even think about that, I *will* do an intervention," said Holly.

"*Excuse* me?"

He wasn't planning to hook up with Kendra. All they'd done was talk and, okay, maybe flirt a little. There had been chemistry, he wasn't going to lie. But knowing Kendra, it would never go any further. She wanted more than an ordinary firefighter.

But the hell if he was going to let his little sister tell him who he could and couldn't date. "Why not? Wait." He flung up one hand. "If you say one word against Kendra—"

"Why would I do that? Kendra's awesome. She comps us free burgers at the Blue Drake if we get an A on something."

"Yeah, and she gave me some purple Fudge hair color for my birthday, right after I came out, and it was like, the nicest thing anyone ever did for me. I mean, grownups. Not you guys," Kayla added quickly as Holly bristled.

"Kendra's the bomb diggity, so you can't go out with her right now," Chloe explained.

"Right." Jason nodded, hiding his hurt. They were just kids. No need to take it personally. "I'm not on her level is what you're saying. I know that."

"What? No, that's absolutely not what we're saying. You're still grieving your relationship with Gretchen. If you're going to have a rebound, it can't be with someone as great as Kendra. That's a waste!"

"A waste?" He was lost. Holly wasn't making any sense. "A waste of what?"

"Of a potentially solid relationship. You have to wait until you're ready, then you can date Kendra. There has to be a bridge relationship that leads you out of the depths of heartbreak back into a social life. But that person is just a springboard to the next relationship, the really good one."

"Jesus, Holly, where do you get this stuff? You've never had a single serious relationship." Bemused, he scratched at the back of his neck. All her theories seemed absurd to him.

"By choice. Which proves I take relationships seriously. You don't, and that's your problem. That's probably why Gretchen ditched you."

"Or it could have been because he's the classic commitment-phobe," said Chloe wisely.

"No, he's okay with commitment." Finally, his sister was actually defending him. "He's the only pseudo-parental figure who's still around. He just doesn't take things seriously."

"I take fires seriously." He felt compelled to point that out.

"Do you though? Didn't you just fill Brent's boots with glow-in-the-dark worms? They say people could hear his screams all the way from the lake."

"Pranks are a time-honored part of being a firefighter. They release tension, create unit cohesion, boost morale."

Holly clapped her hands together. "You've been prepping for your fire chief interview! Yes! You're going for it!"

"I still haven't decided," he said quickly. She'd been pushing him to apply ever since he first mentioned the possibility.

"See? If you really took things seriously, you'd already have that job. How do you expect someone like Kendra to want to date you—I mean, one girlfriend from now—if you don't even apply for a job that's perfect for you?"

"That's easy. I don't." He shrugged. Dating Kendra wasn't on his agenda. Or it hadn't been, until tonight.

"Booo." The three girls heckled him as he put his water glass in the sink and dodged around Kayla toward the stairs. "Scaredy-cat"... "cluck cluck"... "don't be a pussy" ... "Girl, pussy should be a compliment"...

He tuned them out as he hit the stairs.

But Holly had given him something to think about. *If you want to date Kendra...*

Did he?

Damn, he did. He really did. She was beautiful and brilliant and big-hearted and he found her absolutely fascinating. She thought he should apply for fire chief too. But would that really make a difference to her? He'd still be a small-town, simple-life guy. That wasn't going to change. If he wasn't good enough for her as he was...

Just do it. Push yourself. Take something seriously. Go for it. All the way. Prove to yourself you can do it.

Shocked, he stopped at the top of the staircase. That thought hadn't come from his sister, or from Kendra. It was all him.

Damn. He was going to do it. He was going for fire chief.

On his next day off, Jason went to visit Thomas Cooper, the former fire chief. He'd lost his job in a confrontation with the board of aldermen, then turned around and run for an open seat on the board—and won. He knew all about Lake Bittersweet town politics.

Thomas opened the door and put a finger to his lips. From upstairs, the faint sound of a lullaby drifted down. Carly must be trying to put Teddy to sleep. Making as little noise as possible, they tiptoed out to the redwood deck. It had a view of the lake, if you squinted past scrub pines and eelgrass. Laundry hung from a line strung from an upstairs window to one of the deck posts. It seemed to be filled exclusively with tiny onesies.

"Good to see you, man," Thomas said once they'd both settled into Adirondack chairs on the deck. An old apple crate served as a footrest. "Tell me something good. I need a distraction."

Jason cut right to the chase. "Is there any reason Kendra Carter shouldn't apply for the town manager job? She doesn't want to waste her time if she doesn't have a chance with our board of town fossils."

"No reason, if she really wants the job. Why would she?"

Jason shrugged. "She likes being in charge of things. She'd be good at it."

"If she likes pushing boulders uphill, she should go for it."

Jason texted that to Kendra, then looked up to find Thomas' penetrating gaze on him.

"How about you? Rumor has it you're considering going for my old job."

"Yeah. I might. I mean, I am." God, why was he stammering? It felt strange, saying out loud that he was aiming for fire chief. "I, uh, just filed the application this morning."

Thomas stretched his legs out and crossed them at the ankle. "What took you so long?"

"I know, I know. Took my time deciding, what can I say?"

"I'm serious. It's a serious question. What held you back? The aldermen are going to want to know if you really want it. They don't want to do a new search in a year."

Well shit. That wasn't the welcoming reaction Jason had expected. "I wasn't sure I was the fire chief type."

"And now you are?"

The edge in Thomas' voice made him draw back. "I hope so. I'm a good firefighter. The crew respects me. The community knows me."

"They know you as a friend. A jokester."

Jason drew in a breath. Maybe mentioning this to Thomas had been a mistake. He started to rise to his feet, but Thomas stopped him with hand on his arm.

"I'm giving you a taste of what you might get from the board of aldermen. They usually hire laterally, you know. They like people who already have some leadership experience. You're going to have to convince them you have what it takes."

He sank down onto the chair. This close to the lake, the earthy scent of thawing mud surrounded them. He had his mud boots with him in his truck; maybe he should get out of here and go cast a line. Stick to the simple stuff.

Thomas shot him a curious look. "Seems like you might have to convince yourself first."

He shrugged. "Maybe. I'm not like you. I'm just a guy."

"Bullshit."

That quick response took Jason by surprise. "Huh?"

"No one's 'just a guy'. But especially not you."

While Jason was trying to figure out how to respond to that, Thomas switched gears. "How are your parents doing?"

"Good. Yeah. Business is booming. Lots of hipsters in Minneapolis wanting to learn swing dancing and conga."

"You used to work for them, didn't you?"

Jason squirmed in his seat. He hadn't had a choice. His parents had needed him to play dance partner when there weren't enough men signed up for the classes, or an uneven number, or they simply wanted someone younger to help out.

Not that he didn't like dancing. He enjoyed it, and those skills had actually helped when it came to firefighting. Firefighting had an element of choreography to it, as well as coordination and controlled movement.

"Yeah. Until sometime in high school, when I didn't have time anymore. Why?"

"You could have taken over their business. That would have been the easy route. Becoming a firefighter ain't exactly easy. Especially with a learning disability. Makes the exam a lot harder."

Jason froze. A sense of shame flooded him. He'd tried so hard to hide it. He knew how to compensate. Some things, like reading, just took him twice as long. The upside was that once he'd read something, he knew it. There was no such thing as skimming for him.

"How did you know?" he managed.

"I just figured it out after a while. Don't worry, it's your business."

"Then why...why even..."

"Bring it up? Because I kept waiting for you to throw your hat in the ring, and you didn't. I wondered if had to do with your learning disability. I just want to point out that you became a firefighter by working twice as hard as most people. I admire that. You underestimate yourself."

Now he sounded like Kendra.

Thomas lifted his eyebrows, and Jason realized he'd mumbled that out loud. "Well, she's usually right. You should listen to her."

Jason let out a sigh and leaned forward, resting his elbows on his knees. Kendra knew a lot of things, but nothing about being a firefighter. She didn't know about his learning disability, either. He would have rather died than tell her.

"Seriously, Cooper, you think I can do the job?"

"Yes. But things would change. You'll have to cut back on the pranks and all that shit. You can't be one of the guys anymore. You have to set the tone. That's what leadership is all about. Some people are just natural-born leaders, but other people have to work on it, like a skill. I'm not sure which one you are. My theory," he squinted at Jason, "is that you're a leader in hiding. There's something holding you back."

A cry floated through the air. As they both looked up, an upstairs window was flung open. Carly poked her head out. She held a tiny black-haired baby against her chest. "I need a break," she called down to Thomas. "It's either a break or some vodka, and since I'm still breast-feeding..."

"On it."

Thomas leaped to his feet. Carly lifted a hand from her baby's back to give Jason a wave. He felt an almost proprietary concern for her little guy, because he'd been the one who took her to the hospital. She'd nearly fainted at the hardware store. He'd been picking up supplies for the firehouse, but abandoned that job and whisked her off to the hospital. It turned out that she was already in labor, and she'd been so busy wrapping up loose ends at the Blue Drake that she'd ignored the contractions.

"I'll show myself out," Jason called after him.

As he headed for his truck, he realized his gut was roiling with anxiety. He hated talking about his learning disability. And Thomas' mention of the dance studio...he hadn't thought about that in a long time. His parents had been so disappointed when he'd told them "no" to their offer.

"Querido, we really wish you'd reconsider. This business is perfect for you. It's entirely physical. You can hire someone to do the parts that are hard for you. You can hire an accountant, a front desk clerk, someone to keep records. All you have to do is spin around the room with one girl after another." His mother demonstrated with one of her graceful moves.

"Not so hard, is it, buddy?" His father gave him that big old charming smile that he beamed down at every woman he twirled across the floor.

"I don't want to run a dance studio. I want to do something different than that."

"Different how?"

He thought hard about how to put it. "Life-saving."

"Mi caro, you'd never get through medical school. This is not an option for you."

"I didn't say I wanted to be a doctor." But he wouldn't have minded it. Doctor, or maybe a nurse. *On camping trips, he was always the one who knew what to do if someone sprained their ankle or burned themselves on a smoldering log. He'd even splinted his buddy's broken arm after he'd fallen into a ravine. Then he'd helped get him up the rocks back onto the trail. Maybe he could be an ER doctor. He was good in a crisis. Everyone else freaked out, but he never seemed to.*

"You need to be realistic," said his father, serious now. "With your issues in school, you need to lower your expectations, son. Not everyone can be a superstar. Some of us just try to bring a little fun into the world. That's what we do. Why can't you be happy with that? Everyone loves you. Be happy with that."

Well, he was happy. But he'd also proven his parents wrong. Just like Thomas said, he'd done the work it took to become a firefighter, and he was really fucking good at it. But it was hard not to take those long-ago lectures from his parents to heart. *Not everyone can be a superstar. Some people are just here to bring a little fun into the world.*

Was that where it began and ended for him?

six

Kendra's first meeting with the hiring committee didn't go well. They kept coming back to her lack of experience planning big events.

"Let me prove I can handle it," she offered. "Give me an event. Any event. A square dance. A silent auction. A five-mile run. A blood drive. Anything. Watch me in action."

"Do you even know what events the town sponsors?" Betty Bannister asked. Betty was nearly eighty, which made her one of the younger members of the board.

"Of course I do." She'd rattled them off, starting with the iconic Sunburn Fest in May and going all the way through the Winter Carnival. "But I think we should have even more. If I get this job, I'll be researching more potential events for the winter season. I've already started a list. I know what it's like here in the winter, it's very bor—I mean, quiet. A lot of businesses struggle to make it to spring. There's no reason we can't be drawing tourists here year-round. It would be good for business, good for the tax base, good for the kids who grow up here."

She deliberately emphasized her local roots, since rumor had it her competitors were all from out of town.

They exchanged glances that ranged from impressed to amused. "You have a lot of energy and ideas, don't you?"

"I do." She paused. "I hope that's not a problem."

"No no, of course not."

But it was. She learned that fact when she ran into Jason at the SweetBitter Café. In his work pants and dark blue Lake Bittersweet FD t-shirt, he looked as delicious as the fresh pastries.

He told her that his spy had informed him that more than one member of the committee was worried that she might shake things up too much.

"Shoot. I should have known I was coming on too strong. I tend to do that when I'm nervous. Right before I went in, my mother called and warned me about that. I should have listened." She bit her lip as she took her blackberry muffin from Rick Sanchez, the café owner.

"No charge, buttercake." Rick blew her a kiss and a wink. "Not when you're looking so blue."

"Buttercake?" she murmured to Jason as they left the café and stepped into the heat of the last day in June. "I seriously can't tell if that's a compliment or an insult."

"Everyone loves butter and cake, so I'd go with compliment." His tall form paced easily next to her. Ever since that night at Mariano's, she'd been hyper-aware of Jason. Every time a fire truck rolled past, she perked up and checked to see if Jason was onboard. It was pretty ridiculous and made her feel like a teenager with a crush. She hadn't been like that with Dominic. They'd simply slid into a relationship as if it was destined.

"Should I have toned it down in my interview?" She broke off the top of the muffin, then offered the bottom part to Jason.

"No way. It's only the old relics who are afraid of change. The

62

other people on the committee think you're great. Just so you know, Thomas had to recuse himself from the decision because you're so close to Carly. But he's keeping tabs on it for me."

He took the muffin from her and looked at her oddly. "Something wrong with this part?"

"Yes. It doesn't have sugar sprinkles." She wrinkled her nose at him as she bit into the top. "Generally I give my muffin bottoms to my dad, because he's not supposed to eat too much sugar. But you're here, so..." She shrugged.

"Wow, can I get that on my tombstone? 'He was there, so...'" With a laugh, he bit into the muffin.

"Oh my God, I didn't mean it that way! You're much more than just 'there.' What I mean is, I wouldn't share a muffin with just anyone."

"Nice. A compliment for me, too. Thanks, Buttercake."

It occurred to her that she'd never offered half of a muffin to Dominic. For one thing, he didn't eat carbs. For another, he paid very careful attention to everything she ate, too, so she tended to only indulge in baked goods when she wasn't around him.

"So what should I do, Jason? You're good at that sort of thing. I'm open to advice, and believe me, I don't say that very often."

"What sort of thing are we talking about? Not muffins anymore?"

"The job. How can I get them to like me and want to hire me?"

"Why do you think I'd know?"

"Because people like you!" She gestured at the busy street, where the first tourists of the season mingled with locals running errands. "How many people have you said hello to while we've been walking?"

He shrugged, even as he waved at Mrs. Halliday as she pushed her folding shopping cart down the street. "Need a hand over there, young lady?" he called.

"Maybe later, smokeshow." She grinned from under her crocheted hat.

"*Smokeshow*?" whispered Kendra.

"Hey, I get nicknames too." They both laughed. "But what she's actually referring to is when I put out a grease fire in her kitchen, and I used the term 'smokeshow' to explain what was happening."

"Huh. So if I counted right, Mrs. Smokeshow over there was the seventh person you said hello to in the fifty steps we've taken between the café and here."

"It's a slow morning. A lot of people are sleeping in."

"How do you do it? How do you get all these people to fall at your feet?" She paused, thinking further. "Actually, that would be annoying. I just want the board to respect me enough to hire me."

"Kendra, believe me, everyone in this town respects you. You don't have to do anything. Just be who you are." He took a bite of the muffin bottom and chewed for a moment. "Didn't you offer to handle a big event?"

"Yes, but someone's already doing the SweetSummer Fest, which is the next one coming up."

"So add on to it. How about an outdoor concert at the Blue Drake?"

She stopped dead in her tracks and stared at the fireman next to her. "Jason, you are a freaking genius."

He laughed. "Funny thing to say to a guy you once tutored in history."

"Oh my God, I forgot about that."

He'd been struggling in the class, so she'd offered to help get his grade up. Then she'd been surprised by how interesting their discussions had been. He had no trouble with the concepts of the class. It was the amount of reading material that hampered him.

"You know," she said sternly, "there are many forms of intelligence that don't involve doing well in school. You probably have many of those."

He finished the muffin by popping it into his mouth. "Is snack acquisition intelligence one of them? I've got that."

"I'm pretty sure turning everything into a joke is a sign of *lack* of intelligence."

"That's too bad, since it's my superpower." His grin was so infectious, she had to laugh. They reached the corner where their paths would diverge, the Blue Drake one direction, the firehouse the other. She found herself slowing down so they'd have more time together.

"That concert idea is fantastic, but I'm not sure where I could find a band at this late date. Oh!" She snapped her fingers. "My dad's jam session group. Didn't you say you play with them?"

"Oh hell no." He backed away from her. After a quick check of traffic, he bolted across the street. "Byeeee!" he called from the other side, then disappeared inside the firehouse.

She laughed long and hard, then hurried in the direction of the Blue Drake. Her father was in charge of that group, and she could get a "yes" from him with a snap of her fingers. Being a daddy's girl had its advantages.

The biggest festival of the summer season in Lake Bittersweet, known as the SweetSummer Fest, was held on the first Saturday of July. The town always closed the downtown area to traffic, making room for food stalls and crafts tables and cotton candy and games and balloon animals.

As with all the town festivals, Alvin's Burgers and Blues planned to set up a grill to serve the world-famous Blue Balls Burgers. Alvin offered to cover the stand until it was time for him to perform at the concert she'd organized for that night. She'd found three local bands willing to play under the stars on the Blue Drake pier; her dad's group would be the headliner.

When he heard that news, Jason had sent her several texts that were basically all freakout emojis.

She sent back some chickens.

She had to admit, the rebound idea was getting more and more interesting. As an adult, Jason still had all the natural charm he'd possessed as a teenager who'd grown up in a dance studio, combined with years of experience with women. It was an incredibly tempting combination.

What if they just...talked about the possibility? What if they both went into it with eyes wide open, not expecting anything other than a temporary in-between sort of relationship?

She should see what he thought about it. She imagined the conversation. *"So, Jason, since we're both momentarily single and on the rebound, why not give it a try?"* God, that sounded terribly unromantic. She tended to be pretty practical when it came to relationships, but she wasn't calculating.

How about, *"Remember those two kisses I apparently owe you? Anytime you'd like to collect, I'm available."*

Ugh. There was no need for this amount of awkwardness. This was *Jason.* She'd made fun of the photo of Beyoncé he had pinned to his locker. They'd teased each other over everything from her favorite pre-exam snack (peanut butter crackers) to his attempt to grow a soul patch (disastrous.) *Get a grip.*

Bright and early on the morning of the festival, she ran into Jason in the firehouse parking lot, where she was delivering supplies for the Alvin's Burgers stand. He broke the news that he was on shift that night and therefore would not be playing trombone on the Blue Drake pier.

"Does being on shift include the traditional mandatory dunk tank?"

"Don't you wish." He grinned at her. "You dunked me twice last year. I haven't forgotten."

"It wasn't just me. Didn't you get awarded a prize for most times dunked?"

"Yes, which is why I opted out this year. If you want to dunk me, you'll have to meet me at the pier and do it yourself."

"You're on," she found herself saying. "Why don't you come by after the concert and we'll see what happens?"

See what happens? Not too suggestive.

Okay, pretty suggestive.

"Sounds good. I'm on shift until midnight." If he was surprised that they sort of had a date-ish kind of arrangement, he didn't show it.

"Midnight at the Blue Drake pier. See you then."

He flashed her a thumbs up, and she hurried back to her car. "Walking on air," wasn't that the phrase? That was how she felt, as if she was floating six inches above the pavement.

Not because of Jason, probably. How could someone she'd known since high school make her feel that way? It was probably because she had a plan to win over the hiring committee. She was going to invite them all to the outdoor concert and show them just how well she could pull off a last-minute event with many moving pieces.

And then she'd meet Jason at the pier and they'd...*dot dot dot.*

Kendra spent the rest of the day shuttling between the Blue Drake pier, getting set up for the night, and the Main Street pedestrian zone, to bring more supplies to her father. With a clipboard in one hand, earbuds in place, phone ringing nearly constantly, she was in her damn element. She looked so official that strangers kept asking her questions about bathroom locations and raffle prizes.

Were the aldermen watching?

Her biggest mistake so far was letting Alvin be in charge of the grill. Their stand was set up smack in the middle of Main Street and had by far the longest line, thanks to her father, who chitchatted amiably with each customer. Everyone in town loved her dad for his music, his kind nature, and his mind-blowing burgers, and of course they wanted to chat with him.

She loved him too, but she was also intensely proud of him and extremely protective. If her mom was around, she could keep him on track, but she was back in Arkansas taking care of Kendra's grandmother as she went through chemo.

It was up to her to explain to her dad that he needed to pick up the pace if they were going to break even on this event.

She slid into the booth, which was little more than a table on sawhorses and a portable propane grill. "Pop," she whispered in his ear. "You don't have to chat with every single customer."

"Well, why the heck not? Usually I'm back in the kitchen and don't get to see no one. This is good for marketing, sweet-pea. Don't you worry about it."

Even though she groaned, she had to admit he had a point. The whole purpose of the booth was to build community goodwill, and what better way than having her father shine his light on everyone he met?

"Fine. Have it your way."

"Wait. Don't leave yet. Want a burger?" He cast an apologetic look at the man at the head of the line, someone Kendra didn't recognize. "Sorry, mister, this here's my daughter and she's busy keeping everything going. Mind if I feed her real quick? It'll only take a minute."

The man nodded amiably enough, but Kendra picked up on his irritation. She wondered who he was. The SweetSummer Fest was a casual event, with flip-flops, shorts and sunglasses the most popular outfits. This guy was wearing a damn business suit and a tie. Tall, blond, impatient. Important. Whoever he was, he was used to being catered to.

"Pop, it's fine. I'm not hungry. I'll grab something from the kitchen." She beamed her best smile at the man. "You go ahead and order."

"Kendra, right?"

She gave a double-take. "Do I know you?"

"No, but Dominic said you'd—" Before he could say another word, Kendra grabbed him by the arm and hauled him off to the side. Any conversation involving Dominic needed to happen in private. Too many curious locals were wandering around.

"Who are you? How do you know Dominic?"

He smirked. "Still touchy about the breakup?"

"*Excuse* me?" Whoever he was, Kendra already disliked him.

"Dominic told me I should say hi if I saw you. So, hi. I'm Mark Jordan." He offered his hand, which she shook numbly. "My sister's married to his brother Liam."

She knew Liam Robb. He'd never liked her, and she'd never liked him. She could barely summon up an image of his wife, Amy. Blond, just like Mark. Very uninterested in anything to do with Kendra.

"What brings you to Lake Bittersweet, Mark?"

"I'm in town for a job interview."

A sinking feeling came over her. If he was going for the town manager job, she'd have to do something drastic. She couldn't bear it if this smug stranger got the job over her. "What's the job?"

"I'm a firefighter. This town's looking for a new fire chief. I'm pretty sure I have it in the bag. I'm overqualified, but I'm looking for a change of pace."

He smoothed his tie. Figured a friend of Dominic's would be wearing one to a festival.

This was even worse. Mark with the Tie was competing with Jason, not her. She had to tell him that he had some serious competition. He needed to step up his game if he was going to get the fire chief job. Jason was too laidback. Whit wore a blazer that fit him perfectly and had a smooth-talking manner that probably went over great at fundraisers and budget meetings. He was also pretty fit, broader in the shoulders than Jason, maybe a little bit taller.

How could Jason ever compete with someone like this?

"Well, Mark, as someone who grew up here, you should probably know that it's a tough place to live. The winters are *long* and they can be boring. If anything exciting happens, it's usually life-threatening. If you're looking for peace and quiet, that's not exactly what you get here. It's more like tedium and bad internet access."

"The wifi seems to work pretty well."

"Sure, now. But it often goes out in the winter. The snow can get so deep you have to ski out of your second-floor window." That had only happened once in anyone's memory, but it made for a good story. "And I hope you like burgers and pizza, because that's about all there is to eat in terms of restaurants after the summer ends."

"How's the pizza?"

"Excellent," she admitted. "So are the burgers, since my dad makes them. I'm just saying, the pace is really slow here, so you might want to look into a job in a bigger city."

Mark looked irritated. "I get it. You don't want me here. If this is because of the Dominic connection, I'll stay out of your way. Your breakup is your business."

It wasn't that. It was Jason. She didn't want him to lose out on the job he deserved. She didn't want some out-of-town dude cutting him out—especially one related to Dominic. She was Team Jason all the way. And when she was on someone's team, she went all out.

A scheme formed in her mind, the kind of thing she and her crew used to do back in those long-ago summer days. Did she still have it in her or had the breakup ruined her sense of adventure?

She thought about the pool hall, and Brooke, and WWBD.

"Not at all, Mark." She beamed her best smile at him. "How about I show you around town a little?"

seven

By the end of SweetSummer Fest, Jason had given so many tours of the ladder truck to local kids that he seriously considered riding his bike to the next fire. He was that sick of the thing. But it was always fun watching kids' faces light up when they got to try on a helmet or sit in the engineer's seat.

This stuff was right up his alley. If he became fire chief, he'd try to increase outreach to the younger population of Lake Bittersweet. Getting them involved in junior firefighter drills or painting projects at the firehouse could help keep kids out of trouble. Like a lot of small towns around here, there wasn't much going on and teenagers tended to get bored. And that was when bad things happened.

After his volunteer shift was through, he started his real shift patrolling the fair. He wandered through the crowded streets, sent a drunk tourist back to his hotel, broke up a fight between Dickie Brown and Sven Cavendish, who'd been feuding for the last sixty-seven years. He inhaled the scent of cotton candy, sunscreen, and the ever-present pine trees. Ah, summer. God, he loved Lake Bittersweet in the summer.

As night closed in, he decided to see how things were going down at the Blue Drake. Most people were headed that way anyway, drawn by the thump of the bass line reverberating down the street and off the brick-faced buildings. As he reached the back terrace, which looked out over the pier, he saw that the place was packed. He could barely see the band at the end of the pier through all the bobbing heads and raised Solo cups.

This party was hopping. Good for Kendra.

The night was soft as velvet. The violet remnants of the sunset lingered above the forest that surrounded the lake. The music floating over the water plucked a chord of joy deep within him. He wanted to dance, sing, swing someone around. He wanted that sparkle and fizz he felt only with Kendra.

The end of the Blue Drake pier had been transformed into a stage with a white canopy tent overhead in case of rain. He spotted Kendra near the far end of the pier, adjusting the position of a speaker, busy as always.

Glancing around, he saw mostly younger people. Would any of the aldermen get to see Kendra's hard work? Since their average age was seventy-nine, they might be done for the day.

He had to do something to help her out. If she got the town manager job, maybe she'd stay in Lake Bittersweet. It would take something big like that, something interesting and challenging, to inspire her to stick around.

And damn, he wanted her to stay.

On a mission now, he headed back to the main street, which had been closed off for pedestrians. *Find an alderman, any alderman.* He'd drag one out of their house if necessary.

Fortunately, he was spared from trespassing and kidnapping when he ran into Betty Bannister. He knew Betty from the swing dance lessons she used to take with her husband. The Bannisters were third generation Lake Bittersweeters and very influential in town politics. If he could get Betty on Kendra's side, she'd be a shoo-in.

Always the eccentric dresser, she wore a brocade vest over a billowing floor-length cotton muumuu. Her general vibe was "Bannisters can wear whatever we want."

He flashed her a grin along with a little bow. "Evening, Betty. What a great SweetSummer Fest. I had so many kids come through the ladder truck I could have opened a preschool."

"Well hello, Jason." She looked a little flustered under the full force of his smile. "It was one of our best fests yet, if you ask me. And try saying that fast three times in a row."

Betty had always had a quirky sense of humor. She reminded him a little of his infamous Irish grandmother, though he'd never tell her that.

He presented his elbow to her. "Are you headed my way? I'm going to check out the Blue Drake concert. Looks like just about everyone in town's headed down there."

"Well, with an offer like that, how could I say no?" She tucked her hand into his elbow and they strolled down the sidewalk. The volunteer cleanup crew fanned down the street, picking up trash. "Mind you, I have nothing to do with the fire chief decision. I'm not on that committee."

He laughed at her wry warning. She had no idea that he'd forgotten all about his own job goals, and was totally focused on helping Kendra achieve hers. "Yes, I do know that. I'm not trying to win your vote. Although I'd be a damn good fire chief."

"I'm sure you would. A very handsome one, too."

"You're a flirt and a menace, Betty Bannister." A group of kids darted past them, racing toward the Blue Drake, waving balloon animals they'd picked up at the fair. He steadied her against the flow of young people.

"Thank you, " she said. "Now why don't you tell me what you're up to, young Jason?"

"Up to?"

Glancing down at her, he caught her knowing gaze. He should have known he couldn't fool Betty.

"I guess I'm busted. I do have an agenda. I wanted you to see what a great job Kendra Carter did putting the concert together. She's going for the town manager job, you know."

"Oh, I know." Her tone didn't sound promising. "She's a real go-getter, isn't she?"

"Yes. She's also smart and hardworking and dedicated. She'd be great for that job."

"I'm not so sure." Betty picked her way past an abandoned balloon animal. Was it a goat? A hippo? Hard to tell. "How do we know she wouldn't use the job as a stepping stone to something bigger? Kendra has always been ambitious."

"Well..." Jason was at a loss for words. "Isn't that how jobs work? Do you want her to commit to the position for the rest of her life?"

"No, no, of course not. But look at you. You've lived here all your life and never shown any inclination to go anywhere else. You're committed to this town. Kendra, on the other hand, has been away more than she's been here."

"That's a good thing. She's learned things out there in the big wide world."

"But we don't want those things to come here. We like our boring little town the way it is."

Resistant to change, he realized. She probably wasn't the only one. His heart sank. Kendra would be up against some powerful forces, and those wouldn't go away even if she got the job. Did she know what she was taking on?

"If Kendra commits to a contract, she'd never walk away."

"You sound very confident in her."

"I am. I've known her a long time."

"Well, I'll take that under advisement. Now why don't you show me what your girl can do."

"She's not my girl. Kendra is her own woman."

"Everyone's so independent these days," Betty grumbled. Jason wondered if he should have fed her some cotton candy to get her blood sugar up before dragging her to the pier.

He led Betty to a spot on the terrace with a view of the pier and the white canopy tent adorned with fairy lights. "Notice the tent? Kendra thinks ahead and plans for all possible problems. She knows there's always a chance of rain around here."

"My goodness, you really are a fan, aren't you?"

A swing band was playing a fast-paced song, and a few couples were dancing along the length of the pier. Others milled around on the terrace and the back lawn; there were even a few people listening from their boats. The strings of fairy lights scattered sparkles across the surface of the lake. The atmosphere was pure magic.

He felt his feet move automatically to the music. That was what happened when you grew up in a dance studio. When he noticed that Betty was tapping one ballet-slippered foot, he offered her his hand. Just like the old days in his parents' studio, he swung her in a gentle two step.

As they danced, he scanned the crowd for Kendra, but didn't see her. Maybe she was inside somewhere, getting the next band ready for their slot.

Nope—there she was. He finally spotted her close to the stage, in the company of a tall blond stranger in a business suit, of all things. The guy looked absolutely wasted. He was swaying to the music, completely missing the beats. He kept sipping from a large clear plastic cup.

And Kendra....well, she kept filling it up from a flask stashed in her back pocket.

He squinted at them in confusion. Since when did Kendra

push alcohol on people? That wasn't her way. She was usually the one cutting customers off as soon as they showed any hint of being impaired.

Was she deliberately trying to get this guy drunk? It seemed so, but he couldn't imagine why.

Sure enough, as he watched, Kendra added another splash of liquor to the stranger's cup. Was it someone she was dating? Hadn't she told him that things had ended with her ex, and that she was still recovering?

The stranger was getting sloppier. The way he danced looks more like a full-body spasm. Every step he took brought him closer to the edge of the pier. Even though it had a railing, people had been known to go over the edge and end up in the lake.

"What are you looking at?" Betty asked. He realized he'd come to a standstill. "Oh my, is that Kendra?" She dug in her quilted cross-body bag for her glasses, and peered through them at Kendra and the stranger. "What *are* they doing?"

The stranger's foot hit the edge of the pier. He windmilled his arms to catch his balance, but he was too drunk to manage it. His hip hit the railing. Good, at least he wasn't going overboard.

"Look at that, Kendra's got it under control," he said. "Of course she does. That's Kendra for you."

"Noooo..." said Betty, squinting to see better. "She's...oh dear, I don't think she's helping."

Jason saw it too. As she pretended to applaud the band, she took a step backwards, then deliberately jammed an elbow into the stranger's ribs and boom, his butt hit the railing and he toppled over it, plunging head over heels into the cold lake water.

He surfaced right away, coughing and shouting. Swearing, mostly. Dammit, Jason knew he should go help him. He was on shift and it was his job. But that lake water still hadn't heated up to its peak-of-summer temperature.

Nothing to it but to do it. He heaved a sigh. "I'll be right back," he told Betty.

"Did you see that?" As he moved to go, Betty grabbed at his arm. "Kendra pushed him off the pier! That doesn't seem very professional to me."

"I wouldn't put it that way..."

"I know what I saw. She shoved him off with her elbow. It was a hit job."

"A hit job? Shit, I gotta go."

The man was spouting water out his mouth as he flailed around. Good God, did he not know how to swim? He definitely wasn't a local, because everyone in Lake Bittersweet grew up knowing how to handle a plunge into the lake.

Jason jogged down the pier, stripping off his outer layer as he went. "Fire department, coming through," he called so everyone would get out of his way.

"Help!" the man in the water screamed. "Someone help me! I'm drowning!"

"Dude! It's not that deep! You're not going to drown!" Kendra called to him.

"What the hell?" Jason murmured to Kendra as he ran up alongside her. Her eyes were wide and shining with mischief.

"You can practically touch the bottom here! He's being ridiculous."

"Help!!"

Jason stripped down to his t-shirt then he executed a smooth dive into the water, landing a safe distance from the splashing man overboard. Goddamn, it was cold. He gave himself a moment for his breath to catch up with the shock.

"Here! Over here, you moron!" the stranger yelled, as if Jason had missed the mark and was supposed to land directly on top of him.

"Don't panic, I got you. I'm a firefighter. Stop moving your arms like that, you're only making things worse."

In a moment, Jason had him in a lifeguard's hold and was frog-kicking toward the shoreline. The onlookers broke into applause as the two of them staggered onto the pebbly beach, where the man collapsed into a shivering heap. "Firefighter, you said?"

"Yeah, but around here we end up doing our fair share of water rescues too. You okay, man?"

"Looks like I'm alive." He shuddered and wrung lake water from his tie. A tie. Who was this guy, anyway? He looked up at the audience lining the dock, and gave a resigned sigh. "Not a great first impression. Tell me something, firefighter. Who's up there? Anyone important?"

Weird way to put it. Wasn't everyone important? "Much of the town," he told the drenched stranger. "It's okay, no one's going to hold it against you. You wouldn't be the first to drink a little too much and end up in the lake."

The man shook water from his hair. "Help me up, man. I need to say a thing or two to that bitch up there. She fucking knocked me overboard."

"Oh yeah? How much have you had to drink? Should we check your blood alcohol level?"

"I'm sobered up now," he growled. But his attempt to get to his feet went nowhere except back on his ass.

Jason put some steel in his voice. "I'll help you stand up, but don't go picking any fights. Just go back to wherever you're staying and take a shower. That's my advice."

The man took a swing at him—he really got aggressive when he was drunk—but Jason caught his arm by the wrist. "You'd really better get a grip on yourself, dude. Around here, fire-fighters are frontline law enforcement. I can bring you in to the lockup if you keep acting like an idiot."

"Are you threatening to arrest me?" he hissed. "You're going to regret that when I'm your new boss."

"*What?*"

"New fire chief. You're looking at him."

Jason watched him stagger upright, then lurch toward the terrace. At least he wasn't going in Kendra's direction anymore.

So they'd gone and hired someone without even giving Jason a chance to interview. Sharp disappointment shot through him as he slowly got to his feet. Now that it was off the table, he realized that he really, desperately, wanted the fire chief job.

What did that guy have that he didn't?

Well, a silk tie, for one.

A gut full of lake water, for another.

"Jason!" Betty called his name as she clambered down from the terrace to the beach. "I saw everything, and I have some questions."

eight

Kendra had never seen Jason like this before. Usually he was so even-keeled. But now he was pacing across the dock, prickly energy pouring off him. It had taken an hour to break down the stage after the last performer wrapped up at ten. The concert had been wonderful, a smash success. Everyone in town had enjoyed themselves—except for a certain unwelcome stranger. And she knew for a fact that Betty Bannister had witnessed her triumph.

"So you got him drunk, then made sure he fell off the pier, am I getting that right?"

"Yes! While I was showing him around town, he told me he didn't know how to swim, and to me, that should be a deal breaker for anyone trying to be fire chief in Lake Bittersweet. But how would the hiring committee ever find that out beforehand? Now they know!"

Watching his awkward plunge into the water had been extra sweet because of his connection to Dominic. If only she could have pushed *Dominic* off a pier. It was wildly empowering.

"He could have been hurt."

"I knew he wouldn't, the water's not that deep. And the entire town was right there. And then you rescued him, and it couldn't have been more perfect!" She clapped her hands together, still fizzy with glee. "He looked like a clown and you looked like a hero."

"So you did this for me?"

"Yes. You're welcome. Believe me, no one's going to want to hire a fire chief who got drunk on his first night in town and fell overboard. There's absolutely no way he's getting the job now."

"Does he know that?"

She took his hand, noticing that it was still chilled from his time in the lake. She didn't regret what she'd done. Jason deserved a little boost. And Mark deserved a dip. Win-win, and she'd pulled it off flawlessly. The only downside was that she'd had to stay close to him all evening to keep putting vodka in his drink. It was worth it, knowing that Dominic's smug jerk of a relative was going to end up in the water.

So very satisfying.

She smiled up at Jason, wondering when he'd stop fretting and start praising her. Why was he so upset? Maybe it was because his public safety sensibilities had been offended.

Fair enough.

"I knew he'd be fine," she said again. "In the entire history of Lake Bittersweet, no one has died from falling off the dock."

He scrubbed a hand through his hair. "That's not the problem."

"Okay, what then?"

"Betty saw you push him. We were dancing together. I brought her *specifically* so that she'd see what a great job you did with the concert. Then you screwed it all up with that stunt."

Her heart plummeted right down to her feet. How on earth had Betty spotted her little maneuver? No one else had noticed. "Are you sure?" she managed.

"Yes. She said, 'did you see what Kendra did?' And then she used the word 'unprofessional.'"

Kendra gasped, since she could barely imagine a worse insult. "*Unprofessional?*"

"Or 'not very professional,' something like that. I tried to play it off, but she knew what she saw. She *lectured* me." He kicked at a loose plank on the pier. "I should never have brought her to the concert. Fuck me. I was trying to help you."

"I was trying to help *you!*" Butterflies rampaged through her stomach. How badly had she messed up? Could she explain it away somehow? Claim it hadn't been intentional, just a random arm spasm?

Then the irony of the situation sank in. "Wait. I was trying to help you. You were trying to help me. We were both trying to help each other, and we both totally screwed it up?"

They gazed at each other in the starlight. He looked gorgeous to her, the planes of his face molded in light and shadow, his eyes a dark shimmer.

At the same moment, they burst out laughing.

"We couldn't have planned it worse," he said.

"A perfectly executed disaster," she agreed.

They laughed until Kendra felt tears squeeze from her eyes. She remembered all the times she and her crew of fellow chambermaids had laughed like that on this very spot. The Blue Drake pier had been their favorite place for sunbathing and goofing around.

Something shifted inside her, a kind of tension releasing. She hadn't known she'd been carrying it—or maybe she had, but she'd gotten so used to it that she didn't think about it any more.

"I guess all you can do is laugh about it," she finally said, wiping her eyes.

"Pretty much my motto in general."

Spent from her laughter and the long day of scrambling, she

sat on the pier and rested her back against a post. Jason stretched out on his back, crossing his long legs at the ankle and interlacing his hands behind his head so he could look up at the stars.

"Nice night for a disaster," he murmured.

She tilted her head back and took in the panorama of merrily sparkling stars overhead.

"Yeah, if you're going to torpedo two careers in one night, why not make it a pretty one?"

He chuckled softly. "You know something, even if I do end up with a boss who has a grudge against me, it was worth it. The one and only Kendra Carter tried to help me. That's almost better than getting the fire chief job."

She stuck out her foot to poke him in the thigh. "Don't say that. You deserve that job."

He turned his head to look at her. "You think people always get what they deserve?"

"No. Obviously not. But they get what they fight for. Sometimes." She could think of many examples of that not happening. "How about, you don't get what you don't fight for."

"Unless you're part of the good-old-boy network. Then you get what you suck up for."

"Wait wait wait. Aren't you part of any network like that?"

"Me? Why would I be?"

"You know. White boy that everyone likes."

"First of all, I'm not all-white. My father is, but my mother's half-Argentinian. She grew up in Buenos Aires."

That explained his dark good looks. "How'd she end up here in Random, Minnesota?"

"She met my father on a movie set. She was an extra, and he was a stuntman from LA. They were filming a dance scene. One dance together, and that was it. When they first moved here, it was really hard for my mom. The whole Scandinavian Minnesota-nice vibe is very different from how she grew up.

They'd bought the dance studio sight-unseen and were kind of stuck with it. Stuck *here*. For most of my life, until they finally figured out how to run the business, they had no money. Between that and," he broke off, as if he'd been about to say something he wasn't ready to, "my school struggles, I always felt like an outsider. So I compensated by being Mr. Likable. That doesn't make me part of any network, though."

There were so many things about Jason that she hadn't really paid attention to, she realized. That easy smile hid so much. She wanted to know more. She wanted to challenge him.

"Okay, as a dude of some color, here's the million-dollar question. Do you think there's any racism here? Like, racism that might keep me from getting that job?"

"Ooh, the 'r' word. People don't like to use that word around here." He laughed. "What do you think? You're Black, you grew up here."

"I already know what I think. I want to know what you think."

"Why do I feel like this is a trap?" He groaned and stretched his arms over his head, then sat up. "Okay, here goes. Yes, it's a mostly white world here. So that's the starting point. Everything's tilted toward white. On an individual level, I'd say most people in Lake Bittersweet take a person as they are. They judge according to your actions. But not everyone. One old geezer didn't want me coming on his property even though his freaking shed was on fire."

"That's messed up."

He nodded in agreement. "It hurts when that shit happens. So yeah, I think there's some racism, but no, I don't think it'll keep you from getting the job. The fact that you pushed the new fire chief in the lake might be a bigger issue."

She groaned. "Don't remind me."

He whooshed out a long breath and gave her a nervous look. "Well, how'd I do with the R word?"

"Not bad, Jaybone. Not bad."

"Really?"

"Yes, I basically agree. My parents had some hard moments when they first moved here. But my dad says most people here are down-to-earth and fair-minded. He says he still keeps his guard up sometimes, but not as much."

"What about you? You keep quoting your dad."

"Hmm." She let her eyes drift half-closed as she thought about it. The wind off the lake felt like a cool breath on her face. The moon was just starting to rise over the pines to the west. Such a beautiful night, and here they were talking about "the r word."

Funny. Especially when you considered that she'd had a very different "r word" in mind.

Jason stretched out on his side so he could watch her. He was so sexy with his long limbs and relaxed manner. Like nothing could really faze him. What did it take to become that comfortable with yourself—and with the rest of the world? She had no problem loving herself. Her parents had instilled that in her from an early age. But sometimes she struggled with some of the bullshit out there.

"To be honest, it pisses me off that we even have to have a conversation like this. I wish racism never existed. Or that it's like thinking the Earth is flat. Like you can't understand why anyone ever believed that."

"Damn right. I bet we'll get there. I don't know when."

"Maybe next week?" she said hopefully.

As he laughed, she watched his chest rise and fall. She wanted to touch him, but she resisted the urge.

"It's weird, but it feels good to talk about this stuff," he said.

"I don't usually have conversations like this. We tiptoe around it, all Minnesota-nice."

"Maybe that's part of the problem. Isn't it better to talk about it?"

"There you go, being right again. Damn you, Kendra Carter."

"Shut up." With a laugh, she reached forward to swat him on the chest. The desire to touch him was just too irresistible, and this seemed like the perfect excuse. His chest was hard and muscular, just as she'd imagined.

When she tried to withdrew her hand, he caught her wrist and kept it where it was. "Where are you going?" he murmured.

"I don't know. Where are you going?"

"Wherever you are." He grinned at her. God, he looked good in the starlit darkness. He was like liquid sex poured into a six-foot body. "By the way, I always liked it when you got riled up. It was hot."

"Oh, you thought it was hot?" Her heart was doing this odd skipping thing that made her voice sound husky. "Even when I was lecturing you about studying harder?"

"Especially then. Because you'd be aiming those gorgeous eyes at me. You have the brightest eyes in the world, do you know that?"

"They're basically...brown. Dark brown."

"No. They shine and sparkle and glow. It's like there's all this fire inside you, and it's right there in your eyes. It's a beautiful thing."

Wow. She'd been complimented before, of course, but never in such a heartfelt way. Jason had a sincerity about him that Dominic, for instance, couldn't begin to imitate. "Thank you. That's...nice."

Her hand was still pressed against his chest. She felt the steady thump of his heartbeat. The same rhythm seemed to echo in her own eardrums, as if their systems were synchronizing with each other. "You're welcome. But it's just the truth. You're a star, Kendra Carter. You always were."

She scooted closer to him, curled herself into the shelter of his stretched-out body, and rested her elbow on his hip.

"You know, sometimes you sound like you had a crush on me in high school."

"I wouldn't say that. I looked up to you. I thought you were incredible. But it wasn't really a crush. Maybe I would have, but there was…"

"Gretchen." She finished the sentence for him. She'd almost forgotten about Gretchen. But of course he hadn't. He was probably still in love with her. You didn't switch gears that fast.

"Yeah. And, you know, she had sex with me." He grinned widely. "It's hard to beat that when you're a teenager."

"You were each other's firsts?"

"Yes. Ironically, that was one of our problems. FOMO. You know, who else is out there? What are you missing out on by staying with the first person you sleep with? I mean, it works for some people, obviously. In the end, I guess we just didn't love each other to that extent."

"I always thought you'd get married and have a bunch of kids by now."

"Yeah. I can see why you would think that. But no. I hope she gets pregnant soon," he added thoughtfully. "She always talked about wanting kids. And I was always like, yeah, sure, someday. I guess she got fed up with me."

"So you don't want kids? I'm confused."

Amazing how this conversation was covering all kinds of ground. Usually she avoided the big topics in the early stages of getting to know a guy. But of course, this was different. She knew a lot about Jason already, and besides, this wasn't on track to be a "relationship." If it was going to be anything, it would be strictly a rebound.

"Sure. Kids are awesome. I have a niece and two nephews, they're pretty great, plus I work with kids a lot. I guess I just don't plan ahead like that. When it's time, I figure I'll know."

And that was one huge difference between them. In her book, the more you could plan for the future, the better. Too bad her biggest and best plan, the business with Dominic, had blown up in her face.

But none of that mattered when it came to her and Jason. This was nothing but a..."rebound," she said out loud.

"Excuse me?"

Welp, she sure had blurted that out of nowhere.

"Just wondering if it's the only relationship terminology that's also in basketball. You know, just randomly. Apropos of nothing."

He scanned her face in the darkness. She lifted her chin to hide her unaccustomed embarrassment.

"It's not."

"Huh?"

"It's not the only one. There's also 'slam dunk.'"

nine

Jason watched that sassy smile spread across Kendra's face. The moon had risen enough so that he could see her more clearly. Her eyes were still full of fire, but it was a softer glow than usual, banked embers instead of a brilliant flame.

"Are you saying you're a slam dunk?"

"Nothing but net, baby."

Holly would be furious with him, but he didn't care. She was only seventeen, she didn't know everything. If there was any chance of something with Kendra, he was going for it.

"Okay, but we should talk about it first."

"We've done a lot of talking already," he pointed out. They'd covered a lot of ground, too, topics he didn't usually discuss. He was starting to get cold on the dock out here after midnight.

"I mean about, you know, being on the same page. Our situations aren't so different. We both recently broke with someone we were serious about. Neither of us is recovered. I know I'm not. Do you know I looked up the definition of a 'rebound?'"

"Why does that not surprise me?" he murmured.

She made a face at him. "It means getting into a new relationship before you've totally recovered from your last breakup. In other words, it's doomed to failure because you're still all messed up. But at least it's something."

"Wow. And you thought of me. I'm so flattered." His dry tone didn't quite hide his hurt.

"Boy, don't act all wounded. We both deserve love and a solid, long-term relationship. But are you ready for that right now? Aren't you still mourning over what happened with Gretchen?"

"Yeah. I saw her the other day with her husband and had actual fantasies about how I could sabotage their fancy-ass boat. It got quite specific. Rope in the engine prop, that kind of thing."

"There you go. I have the same thing. Except in my case, it's more like I schedule a meeting with his new bosses and present them with a PowerPoint of all the reasons they shouldn't trust him."

"I bet it's very comprehensive."

Her lips quirked in amusement. "You know it."

"Okay, so, revenge fantasies. Check. What's your point?"

"That we're not fully recovered. Either of us. We're both in a rebound-prone phase. But maybe that works out better. If we're both on the rebound, then neither of us can really get hurt."

"How do you figure?" He couldn't wait to hear her explanation for that theory. The way her mind worked, it was really something. Those wheels were always turning.

"It's like this." She sat up, and he instantly missed the warmth from where she'd propped herself against his hip. "In a rebound, part of your heart is still with the previous relationship. Therefore it can't get as hurt if the new one goes wrong." She brushed her hands together briskly. "And I know neither of us is trying to get hurt again."

Fair enough. Jason had no idea if her theory was correct or not. But he wasn't going to argue. Kendra was the kind of person who wanted lots of logical reasons for anything she did. Him, not so much. He didn't analyze things the way she did. Of course, that probably meant they weren't a good match, but for the purposes of a rebound, did it matter?

"What else did you find out about rebounds?"

"What else?"

"Benefits, pitfalls, that sort of thing. I know you. I bet you dug deep into that research."

"Of course I did." She cocked her head with that "take on the world" attitude that he would always associate with her. "Are you sure you want to hear it?"

"Why wouldn't I?"

"Well, if you're not considering it, why waste your—"

"I want to hear it," he said firmly. How could she possibly think he wasn't considering it? Had she missed the "slam dunk" reference?

"Okay. It's complicated, like everything emotional. A rebound can be very healing, as long as you're aware that you're in a rebound, and that you're still trying to work through things from the previous relationship."

"So calling it a rebound right off the bat is a good thing."

"It might be." Her lips curved in a smile. It reminded him that she still owed him two kisses. Couldn't they kick off this rebound with those? Like, soon? But she was Kendra, and Kendra approached things a certain way. With a lot of analysis and preparation. He could be patient. "The downside is that a rebound can prevent you from learning everything that the breakup could teach you. Breakups can be important growth experiences."

"Fuuuck that." His heartfelt exclamation had her laughing.

"I hear you. When I first read that, I had the same reaction. But seriously, they can be. Sitting with negative emotions, learning to be alone again, being independent. I mean, if I'm going to get dumped, I want to ninja that shit into being a better, stronger woman."

He burst out laughing. Who else besides Kendra would insist on maximizing the growth potential of her breakup? And by the way, who on earth would break up with someone like her? Whoever this Dominic was, he hoped never to meet him, because he'd have a hard time keeping his insults to himself.

"I don't mind being alone. It's just that it doesn't happen very often."

"Because there's always another woman ready to step in?"

He nodded, then added a wry shrug. "Maybe there's a man shortage in Minnesota."

"Oh stop. You know you're a catch. Name me one cute fireman who has trouble finding a girl."

Did he mind being reduced to a "cute fireman"? Nah.

"But seriously, Jason, did you ever think that maybe you're in a constant loop of rebounds and it's preventing you from really going deep?"

"Damn, Kendra." He tugged her arm, destabilizing her so she tumbled on top of him. "Can't we put the therapy session on pause and get to the good stuff?"

She smiled down at him with those brilliant eyes that seemed to gather all the starlight and shine it back just for him. "We can. But should we?"

He cupped her face in his hands. Her skin felt like lush velvet. "You might be overthinking this. We're both available. I'm crazy attracted to you. You just called me a cute fireman. We're both grownups who can decide if we want to take a chance or not."

Tentatively, ever so lightly, as an experiment, he brushed his lips against hers. He just wanted to know what that contact would feel like. Her lips were so beautifully shaped, so generous with their laughter and their moods. He'd seen them tighten when she was upset, lift with scorn when something irked her, quiver when she was trying not to laugh. Now he wanted to see what they felt like.

So soft, and so so sweet. Her lips parted against his and he felt her warm breath. Kendra was such a self-possessed person that maybe he'd expected something different, nothing but strength and confidence in her kiss. But she was just as tentative as he was, as if they were both taking a tiny baby step across quicksand. Just feeling it out. Is it safe? Is it worth it?

Safe was debatable. "Worth it" wasn't.

He touched his tongue to her pillowy upper lip. Her taste made him think of the top-shelf brandy he'd sneaked from his parents' liquor cabinet as a kid. Not because of the rich flavor, but because of how *adult* it felt, how new and intoxicating. Maybe it was just a kiss, but he was sharing it with *Kendra*, and that put it in a category all its own.

She pressed against him, parting her lips so his tongue slipped inside. The heat and sleek wetness of her mouth made him dizzy.

Adrenaline coursed through him, all the way to his fingers. He was still cupping her cheeks and he wondered if she could feel the energy zapping from his fingertips. He felt alive and energized and ready to tumble her onto her back and strip the clothes off her beautiful body.

Get a hold of yourself, he scolded. But it was hard. He hadn't felt this kind of wild desire for a long time. *Ever?*

A moment later, they were kissing each other with a kind of franticness that made him forget they were in a public place. He plunged his hands into her hair, loving the way her soft natural curls felt against his palms. Kendra could be very creative in how she wore her hair, and he always admired that, but for now, for tonight, he was glad it was loose so he could immerse himself in the sensual texture.

She was still lying partly on top of him, partly on the dock.

He gathered her against him to cushion her from the wooden planks. She murmured something against his mouth, and eagerly fitted her body against his. What had she said? Did it matter? As long as neither of them was stopping, she could recite the Declaration of Independence for all he cared.

But the next time she murmured, he reluctantly dragged his mouth away from hers. "What?" he managed.

"You really know how to kiss."

"You interrupted our flow for some commentary?" As the lust cleared from his vision, he laughed. He stroked his hands down her back, reveling in each delicious curve.

"Yeah, I'm annoying like that." Her rueful tone made him think she'd gotten that complaint before.

"It's not annoying. One thing about Kendra Carter, she's always going to have something to say. And it's always going to be worth hearing."

Her eyes gleamed down at him, more dazzling than the panorama of stars behind her. "No wonder you get all the girls. You know just what to say."

He didn't respond to that, because it didn't really sound like a compliment. Maybe it was one of the dreaded compli-sults. And besides, it wasn't accurate. He was saying what he thought, what he knew to be true. Why did she have to turn it around on *him* like that?

"Sorry," she murmured. "I don't mean to make you sound like a man-slut. I know it's not like that."

"Good, because it's really not like that. Even if I date a lot, it doesn't always end up in bed or in a relationship."

"It doesn't?"

"No. I mean, you have to find out if the chemistry is there. Sometimes it is, sometimes it isn't. Then you have to find out if it's going to be fun hanging out with someone or not. Usually, one of those things doesn't pan out and we agree to not take it any further."

She was quiet for a moment as she scanned his face. "So where do we fall?"

"How about we kiss some more and then have more commentary and decide?"

Her gorgeous smile flashed across her face. That smile could light up the entire lake. "Have you always been this funny? Never mind, don't answer. You have. You always made me laugh. I used to think, it's a good thing my locker is next to his because it helps me start the day off with a smile."

"Awww. That deserves another kiss, don't you think?"

"Okay, but that'll be two. That's how many I owe you. Anything more than that, you'll have to work for."

"I am up to that challenge."

The next kiss, he didn't start slow. None of the gentle brush of skin on skin. He dove deep right away, devouring her mouth, twining tongue against tongue, tasting, savoring, arousing. He felt her body move against his, a slow grind that brought his cock to immediate hardness. He'd been aroused the entire time, but that firm pressure of her hips made the blood surge into his erection.

Her breasts pressed against his chest. Full and generous, so close but so far, trapped behind her jacket and her top. If he could just...he slid his hand under her clothing and touched the smooth living satin of her skin. A silent sigh escaped him, an acknowledgement that this was where he'd longed to be for some time now.

Maybe ever since she'd gotten back from Minneapolis and he'd spotted her laughing with Gina Moretti in the pasta aisle of the grocery store.

Want. The emotion had flashed through his brain with no warning.

And now here he was, his hand sliding around the curve of her breast. He was breathing in the heady scent of her skin, savoring the pressure of her thigh against his bulge.

Want. More. He moved to fill his hands with her breasts, desperate to find her nipples, which perked against his palms with a quickness that thrilled him. His breath clogged in his throat and images cascaded through his brain. He wanted her clothes off, her breasts exposed to his greedy gaze, his mouth on her nipple—

A sound from somewhere out there, somewhere not in the intimate space between the two of them, snagged his attention.

Someone was on the lake. Yodeling? Catcalling?

He pulled away from her with a gasp and put his finger to her parted lips. "I think someone noticed us."

"Do I even care?" she asked, adorably breathless.

"You will tomorrow. Especially if it turns out to be anyone from high school. Or Betty Bannister."

"Is Betty *everywhere*?" She rolled off him. He sat up and squinted into the darkness. Except it wasn't as dark as it should have been. Was that...fire?

Holy shit. A boat was on fire out there on the lake.

ten

Normally, Kendra wouldn't be too crazy about being dumped on her butt on the pier. But she made an exception in this case. Jason swore as he scrambled to his feet.

"Call 9—"

"I got it," she told him as she grabbed her phone.

He was already ripping off his jacket for the second time that day.

"You're really going to swim all the way out there?"

"It's not that far. There's no boats tied up that I can commandeer. Anyway, I'm hoping the crew shows up and I can hitch a ride the rest of the way."

"Then go. Or do you want me to push you off like we planned?"

Even though he laughed, he already had his game face on. She'd never seen him in firefighter mode, at least not in an emergency situation like this. Every hint of his usual lighthearted manner dropped away. He was all business now, focused, planning. He gave her one more nod and dove into the water. A moment later, he surfaced a short distance away and struck out across the lake.

The dispatcher finally answered. Kendra recognized the voice of Eileen Iverson, because she used to work as an auctioneer and still had that certain cadence to her voice. "Lake Bittersweet Dispatch, please state your name and emergency," she said, fitting all the words into about half a second.

"This is Kendra Carter. There's a boat on fire on the lake. I'm on the Blue Drake pier and it's maybe two hundred yards away. I think they were heading this way. Jason Mosedale is on his way out there."

"In a boat?"

"No, he's swimming. Just getting a head start."

But he was doing more than that, she saw as she gazed across the dark water. Someone tumbled off the boat and treaded water near the speedboat. That person was yelling at someone else, someone still onboard. The panic in his voice gave her chills. Jason stopped to see what was happening, called something to the man, then kept swimming. She couldn't make out what any of them were saying, but she could guess. Jason was telling him to hang on, help was coming. Don't panic, that sort of thing.

Should she join him out there? She was a pretty strong swimmer herself, but she had no rescue training. She might make matters worse if she got tired out there and someone had to rescue her.

There was something she could do, though. Back in her chambermaid days, they used to keep extra blankets in a cedar-lined storage shed near the head of the path. Gina oversaw that sort of thing now, but there was no reason why it would have changed.

She ran down the pier and jumped onto the packed-dirt pathway that connected all the cabins. The storage shed had a padlock fastened with a combination lock. Recalling the old numbers, she twirled the knob, and incredibly, it worked. Gina must have kept the same number for sentimental reasons.

Inside, she grabbed a pile of blankets, then ran back along the pathway. From here she got a different angle on the burning boat. The flames soared higher, dragon's tongues licking the air. Had the other person onboard jumped off? Were there only two people onboard? After the concert, a few boats had set off from the pier, heading back to their homes on the other side of the lake. It was much quicker to boat across than to drive around. Maybe one of those people had run into engine trouble?

She dumped the blankets on the end of the pier, then thought of something else. Binoculars. Her father kept a pair in the kitchen of the Blue Drake for those oh-so-exciting bird sightings. Personally, she had no patience for birdwatching, but she'd take the binocs, thank you very much.

Another dash back up the pier, into the kitchen. She grabbed the binoculars and a DeWalt flashlight so she could see better. Back on the pier, she used the binoculars to scan the area for the arrival of a crew of firefighters, but saw no one. The fire department didn't own a boat, but several of the volunteer firefighters had contracts with the department for use of their boats in emergencies.

There had to be better options for water emergencies. If she got the town manager job, she'd come up with a proposal.

Not that she had a chance now. The reminder of her stupid—and uncharacteristic—screwup made her stomach hurt. Betty could easily tank her application. And to be honest, her actions had been reckless and immature. Unbecoming of a town manager. Should she pay a visit to Betty and formally apologize? Maybe explain her very wrong-headed thinking and promise never to get anyone drunk and push them off the pier if she was town manager?

Unless Dominic himself came to town. Then all bets were off.

Out on the water, she saw Jason reach the first man who had jumped off the boat. And there, Kendra spotted another person. A woman, perhaps? Someone smaller. She raised the binoculars to her face. The second person grabbed onto Jason by the neck and hung on. He or she seemed to be sobbing. It was a young kid, she realized, but not anyone she recognized.

Behind them, the boat was beginning to founder. It was too late for the fire department to save it. The most they could do was rescue the people onboard, and Jason had already done that.

But how was he going to get them to shore? He must be tired himself, and that kid was about to drag him under. Was he supposed to transport both of them to shore by sheer force of will? She couldn't just stand out here. She had to do something.

And then it hit her.

A rental kayak. The resort owned a few they offered up to guests. Why hadn't she thought about them before? Those kisses must have really scrambled her brain. They were stored on a rack near the top of the pier, hidden in the shadows of the forest. She dashed to the rack and tugged free a two-person kayak, which clattered onto the ground. There was no way she could carry it alone, so she dragged it down the beach. *Sorry, Carly! I know you'd understand.*

When she reached the water, she kicked off her shoes, pushed the kayak into the water, waded in, then climbed onboard. She didn't bother with a spray skirt, which provided for choppier days. Paddling hard, she skimmed across the water, and in a few minutes drew close to the three swimmers.

"I can give someone a ride," she called. "Or two people can take the kayak and I'll swim."

Jason was using one arm to tow the kid, the other to swim. He grabbed onto the bow of the kayak and worked on catching his breath. He looked exhausted, his breathing harsh and rasping.

The other man spoke between gasps. "Take Tyler. My son. He's only eight and he's a better skier than swimmer."

Kendra caught Jason's eye and saw him nod. She looked at the boy, whose face was drenched with both lake water and tears. "Are you Tyler? I'm Kendra. How'd you like a quick paddle back to shore? Does that sound good?"

He nodded, shaking and shivering. "What about my dad?"

"I'll come right back for him. Shoot. I could have towed another kayak behind."

"No, this is good," Jason said hoarsely. "Quicker this way." He pulled his way along the side of the kayak until he reached the front seat. The other man joined them and the two of them maneuvered the kid into the seat. Using her paddle against the force of the water, Kendra did her best to keep the kayak steady until he was safely onboard.

She handed him the extra life jacket. "Welcome aboard, Tyler." She caught Jason's glance again, and noticed that he too was shivering. His dark hair was plastered to his head, and his t-shirt clung to his tight muscles. This was the second time in one night that he'd performed a water rescue, and this water was still icy cold.

"Are you okay?" she said in a low voice, just to him.

"Good," he said briefly, as if he was trying to save his breath.

"I grabbed some blankets for everyone."

"Smart girl."

His approving glance gave her a shiver of pride. Of her many competencies, she didn't count emergency rescues among them. This was her first, in fact. He gave her a quick wink and slapped his hand on the hull of the kayak. "Giddyup. Get that kid to a blanket."

"Should I stay with Tyler on shore or paddle back?"

"I can make it to the pier," called the other man. Jason nodded in agreement, so she dug the paddle into the water and glided away.

Halfway back to shore, Tyler finally spoke. "Our boat burned down."

"I saw that. That must have been scary."

"It's not even our boat. We just borrowed it."

"Well, they'll probably do an investigation and figure out why it happened. Was it just you and your dad onboard?"

He nodded. His thin arms were wrapped around himself and he was leaning forward eagerly as they came closer to the beach.

"Have you ever kayaked before?" she asked him.

"No. But I tried to Jet Ski once. I fell off. My dad said we could maybe try again in a few years."

"That sounds like a plan. So what happens here is, I'm going to paddle straight onto the shore as hard as I can. That'll beach us on the gravel. Then I'll keep the kayak steady while you climb out. Can you do that?"

"It doesn't sound very hard." She was happy to hear some confidence in his voice.

"You might get a little wet."

He gave a hoot of laughter. "I'm already soaking wet!"

"Right, right." As if she hadn't said it intentionally, as a joke. "Okay then, Tyler, are you all set? Ready to beach this bunny?"

All went according to plan, and a moment later they were both onshore. She dragged the kayak onto the grass, then offered the boy her hand. "Let's get you warmed up, how does that sound?"

He clung to her hand, which proved how scared he must have been, considering he was an eight-year-old boy who probably didn't do that sort of thing much anymore.

Once he had a blanket wrapped tightly around him, she scanned the water with the binoculars, which she'd left on the pier with the blankets. Jason and the other man weren't far away, maybe a fifty yards or so. But when she aimed the glasses farther out, she saw that the boat was nowhere to be seen. All that remained of it was debris floating on the surface.

Another boat approached from the direction of the town. It must be the fire department, finally getting their act together. If Jason was in charge, he'd do a much better job, she thought. He was so thorough. And sensitive. And skilled.

Wait, now she was onto a different topic. That kiss. *Those kisses.* Honestly, it had come out of the blue, how amazing it felt to kiss Jason. Kissing was very important, in her opinion, and people didn't always take the time for it. Dominic, for instance, always seemed to consider kissing to be just a stepping stone on the way to what he really wanted. And towards the end, they generally skipped that part and went straight to the sex. Which also ended pretty quickly because they were both so busy.

But Jason kissed as if it was the ultimate destination, not a stopping point along the way. She'd gotten no hint that he wanted to rush through it or that the kiss wasn't wonderful in and of itself. Those kisses had left her feeling the oddest mixture of arousal and peace. Weren't those two complete opposites?

That was just like Jason, in a weird way. Simple, but complicated. Familiar, but unknown. Relaxed, until he needed to take action. Unhurried, until an emergency hit.

What was sexier, kissing him or watching him swim to the rescue of a boat on fire? Not that she had to choose...both things made him sexy. Added together, they turned him into a rock star.

"Here they come!" Tyler scrambled back onto his feet and jumped up and down. "Dad! Dad! This way!"

"Here, do you want to shine a light for them?" Kendra handed him the flashlight she'd grabbed from the kitchen. "Try to aim it in front of them instead of at them. You don't want to blind them."

"Okay." He held it with both hands and focused the beam on the dark rippling water a few feet ahead of his father. "Can you see us, Dad?"

"Yah," he gasped. His strokes, which had been flagging, picked up speed, as if the mere sound of his son's voice gave him new strength.

Kendra was more worried about Jason. He'd swum all the way out there, then part of the way back with the added burden of a terrified child. He was moving even more slowly than Tyler's father, and she fought the urge to jump in the water and help him the rest of the way. She had no lifeguard training and the two of them might end up drowning each other.

Instead, she tossed sassy words to him like a lifeline. "You got this, Jaybone! I know you can do it, just like you passed that public speaking class after I coached you. Or when you won that dance contest you didn't want anyone to know about? Get your butt onto this pier before I tell young Tyler here the whole story. Didn't you have to wear a shirt with ruffles that made you sneeze? And you looked like a bullfighter? It's one of the biggest tragedies of my life that I didn't have a phone with a camera back then. Tyler, want me to show you his ending pose? It was awesome."

Maybe it was unorthodox, but it was working. Jason's pace just about doubled as he raced toward the pier. "You got this, Jaybone!! Go, go, go!"

Tyler joined in and the two of them jumped up and down, cheering on the two swimmers.

Finally, Tyler's dad reached the ladder at the side of the pier, where Kendra directed Tyler to shine the light. She reached down to help him climb the metal rungs, then stepped back to give him space to wrap his arms around Tyler. She draped a blanket over his shoulders, then added another one just in case.

Then she turned her focus to Jason's weary climb up the

ladder. He practically fell into her arms when he reached the top. His body sagged against hers, and she wondered if he'd lost consciousness. But no—he was just murmuring in her ear. "I didn't look like a bullfighter. I looked like a pirate."

She laughed with so much relief that she just about cried.

She helped him toward the pile of blankets. He sank down onto his knees on the worn planks of the pier, then lost steam. She plucked a blanket off the top of the pile and wrapped it around him, adding a tight hug and a kiss on his cold cheek. "That was some hero shit out there."

"Oh stop. Just doing my job. Pirate style."

She laughed softly and rubbed her cheek against his to warm his skin. The search light of the oncoming speed boat glared in her eyes.

"Looks like the rest of the fire department's finally showing up." She stood up and waved at them. "Everyone's here and safe," she called.

The next few moments were all hustle and bustle, as Tyler and his father got quick medical checkups and were handed space blankets and water bottles. Jason waved off all help except for a long drink of water.

"Do you know what started the fire?" someone asked Tyler's dad, who introduced himself to everyone as Brent Caldwell.

"No idea. I heard a noise and then smelled smoke and saw fire coming from the engine compartment. It's not my boat, so I can't vouch for the maintenance. We barely had time to grab life jackets. Tyler lost his when he jumped. We might have drowned if it hadn't been for him." He gestured at Jason, who didn't argue, possibly because he was too tired.

The firefighters decided they didn't need to take either of the two fire victims to the hospital. Instead they loaded them onto the temporary fire boat and zipped across the lake toward the house they were renting.

Colleen Hopper, who ran a juice bar when she wasn't being a volunteer firefighter, stayed behind to tend to Jason.

"Do you have any idea who that is?" she asked as she crouched down next to him.

"No."

"He's a freaking billionaire. Caldwell Industries? That was his grandfather. I heard they're having a big family reunion at Sans-Souci. My mom's doing some of the catering."

Kendra whistled. Sans-Souci was the most lavish estate on Lake Bittersweet, and the only one with a fancy name like that. The locals didn't bother to pronounce it the French way, just referring to it as "Sansussy." But apparently it meant "no worries," which certainly didn't fit what Tyler and Caldwell had just gone through.

"Just goes to show, even rich people need firefighters now and then." Jason sounded as if his throat was raw, but at least he was spitting out full sentences now.

"That's right. I gotta tell you, Jason, this might put you over the top for the fire chief job."

"No, it's probably too late for that," said Jason.

"Are you talking about that douche who fell off the dock?"

"Yeah, he said he was the new fire chief."

"Bullshit. Especially after I write up my report and make you look like Superman."

Kendra laughed and exchanged a high-five with Colleen. "Now that's how you do it. Seriously, he *was* a superstar. We heard the shouts and as soon as we figured out what was going on, he dove into that water and took care of business."

"You were amazing too," Jason said. He still had the blanket wrapped around his wide shoulders, and his arms looped around his knees. "She picked up the kid in a kayak," he explained to Colleen. "And she called dispatch."

"So uh...what were you two doing out here so late, anyway? Pretty lucky break for the Caldwells."

"Well, you know, we had that concert, and there was a lot of cleanup, and..." Kendra realized she was starting to stammer.

Colleen laughed and waved off her explanations. "I'm teasing. You kids do whatever you want. Just take care of him, Kendra."

It's not like that, she wanted to say, but Colleen was already hurrying down the pier.

When she looked back down at Jason, she saw his eyes were drifting shut. Time to get Superman into a bed.

eleven

When Jason woke up, he couldn't stop sneezing. He also didn't know where he was. He seemed to be in some sort of a cozy cabin. He was staring up at an A-frame ceiling made of raw pine boards. As he dragged himself into a sitting position, he noticed a piece of lined notepaper pinned to a nightstand by a paperweight shaped like a loon.

At least he was still in Minnesota.

The note was from Kendra.

Bad news: you have a fever. Good news: you're kind of famous. There's chicken soup and multiple hot dish casseroles in the kitchen. Holly will be here later. I'll check in on you as much as I can. Kendra.

He sneezed ferociously and stumbled his way to the bathroom. He didn't bother to check the kitchen for soup because his stomach would have thrown a full-on rebellion.

Instead, he went back to bed and didn't wake up again until the door creaked open and Holly peered in. She wore flip-flops and torn cutoffs, making him wonder if he'd slept until summer.

"Oh good! You're awake. You must be dealing with some major trauma from last night."

"No therapy-speak," he croaked. "Water."

She disappeared and came back into the room with a tall glass of ice water. It helped. The fire in his throat eased, and he was left only with the fire in his head. Were his brains burning up?

"I have so much to tell you." Holly sat cross-legged on the foot of the bed. "Where do you want me to start?"

"Uh...where am I?"

"The Harlequin Duck Cabin. Gina rearranged some reservations so you can stay here as long as you want."

"Why not home?"

"Kendra said you were too exhausted to go home last night, and this morning you were running a fever so she didn't want to kick you out."

That made sense. But where was Kendra? He ached to see her. He had vague memories of a tender touch on his cheek and a warm blanket coming around him like grace itself. She hadn't left his side, he knew that much. So where was she now?

Holly seemed to understand. "Kendra will be back later. She had an interview or something."

The town manager job...did that mean she was still in the running? Maybe she hadn't ruined her chances with that stunt last night.

Holly's knee was jiggling up and down the way it did when she had something extra important to say. His head pounded, but he ignored it. "You okay on your own?"

"What? Of course I am. I'm great." And then it burst out of her. "You saved someone rich and he wants to give you lots of money!"

"Huh?" His fever must be making him hear things wrong.

"It's true! Mr. Caldwell came to the house to find you. When I said you were still recovering, he left a certified letter that I opened even though I probably wasn't supposed to. He says he's going to gift you half a million dollars as a thank you! We're rich, Jason!"

"I'm not taking his money." The idea offended him to the core. He hadn't done anything that amazing. He'd just gone for a swim, more or less.

Besides, there was something Holly didn't know. Something he hadn't told her yet. It swam to the surface of his feverish brain, but he shoved it away.

"You have to!" Holly wailed. "I've already upgraded what college I want to go to."

He frowned at her`. Holly had stellar grades and deserved to go to whatever college she wanted. All of them—him and their parents—had told her over and over that she should aim as high as possible. Was she still holding herself back? "I told you not to worry about the money."

"Like I'm not going to worry," she scoffed.

"You didn't tell me you were worried."

"Well, now I can tell you because you're rich! Also, you could get an electric car. Don't you care about climate change *at all*?"

Unfair. Of course he cared about climate change. Every year, the wildfire season got worse because of it. Climate change was a big voting issue for him, and not just because Holly had been lecturing him ever since grade school. But was that really a reason to accept half a million dollars from a stranger?

What about taxes? What if it was dirty money? He didn't know anything about Caldwell. Had someone sabotaged that boat on purpose? What if there was more to the story?

His head was hammering as if piano keys were thumping double-time in his skull. "We'll talk about it later. We don't need that money."

"What are you talking about? Are you delusional?"

He groaned, knowing he'd have to explain himself. But not yet, not until his head stopped trying to kill him. "Later, Holly."

"Oh, also? Everyone is saying you're the front-runner for fire chief. There was some other dude from out of town who had it on lock, but I guess he dropped out. I was picking up a latte on the way to school and I heard Betty Bannister talking about how last night was your interview, and you passed with flying colors. But do you even want that job anymore, now that you're rich? I don't mind if you want to quit and stay home and, you know, invest or whatever. You could invest in some house renovations so I have my own suite and we could maybe put in a swimming pool or a hot tub, and—"

"Holly," he groaned, holding his head with both hands. "I'm not taking that money. Go away."

"'Go away' is not a valid argument."

He had to put this into Holly-language so she'd understand. "I need to process my trauma from last night."

It worked. "Oh my God, I'm so sorry." She slid off the bed and got to her feet. "Do you want anything before I go? Kendra said you might want some food."

He didn't want food. He wanted Kendra.

Holly left then, and he sank back into a half-sleep. He was dancing across the lake, spinning in grand circles across the dark water. It held him up as if it was frozen, even though he could feel the water on his bare feet. The woman he was dancing with kept changing, shimmering from one identity to another. He didn't recognize any of them, they were all strangers to him. They spun faster and faster, until the stars blurred together and hands reached up from the lake to grab him and drag him under.

He woke up with a start to find the room darker than when he'd fallen asleep. His heart was pounding. Night again? What time was it? How long had he slept this time?

Kendra's husky voice cut through his panic. "Hey, you," she

said softly from the open door. She flicked on the light, and he squinted against the sudden brightness. "How are you feeling?"

"You're here," he said stupidly. He feasted his weary eyes on her. She wore skintight brick-red jeans that made his mouth water. One shoulder was propped against the doorjamb, her hip cocked in a sassy pose. Had she thought about their kisses at all, or had all the drama wiped those magical moments from her memory?

Fever, he reminded himself. They were probably just regular, ordinary kisses. Not fiery brands on his very soul. That was the brain fire talking.

"Yeah, sorry it took a while. I had to go make a fool of myself for a job I probably won't get, you know how it goes." Her tone was jaunty, but her mouth showed the truth; her full lips trembled a bit around the edges.

"Sorry."

She shrugged. "Their loss. I have a freaking business degree, and they're obsessed about minor little details like dunking fire chief candidates in the water. You'd think they'd be grateful, since now they can hire the best possible guy for the job." She gave him a smile so incandescent, it put the overhead light to shame. "They want to interview you as soon as you can manage it, but basically, full-on riots might break out if they don't hire you."

"We trained for that. Patty said we'd better not have any because we sucked."

Kendra laughed. "Are you hungry?"

"God yes."

She held up a finger in a "wait a sec" gesture, then disappeared. When she came back, she was carrying a tray with a steaming bowl of soup, a mug of hot tea, water, and a bottle of Tylenol.

He popped a couple of Tylenol tablets, then tucked into the

soup. She perched on the end of the bed, where Holly had sat. But instead of chattering away, she let him eat in quiet.

"Never had dinner last night," he explained through spoonfuls of broth. "Just cotton candy and roasted peanuts."

"You mean the night before last. You've been here two nights."

"*What?*" He paused between spoonfuls. "No way."

"Yeah, you were *out*. I consulted with a doctor and she said just to keep an eye on you, that it would be normal to need lots of sleep after an event like that."

He went back to his food, which had that telltale Alvin Carter flair. "Did your dad make this soup? Either it's freaking incredible or I'm literally starving."

"Yes. He says he needs his favorite trombonist back in action."

He corrected her. "Only trombonist."

"He's being nice, eat the soup."

"Yes ma'am."

She leaned forward and plucked a paper towel off the tray to wipe away a dribble of soup from his chin. He rolled his eyes at himself. "Guess I am literally starving."

"An appetite is a good sign. So, are you ready for a big old dose of news?"

"Holly already filled me in."

"Oh really? Did she tell you there are news crews lining up to talk to you?"

His head jerked up. "What are you talking about?"

"It's a big story. A billionaire and his son rescued by a lone hero firefighter. There's even visuals. Some teenagers having a campout saw the flames and got out their iPhones."

He groaned and pushed away the food. Then remembered that he was still ravenous and took it back. "I'm not going on the news or any of that shit. Not feeling like this."

"Don't tell me, I'm not your PR agent." She leaned backwards to grab a messenger bag she'd brought with her. "But Peggy showed me some of the emails the fire station is getting. Most are favorable, but there's always someone who isn't happy. Some people think you should have let the billionaire drown."

He took the printouts she handed him and scanned through them. Fan mail. Huh. The closest he'd ever gotten to fan mail before was the occasional heartfelt kid's drawing after he rescued a cat from a tree.

Speaking of which...he longed for his dog right now. He'd even allow him to spread his hairy bulk across the foot of his bed. "Rusty hasn't gone after any reporters yet, has he?"

"Not that I know of."

"Is it safe to bring him here?"

"You miss your dog, huh?"

"I'm a nine-year-old boy at heart."

Kendra cocked her head at him. Sympathetically, he thought? But he couldn't be sure because the Tylenol was kicking in and his eyes wanted to close. "I can bring Rusty to you. Are you saying you want to hang out here for a while longer? Are you in hiding?"

"Until I'm up to facing news cameras, if it's okay."

"It's fine. Gina worked it out."

An idea came to him. Another chance for Kendra to show off her skills. "I wasn't the only one there that night. Why don't you handle the media? You're much better at that shit than I am. Remember our public speaking class, when I started my speech with 'Hello, I'm Jason *Moose*dale?'"

She laughed. "Iconic. But you're better at that kind of thing now. People want to hear from the hot firefighter, not the witness."

"The sexy witness," he corrected as he sank back on his

pillows. "Come on, this is the perfect chance to show everyone how well you can represent the town."

Looking exasperated, she threw up her hands. "How many times do I have to prove myself?"

"To me, none. But I know those older folks. It might take them a while, but they usually end up in the right place. You have to push them, without making it obvious that you're pushing them."

"But they already think I'm *too* pushy and have too many ideas."

He squinted at her. Fatigue was dragging him down again, but she had a point. "Okay, then forget them. Do it for me. You're a star. You'll make us look good."

She scooted closer to him on the bed. "When did you come up with this brilliant plan? While you've been fighting a hundred and two degree fever and hallucinating?"

"How do you know I've been hallucinating?"

"Because you kept talking about me getting naked. And that hasn't happened."

Good God. Had he really talked in his sleep about his Kendra fantasies? "Hallucinations aren't the same as fantasies."

"Are fantasies the same as premonitions?"

That wicked wink could only mean one thing. "Can we just pause this whole conversation until I feel better?" he begged. "So I can follow up with actual actions?"

She laughed and slid off the bed. He looked up at her, so bright and confident. She wore a short fawn-colored suede jacket over a white blouse. Perfect for killing it on the TV news. Some network would probably want to hire her as an anchor after she showed off her skills. "Let's talk later after you feel better. Is there anything else I can get for you?"

"Rus--"

"Besides Rusty. I'll be back with him later."

"One more thing. Holly said a certified letter came from Caldwell. I want to see it."

"About that..." She fingered with the flap of her messenger bag. "I was hoping we wouldn't have to talk about that yet."

"Tell me. Before I drop off a cliff here."

She sighed. "Holly got it wrong. He's donating half a million dollars to the fire department, not to you personally. Hey, are you okay?"

A broad smile was slowly spreading across his face, matching the sense of relief flooding through him. "Good, thanks."

"Good? You aren't disappointed? I didn't want to be the one to crush your dreams, but are you actually happy he's not giving you that money?"

His eyelids were getting dragged down by lead weights, and his speech sounded slurred. "Sssssuper happy."

"You don't want to be a millionaire?"

Sleep knocked him out like someone pushing him into a river, and as he floated off into the darkness, he heard himself say the thing he avoided admitting at all costs, even to Holly. "I'm already a millionaire."

twelve

J ason had always had a great sense of humor, but being
able to joke while falling asleep with a fever was next level.
It kept Kendra in good spirits all the way through her time
in front of the news cameras.

Two stations from Minneapolis had sent crews, along with
someone from a cable news channel. They all rented separate
boats to get shots of the debris still floating on the surface, which
added up to a mini-economic boom for local boat-owners.

She gave animated interviews to each station, describing
what she'd witnessed and showing them the kayak that she'd
dragged into the water to rescue Tyler.

"I was always confident that they would make it, because I
have complete faith in the fire department here in Lake Bittersweet." She made sure to repeat the town's name at every opportunity. "Of course no one knew they were rescuing a billionaire,
because that kind of thing doesn't matter here. Every visitor to
our town is important. We don't let any of them drown."

It was fun making news crews laugh.

JENNIFER BERNARD

"If you guys are interested in more local color, did you know that the Blue Drake was started by the late Steven Gault?"

Everyone ought to know that, but things tended to get lost in the shuffle so it was worth pointing out.

"The Freaks guy?" asked one of the reporters, a sandy-haired kid who was probably actually an intern trying to get some experience.

"That's right. One of his closest friends runs that restaurant. Are y'all familiar with Alvin 'Redfish' Carter?"

None of them were, which pissed her off so much she nearly forgot her real purpose here.

"If you get a chance, check out his catalogue. He's a legend. The point is, I'm not at all surprised that a billionaire would choose to vacation here. I'm just happy we were able to get him to safety, thanks to our stellar fire department, and especially our own Jason Mosedale."

Since Caldwell himself was declining all interview requests, Kendra was in hot demand. By the end of the day, her voice was just about gone, but she was proud to say that she'd given a plug to a very comprehensive list of Lake Bittersweet businesses. The Inn, the SweetBitter Cafe, Dream Getaways, Galen Cooper's wilderness adventure business, the Indigenous Arts cooperative, the maple syrup cooperative, and of course, the world famous Blue Balls Burgers at Alvin's Burgers and Blues.

She had no idea how much of that would make it on the air, but she'd done her level best.

In the kitchen at the end of the day, her father wiped his hands on a dishtowel and shot her a suspicious stare. "Why are you knocking yourself out for those folk? We don't need that much business."

She leaned her butt against the edge of the counter and dropped a leftover jalapeño popper into her mouth. The fiery flavor gave her a little boost of energy. "It's...I'm promoting the town. Don't get wound up, but I applied for the town manager job."

He tossed the towel over his shoulder. "Why didn't you tell me before?"

"In case I didn't get it. Which...I'm not. Getting it, I mean. Jason wanted me to give it one more shot today, so I played Lake Bittersweet cheerleader." She caught his expression. "But don't worry, I'm not going anywhere. I'm still queen of the burgers."

"I'm not worried about that. I always knew you'd find something to suit you better. Are you telling me they turned you down?" His voice deepened the way it did when he was upset.

"It's not official yet, but yes."

"Let me talk to them. If this is because of me, or Gault, or the color of—"

"Pop, no! You stay out of it. It's not because of any of that. It's me. I screwed it up all on my own."

"I don't believe you. What'd you do?" he demanded.

She told him the story, which left him shaking his head. "That's not like you, Kendra. I never used to worry about you. Now you got me staying awake nights, picturing all kinds of scenarios. Where's your man? When's Dominic going to come see us?"

Oh lord. She wasn't ready to inflict another disappointment on him. Maybe he worried about her, but she worried about him even more.

She ate the last jalapeño popper and pretended to check the time. "There's no need to worry, Pop. But I can't talk now, I have to go pick up a dog. Mind if I take the truck? I don't want dog hair in my Lexus."

"A dog? We aren't getting a dog."

"It's Jason's dog, relax."

"How's that boy's fever?"

"Better. Don't worry about him either." Something occurred to her. "Jason isn't a millionaire, is he?"

"A *what?*" Her father let loose that hearty laugh that always seemed to come right from his gut. "Come on now. His parents barely scraped by with that dance studio. He's about the same. Good man, but no millionaire."

As she'd thought.

Ten minutes later, she knocked on the door of the old farmhouse occupied by Jason and his sister.

Holly flung open the door. "Oh. It's you." She sounded so disappointed that Kendra wondered if she should turn around and leave.

"I'm just here to pick up Rusty. Expecting someone else?"

"Yes. No. I don't want to talk about it. Oh! You and Jason aren't a thing, are you? Because people are asking and I need to know what to say other than, 'of course not, because that would be a rebound and they both know better than that.'"

Did they, though? Those kisses on the dock had been haunting her nonstop. "I'll write up a prepared statement for you."

"Funny. See, this is why I told Jason not to date you. You're better than just a rebound. Like, way better. You're possibly even sister-in-law material, but the only reason I'm saying that is I'm pretty upset right now and I'm not watching my words very well."

She flounced over to the couch and sank onto it as if it was a fainting couch. Her baggy shorts left her freckled legs bare. She'd drawn something on her skin, maybe a snake or a dragon? Her faded yellow t-shirt read "F the Patriarchy."

Kendra hesitated, looked around for a dog, and spotted an Irish Setter deeply asleep in a dog bed by a cozy fireplace. She couldn't use him as an excuse to escape, so she might be stuck here with an upset teenager. She didn't know Holly except from all the time she and her friends spent at Alvin's Burgers and Blues.

"Are you upset because of Jason? He's going to be fine."

"No, that's not it."

"Is it the mistake about the Caldwells' donation?"

Kendra watched her reaction closely. If Jason already had millions of dollars, surely Holly would know something about that, and it would affect her response.

"No, I'm over that. Money's the root of all evil," she added morosely. "Billionaires should be abolished."

That settled that, once and for all. There was no way Jason was a millionaire.

"Did you just get dumped by a rich guy or something? Because I know a little something about that."

"Ooh, juicy juice. Normally I'd want to hear everything, because that's my thing, you know. I'm the one everyone confides in because I always give fantastic advice and I'm very trustworthy and I would never sell out a friend, ever ever..." She burst into tears.

Oh shit. Comforting people wasn't really her comfort zone. Carly was much better at that. When she and her friends had been that age, if someone had a crisis Carly and Gina would be empathetic, Trixie would make jokes to make everyone laugh, and Kendra and Brooke would figure out how to handle it. *Where are my girls when I need them?*

"Point of order. Is this the kind of situation where you want me to stay or leave?"

"Thank you for asking! You're one of the best adults, seriously!" Holly wailed. "You can stay."

"Okay. Cool. Groovy." She spotted a footstool and dragged it toward the couch. She cast another glance at sleeping Rusty, who was no help at all, then sat down. "What's got you so upset, Holly?"

The girl wrestled with her emotions for a time. Kendra could practically see them at war on her face. She didn't miss being that age at all, although she'd avoided that kind of drama herself. Her only focus had been excelling at school and getting into a good business program.

"I screwed up," Holly finally said. "I gave bad advice to a friend, and now her boyfriend is being an even bigger dick to her, and it's all my fault."

"How is it your fault? Dicks are gonna dick."

"Oh my God I love you so much, that's awesome." But then she gave a shaky sob. "But it was totally my fault. I lost my cool and I told her she was being a pussy-ass bitch, and that if she didn't stand up to him, I couldn't be her friend anymore. She went to break up with him and ended up telling him what I said, and now he says I'm the one who's controlling. And he had all these videos of different times when I tried to give her advice and it came off as super-toxic."

She waved her iPhone at Kendra.

"And he posted them on his TikTok! I'm like a TikTok trend now. If you hashtag toxic friend, I'm the first person who comes up. And you know the worst part? I wouldn't even care if it was like, a sex video or something. Like, whatever, people have sex. What I do instead of sex is be a great friend. But now I'm famous for being a *toxic friend*. He hit me right where it hurts the most, that prick."

Wow. The world had changed a lot since Kendra had her last teenage drama moment. How the hell was she supposed to handle toxic friend accusations and viral videos? What happened to baby steps? What would Carly do? What would *Jason* do?

Face it, she was on her own.

Cut the drama, girl, she told herself. *She just needs a friend right now.*

"Kinda seems like he proved your point," she said. "You'd have to be a dick to post videos of your girlfriend's friend."

"But did I push him into being a dick? That's what Chloe is saying. That he wouldn't have been such a dick if I hadn't given her that ultimatum. She says he loves her and treats her like a princess and I'm like, red flag, red flag."

"Being treated like a princess is a red flag?"

"It can be," Holly said seriously. "Because if you step off that pedestal and do something he doesn't like, he might get nasty. Think about it. Would you rather be treated like a princess or like a respected equal?"

"Can't it be both?"

"*That's* the dream."

Was it? Kendra's dream was nothing like that. Her fantasy wasn't riding in a golden princess carriage waving to a crowd. It was more along the lines of a standing ovation as she accepted an award for Business Genius of the Year. Then a big bouquet of flowers would arrive on stage, courtesy of her man. He was in the front row, applauding just as hard as everyone else, with a secret wink just for her, a hint about everything he wanted to do to her later in the way of celebration.

"Let me ask you something, Holly."

"Sure. Yeah." Perking up, she scooted herself higher on the couch cushions. "Do you need advice? Is it about my brother? Because that might take us a while and I should go get us some hot cocoa."

"Uh, no. I'm good. How did you get to be such an expert on relationships?"

"Oh. Are you being sarcastic? You sound a little sarcastic."

Holly wrapped her arms around her knees in what looked like a defensive move.

"I'm not. I tend to sound sarcastic even when I'm not, so I don't blame you for thinking that. No, I'm completely serious. I didn't pay much attention to relationships at your age. That's why I'm curious."

Holly blinked as if she'd never heard anything so ridiculous. "Why wouldn't you? Relationships are the most fascinating thing in the world. I listen to podcasts, YouTube videos from relationship experts. But mostly I just watch my friends go through things. I think I want to be a therapist when I get out of school."

"You think?"

"Know." Holly grinned, and stuck her tongue out a little.

"So you're kind of...practicing on your friends?"

The girl rested her chin on her knees. "I guess you could put it that way. It sounds bad, though. I want to help. But I also want to be right," she admitted in a small voice. "You're right, Kendra. I let my ego get in the way. That's what you're saying, right?"

"Uh—" She hadn't exactly said that, but it didn't sound wrong, either.

"I need more humility. I listened to a podcast about that. I don't have all the answers. God, thank you so much, Kendra. I think I see where I went wrong. You can't tell people what to do in their relationships."

Kendra nodded wisely, even though she was just trying to keep up with Holly's rapid pace.

"So I take it back. There's nothing wrong with you and Jason getting into some kind of rebound thing. You have the official Holly seal of approval, and you know, my friends would kill for that." She mimicked stamping Kendra's hand, like for a concert. "Go forth and rebound."

Kendra had to work hard not to burst out laughing. Little did

Holly know that they'd already ignored her advice enough to kiss and make out on the dock.

"Thank you," she said gravely. "But before I can really feel comfortable going forward, what was that advice about Jason?"

Whatever it was, she intended to tease him mercilessly about it.

"Oh. Yes. It's about his learning disability. It's holding him back emotionally."

Kendra's mouth fell open. His *what?*

Holly barreled ahead without noticing. "Gretchen wanted him to propose to her, and he tried to buy a ring like three times, but he never did it. And other girls kept showing up, but then they'd move on because he would start talking about Gretchen. I think he was using Gretchen as a shield. And the reason he needed a shield..."

She stopped to take a breath. Kendra realized she was holding hers.

"...was because his learning disability messed him up psychologically. My parents used to treat him like there was something wrong with him, and sure, a learning disability is a challenge, but it can be overcome. They didn't believe in special ed assessments and stuff like that. They basically just told him to do his best and stop dreaming about becoming a doctor. I think that's why he doesn't settle with one person, because he'd have to be honest about his disability. There's nothing wrong with Jason in any way, he is a top-of-the-line human being, and I'm not just saying that because he's my brother. Half the time he's also very annoying. I'm not a big fan of the male gender in general, that whole toxic masculinity thing is very real. But Jason is definitely one of the good ones, I made sure of that. I mean, he's been my parental figure for the past few years, the least I could do is make sure he doesn't head down a dick-ish path."

Kendra bristled. "I've never known Jason to be a dick."

"He's not. Partially thanks to me," she added smugly.

"I used to tutor him sometimes. He never told me he had a learning disability."

Holly clapped a hand across her mouth. "Oh shit," she said through her spread fingers, before closing them again. "Jason's going to kill me."

"Don't worry, I'll keep your name out of it," Kendra told her. "I'll call you 'anonymous sources close to the family.'"

Holly groaned and buried her face in a couch cushion. "My biggest flaw," she moaned. "I get carried away and I don't know when to stop talking."

"Honey, why don't you lighten up on yourself?" Kendra got to her feet and stretched her arms overhead. "You're seventeen. Of course you don't have everything figured out. What would you do with the rest of your life if you did?"

"Not helping."

So much for offering comfort.

"Okay, maybe a little," Holly murmured as her phone buzzed.

Across the room, Rusty stirred himself off the dog bed. He surged to his feet and ambled toward them with a yawn. Kendra bent down to pet him. "Ready for a walk, big guy?"

At the familiar word "walk," he trotted toward the door.

Kendra waved goodbye to Holly, who barely glanced up from the text she was reading on her phone. "Kendra! We're friends again! Me and Chloe! She says she knows I meant well and I'm not a toxic friend and she's going to start a new hashtag for me."

Maybe that's what I need, Kendra thought as she helped Rusty into the back of her dad's truck. *A new hashtag.* #HeartbreakBe-Gone. #FuckingDominic. Or how about #I'mGoingtoEnjoyMy-Life? #HotSex? #HottieFireman #IsYourFeverDownYetBecauseI'mIntoThisJasonMosedale?

Then again, hashtag "why didn't you trust me enough to tell me about your learning disability" had a ring to it. As did hashtag "you look like a million bucks even if you don't have any."

But none of that mattered for a rebound. He didn't have to share his secrets with her. She wanted Jason. With or without a disability, with or without a million dollar bank account.

thirteen

"So, locker-buddy." A throaty voice pulled Jason from his half-slumber. He'd been dozing off and on throughout the day, feeling better each time he awoke, but allowing himself to fall back asleep because sleep seemed to be working. The most he'd done all day was shower and brush his teeth. "How's the pain on a scale of, um, public speaking to winning a million dollars?"

He opened his eyes to see Kendra posing next to his bed, hip cocked one way, head cocked the other way. The pose did something to his own cock, so that must be a positive sign. She wore shorts that left her long brown legs bare. He reached for her without thinking, and slid a hand up her thigh.

"That good?" That sassy smile brought him all the way awake.

"And more." He curved his hand around the back of her thigh and tugged her closer. She obliged, stepping right to the edge of the bed.

"I know you're glad to see me, but maybe you should spare

some welcome vibes for this guy." On cue, Rusty nosed his way past her and stuck his snout in Jason's face.

"Aw, buddy. I missed you." He scrunched his fingers in the ruff of fur at Rusty's neck, right where he liked it. The dog's back leg slapped against the floor.

"Universal signal for don't stop." Kendra sidestepped the dog and climbed onto the foot of the bed. He moved his legs aside to give her space.

After a few more moments of loving on his old Irish Setter, he gestured to Rusty to go sit in the corner of the room. Since Rusty was getting up there in years, he didn't mind heading off for a snooze.

"So. You're really doing better?" Kendra asked. "Everyone wants an update on the most famous patient in town."

"I think the fever's gone. My head isn't threatening to self-detonate. I haven't sneezed since your dad brought me lunch."

"What'd he bring you?"

One of her smooth legs was bent under her, the other stretched out straight. He set his hand on her bare knee. He couldn't keep his hands off her. "Pulled pork, cornbread and collard greens. I even ate the greens, so I must be feeling better."

"He brought you collards?" She pulled an impressed face. "He doesn't share those with just anyone. I hope you showed them some respect."

"Ate every speck. It's all in here." He pulled the blanket down to pat his bare stomach. All he wore was the extra pair of boxers Holly had brought him.

Her gaze traveled down his torso. She checked him out so thoroughly that it felt practically physical. Then it *became* physical when she scooted forward on the bed and traced a finger down his pecs. "Do you have to be a stud to be a firefighter?"

"No, but it doesn't hurt." He grinned at her.

She touched his jaw, where a good quarter inch of black

beard had sprouted. "And what's with the scruff? Will you have to get rid of that to be fire chief?"

"I'll be making the rules, right?" He winked at her. "Damn, it's good to see you. It's good to feel better." He spread his hand across her knee, seeking the softer skin of her inner thigh, the curvature of her muscles. "Thanks for letting me hide out in here."

"You should thank Gina for that."

"I don't want to thank Gina for that. I want to thank you. Didn't you get me in here before I collapsed? That's how I remember it. Man, I was out of it."

"You sure were. It scared me a little bit, for a while."

"Why, because you didn't think we'd ever get back to doing this?" He reached up to her pretty face, and cupped a hand around her cheek. "There's no way I'd let myself die before I got to kiss you again."

"You think you're guaranteed to get another kiss?" Her sassy words didn't fool him. Her pupils were dilated and a flush darkened her cheeks. She was just as hyped about the next step as he was. Whatever it was.

"I told you I'd work for it."

"And?"

"Where do I start?" He checked off items on his finger. "I rescued a billionaire and his son. I got a half-million-dollar donation to the firehouse, *and* I gave you the opportunity to make the national news. I know *you're* usually the overachiever, but—"

He broke off when warm lips stopped the flow of his words, and a curvy body nestled on top of his. The sudden sensory impact nearly overwhelmed him, especially after all this time alone with nothing but his murky dreams.

She kissed him with a deep and playful fierceness that left him panting for more. Then she drew back, allowing her hand to linger on his chest. "You really did grow up fine," she murmured in that husky voice of hers.

He grabbed her wrist, then brought her hand to his lips and kissed it. "If you had any idea what I would have done back then to hear you say that..."

She chuckled, then shifted her position so one knee was on either side of him, straddling him with her sexy body, with those shorts and those gorgeous legs. "Does this hurt?"

"Fuck no." He shifted his hips to make it very obvious that he felt no pain, only pleasure.

"Good, 'cause Dom—" She folded her lips tightly, as if wishing she could take back that syllable. "Sorry. Wrong person to bring up right now."

True enough. On the other hand, he'd rather know if another man was on her mind. "What were you going to say about him?"

"He didn't like me being on top. If you ask me, he had a problem with a woman having the upper hand."

"Insecure?"

Her eyes flashed to meet his. "You think?"

"I don't know the guy. All I know is that I don't mind you being on top of me. Or under me. Next to me. It's all good, so long as there's a you and a me."

Her full lips quivered into a smile, which dropped away quickly. "That's good, because right now, you're the one on top in every other way. They just texted me on my way over. I didn't get the job. You're going to be fire chief and I just lost my business *and* a job prospect. You're up and I'm down. I think this might be my lowest point, professionally speaking."

"Oh damn. I'm sorry." He spread his hand open on her leg and gently caressed her skin. Going for comfort instead of arousal. "I was really hoping they'd see the light."

"Whatever. It was my own fault. At least there's that." She shrugged, but he could tell it bothered her. Kendra Carter didn't like to lose, or fail, or any of those non-success type things. Especially after what she'd gone through with Dominic.

"Come here," he murmured.

He reached for her and slowly pulled her closer, so her face hovered over his, and her breasts stirred under her low-necked top. The soft shadow between the curves of flesh called to him.

"You're a superstar no matter what."

He lifted his neck to nestle his face just there, where he could breathe in the intimate scent of her skin. When her breath caught, he knew he had the go-ahead to continue. So he tongued his way along the curve of one breast, using his chin to move her bra cup away from her nipple. Ever since the pier, when he'd only had time to feel her breasts, he'd been imagining what she looked like. Now he was finally getting his chance, and her beautiful nipples were even more erotic than he'd pictured. Plump and ready, deep brown morsels that hardened the instant he touched his tongue to one, they brought a moan to his lips.

"You are a goddamn goddess," he told her in between lavish strokes of his tongue. "Have mercy on me."

With a choked laugh, she sat up and stripped off her top. He'd already exposed one nipple, and now as she unsnapped her bra, the other popped free as well. His cock stiffened so much she felt it through her shorts and his underwear, and her eyes flared. "Tell me you have a condom here."

"Why would I have a condom? I've been in bed for the past two days with a fever, and—" He broke off with a laugh as she whipped one from her shorts pocket and shot him a wicked grin. "You're going to pay for that."

"Gonna hold you to that, Jaybone."

fourteen

It's just sex, Kendra kept telling herself. No need to get it twisted. Sex was great. She loved sex, but in her book, there were a lot of things more important than what kind of orgasm a guy gave you. She was perfectly capable of giving herself her own orgasm, if it came to that. It was a lot simpler than bringing a man into the scenario. That's what she'd been doing lately anyway—even before the Dominic disaster. By the end, they'd both been too busy for sex.

So what felt different about sex with Jason? If she broke it down, she'd have to start with the basics. He touched her as if it was the privilege of a lifetime that he got to put his hands on her.

Who could disagree with that?

Also, he had a secret weapon. His hands were pure magic. Whatever those firefighters had to do in order to do their jobs, it resulted in strong hands with the kind of calluses that added that extra *je ne sais quoi*.

It wasn't just his hands, of course. His mouth and tongue were equally skilled, though she had no idea how fireman training affected that kind of thing.

He worked his way, lick by lick, nibble by nibble, from one breast to the other, until her nipples were sending a red flare directly to her pussy. While she was still panting from that, he unsnapped her shorts and sent one long finger on an expedition into her already-slick folds. It didn't take but a minute until he found her clit, and a few strokes later he had that bundle of nerves throbbing right along with her nipples.

She tilted her hips back and forth to give him an idea of what kind of pace it would take for her to come. They'd just started and she was already on the verge. Had some kind of slow-burn simmer been percolating this whole time with Jason? Her body was so ready for him. She didn't want to wait. She wanted release, sweet hot release from all her troubles and worries.

Then he pinched her clit with a firmness, a dominating command—*come now*—and a fierce climax hit her like some kind of avalanche. She rode his fingers, grinding against him, chasing every last electric spasm. God, she *needed* this. And she took it. Every pleasuring second of it.

"Shit, Jason. You don't have to rush me like that," she managed when she could catch her breath again.

"Sneak preview." He winked at her, dark eyes gleaming. "A little thank you for watching out for me. You take care of me, I take care of you."

"Isn't that what mob bosses say?"

"Probably not in bed."

She laughed down at him, her blood humming on high through her veins. All the tension she normally carried with her relaxed with a sigh. "That was...good, Jaybone. Really fucking good. Maybe we should have done this ages ago."

"Like when? In high school?"

"Nah, too soon. Maybe when we ran into each other over Christmas a few years back. At the Morettis', remember? You poured me a glass of wine and I told you all about the business I was launching. I remember thinking what a good listener you were."

"I remember thinking how hot you were. And brilliant and way out of my league."

She scrunched up her face at him. "Don't say that. I never thought that. Look at you. You're a hero firefighter. You're a hot hunk with crazy amounts of charm. Did you know that when you get sworn in, you'll be the youngest fire chief in the history of Lake Bittersweet? That means you're historically successful."

"Historically successful, that's a thing?"

"I'm declaring it a thing. Right now, I'm historically *un*successful."

"I call bullshit. You're successful at the most important thing —orgasms."

She burst out laughing. "You always try to make people feel good, don't you?"

"Is it working?"

"I haven't felt this good since I got my business license. And it didn't make me come."

In a sudden move, he flipped her over and spread her out underneath him. He settled her arms over her head. "Don't move. I'm serious. If you touch me I might lose it."

Her breath stopped and she didn't bother with a quip. This was too good, watching the smooth muscles of his chest flex and tense. She was a sucker for a man's torso, especially all those ridges of abdominals, and the hard muscles along his upper arms. It was shallow to lust after muscles; she knew that. But with Jason, those muscles were just a bonus because there were so many other great things about him. She was drawn to him for those other things—his humor, his intelligence, their chemistry. It was okay to also appreciate his physique, wasn't it?

Even if it wasn't, she wasn't about to pretend he didn't turn her on. Even though she obeyed his request and didn't touch him, she feasted her eyes on his body as he bent his dark head to kiss her breasts, her belly, the insides of her elbows.

Then he shifted lower down her body and pulled her shorts all the way off. With fantastic foresight and some wishful thinking, she'd worn her sexiest pair of panties, deep burgundy lace with strategically placed black roses. The way he hissed when he uncovered them made her smile to herself, and high-five the Kendra who'd bought them at Minneapolis's most expensive lingerie boutique before she left town.

"Oh my God." His heartfelt whistle sent confidence gushing through her. Not that she wasn't confident in general, but Dominic had really put a dent in her self-esteem.

"You like these?" She lifted her hips and did a little dance to show them off. "It's okay if you take them off, I don't mind."

"Hang on. I need to take a mental photo." He gazed at her for so long that she began to ache with desire. To get him out of his trance, she lifted one leg and rested her foot on his shoulder. His eyes flew to meet hers. The heat in them gave her insides a sizzling jolt of excitement.

Still holding her gaze, he moved the crotch of her panties to one side and dragged his finger through the juices he found. Then he licked his finger and moaned.

Hot. So hot. He was making her lose her mind with his smoldering gaze and his slow touch and his blatant lust. She looked down at his boxers, which had turned into an ungainly tent of fabric trapping his erection. "I think you should take your undies off before they tear."

"You're going to tear them off?"

"No, your boner's going to do that for me."

He looked down at himself and laughed. "What, kind of a Clark Kent turning into Superman thing?"

"Is that what you call your Johnson?"

"I definitely don't call it a Johnson." He rolled away from her so he could take his underwear off. More muscles flexing and long limbs stretching. His sheer physical presence made her insides sing with desire. Was that what people meant by chemistry? She'd thought she knew what chemistry meant, but this felt different. All the sparks and lust had something extra involved. She couldn't put her finger on it, but maybe it was "fun." She felt relaxed around Jason, like she didn't have to prove anything.

"What then?" she murmured, rolling onto her side to watch him undress.

He peeled his boxers off his body and her eyes widened as his whatever-he-called-it jumped free. His penis was thickly swollen, a beautiful rod of purpling flesh that soared proudly from between his strong thighs. Jason Mosedale. Who knew?

He glanced up at her and caught her looking. An expression of uncertainty flitted across his face. Not uncertainty in himself, she hoped. It was probably more about what she might be thinking.

"My condom's in my shorts pocket," she told him, to put any possible worries to rest. "Want me to grab it?"

"I got it." He leaned over to snatch up her shorts. The combination of his long body and his thickly jutting penis sure was a sight to see. How the heck was Jason so down-to-earth and easygoing, when he was a stone-cold stud without his clothes? He just wasn't a boaster or a self-promoter, the way someone like Dominic could be. Dominic never missed a chance to tell the world how amazing he was, whether or not it was true.

Jason just...did his thing.

And his thing was off-the-charts amazing.

He rolled the condom onto his penis; at least it fit. Then he shocked her by burying his face between her legs and spending the next few moments licking her back to full-throated, moaning arousal. She dug her fingers into the pillows on each side of her and thrashed her head back and forth.

"Oh God, oh God," she kept moaning. Every stroke of his tongue in her pussy sent her wheeling through clouds of pleasure. One moment he licked her forcefully, the next he soothed and aroused. The way he kept her off balance, even as he stoked the fire inside her...God, it blew her mind.

"You ready?" he murmured as he lifted his head from her thighs. She ached to come again, she was right on the edge, but at the same time, she didn't want to. She wanted to see where this would go, this electric connection they'd generated together.

"Are *you* ready?" she countered. "It's got to go both ways."

He didn't answer, just wrapped her hand around his sheathed penis. The feel of that club between his legs made her shudder with lust.

"You're ready," she confirmed. Her tongue swept across her lips almost compulsively. Her inner thighs trembled and her hands shook. She released him and arched backwards. "Bring it in."

As he positioned his cock at her entrance, she lifted her legs and wrapped them around his hips. It felt more intimate like that, deeper, and she could change the angle in case it wasn't right.

Like a dream, he slid inside her, his flesh swelling against the saturated inner walls of her channel. He entered slowly, smooth and easy, checking to make sure his erection hadn't gotten so large that it was too much for her. The way he constantly thought about her feelings brought tears to her eyes. It felt like...respect.

She liked all kinds of things during sex; sometimes she like wild roughness, sometimes nothing but gentle stroking would do. But the thing she had to have, every time, no matter what else they were doing, was respect. Without that, she would shut down and kick a man out of bed without another thought.

Feeling safe and wild at the same time, she closed her eyes and lost herself in his deep thrusts. He moved inside her like the tide, like the ocean, a constant thrust of in and out. She clenched her legs tighter and lifted her hips. *There.* Deeper. Farther. Her mind went still and her body took over. Sensation led the way, guiding her toward the promised land. *More of that. Oh yeah. Right there.*

And then it all came together in a fireball of emotion and sensation. Like a pair of rockets bursting across the sky, showering sparks in a rooster tail behind it. He went rigid between her legs, every muscle vibrating with strain as his climax ripped through him.

They panted together, breathing synchronized, as if the blood was pumping through their hearts at the same rate.

Then she released her grip on his hips and stretched her legs long. He relaxed and allowed his body to drop onto the sheets beside her. Neither of them had any immediate words to say, so they simply lay there next to each other, letting the afterglow spread peace and satisfaction through every happy cell of their bodies.

Finally, he stirred. "Are you cold? Do you want in on this blanket situation?"

"No, I'm good. Wait. Sure. I'll get under the blanket with you."

He gave her a quizzical glance as he reorganized the bedding so she could join him under the covers. "You're funny. Why the hesitation?"

"I don't know. It's like a couple thing, cuddling under the covers. I had to think about it for a second. Then I realized I was overthinking it and I might get cold if I didn't get under the blankets."

He laughed over at her, his dark eyes holding light deep within them. "You want me to promise I won't assume we're a couple just because we're sharing a blanket and just had phenomenal sex?"

Phenomenal sex...she couldn't argue with that part.

"We've already talked about it, so we both know what we're doing. We're keeping it rebound."

"Is that like keeping it real?"

"Exactly. Look at us, so grown up and mature that we talked it through before jumping into something."

"This is some damn good adulting," he agreed. "Be right back." He rolled out of bed and walked toward the bathroom, his hand on his dick, ready to ditch the condom. Her eyes were glued to his bare ass the entire way. The way his muscles flexed with each step made her want to jump him all over again.

But the poor man was just recovering from a fever. She should probably take it easy on him.

She stretched her body with a feeling of satisfaction that could translate as either a purr or a howl at the moon. Damn, it felt good to have sex again. Fucking Dominic had played all kinds of mental games with her around sex. Sometimes he hinted that she wanted too much sex. Sometimes he made it seem like it was her fault they didn't have time.

Insecure. That was what Jason had suggested about Dominic. Was it true? He'd certainly made her feel insecure. He had a way of keeping her off balance so that she was always looking to him for cues. Was he in a good mood? Did he need some space? If she got it wrong, would he make her feel like shit?

She tried to picture Jason deliberately trying to make her feel like shit, and nearly laughed out loud. It was unimaginable.

Jason ambled back into the bedroom, his partial erection bobbing between his legs. He pretended to stop dead at the sight of her in his bed. "So it wasn't just a fever dream."

"Nope," she said cheerfully. "We had sex. And it was top-notch, in case you forgot that part too."

He climbed into bed and pulled the covers over himself. "Next question. Are you a big spoon or a little spoon? Or anti-spoon?"

She rolled onto her side and plastered herself against his warm skin. Oddly, her mind wasn't already turning a mile a minute, racing onto the next thing she had to do. That was what usually happened after sex. "I don't have an official spoon policy."

"Fair enough."

"Do you?"

"I think it depends on the specific people and how their bodies fit together. Should we test it out?"

"Okay. I'll be big spoon first since I'm already facing that way."

He rolled over and she wrapped her arms around him and snuggled close. His warmth penetrated all the way through the front of her body. She could float there for hours.

"Well?" he asked.

"I like. How is it for you?"

"Your beautiful breasts are pressing against my back so I have no complaints." She liked how the rumble of his voice vibrated into her skin.

"Let's try the other way." It took a few moments of awkward adjustment for both of them to roll onto their other side. His body curved around hers like a shield. His arm came over her, more comforting than a weighted blanket. But... "I like the other way better," she said. "This is a little claustrophobic for me."

Instantly he removed his arm and they shifted back the other direction.

"Better. Thank you." It wasn't just better, it was positively blissful.

"So you don't like to feel trapped, is that it?"

"Something like that."

She could sense him absorbing that, taking a mental picture the way he had of her panties.

"Can you promise me something?" he murmured.

"I can. Don't know if I will."

With a chuckle, he shifted his butt against her groin. Warm comfort surrounded her and she felt her eyelids begin to droop closed. She still had a few things to talk to him about. There was a list she'd composed in her mind on her way over from his house, after Holly's revelation. But couldn't remember it now.

"Can you promise me that if anything I do makes you feel trapped or claustrophobic or any other bad thing like that, you'll tell me? Don't keep it to yourself, is what I mean. I want to know."

"That seems fair."

It seemed like something more important for a real relationship instead of a rebound. But speaking up for yourself was always a good thing. Her parents had taught her that, and she'd always tried to live up to it.

Until Dominic.

That was the worst thing he'd done, she realized in a flash. He'd stolen her business plan and dumped her without a second thought, but even worse than that, he'd made her stifle herself. She'd taken a back seat to him and his charisma and his brilliant future. She'd allowed self-doubt to sneak into her heart and soul.

But Jason had the antidote. Or maybe he *was* the antidote. Right now she didn't even care that she'd bungled the town manager job. She didn't care about Explastica, she didn't care about Dominic. She didn't care if she was a failure at everything except orgasms.

She hugged her body to Jason's, contentment penetrating into every pore.

Sexual healing. Maybe that was what a rebound was all about.

fifteen

wo weeks later, at the height of the summer season, Jason was sworn in as fire chief. Thrown into the deep end, so to speak. Summer was when kids set off unauthorized fireworks, young partiers got into jet ski battles, and campfires sometimes got out of control. He knew the drill, since he'd always loved summer in Lake Bittersweet.

As fire chief, Jason had to choose more carefully when to joke around and when to take things seriously. For instance, when he stumbled across Brent insisting that all new volunteers had to shave a loon into their hair, he had to regretfully put a stop to the prank.

He had to break it to Peggy, the part-time firehouse office assistant, that if she was going to bring her African grey parrot to work, she couldn't allow him to bark commands when people were on the firehouse phone. Callers were getting confused.

"Really?" Her lined face brightened with glee. "Someone really thought Pepper was a person?"

"In emergencies, people panic. Our job isn't to make them more confused."

"Did you hear that, Pepper? You did it!" She gave her parrot a high-five through his cage; he lifted one claw in response. "You sound like a human being! Better than some humans," she added under breath, "because you don't hear him making up crap."

"You understand what I'm saying, right, Peggy?" Sometimes he had to make extra sure the communication loop had been completed.

"I understand that you don't understand how smart this bird is." She offered him a treat, which he grasped in his claw and brought to his beak. "He could probably teach these new kids around here a few things."

"Maybe we can bring him in to assist with some trainings," Jason said gravely. That satisfied her, and she stopped bringing Pepper to the station with her.

Fire chief-ing involved a lot more paperwork than he'd ever imagined. He hated paperwork, for obvious reasons. It probably took him twice as long to do things like budget projections as it had ever taken Thomas Cooper. On the bright side, he did it very thoroughly and meticulously, and caught several errors that the interim fire chief, a retired firefighter who couldn't wait to get back to his fishing, had made.

To help him get through the more mundane paperwork, he hired a part-time assistant. Amber Kenosha was a bright high school student who was training with Gina Moretti to try out for the Olympic canoe sprint team. She needed some extra money and flexible hours, which suited Jason perfectly. All he wanted her to do was summarize reports for him, and occasionally write a rough draft of a presentation. Having a starting point helped him enormously.

Hiring Amber had been Kendra's idea.

"That's what I would have done if I got the town manager job. Did that sound bitter?"

"No. But you don't have to give your ideas away for free, not anymore."

It burned him up that not even her outstanding performance on the news had changed the minds of the hiring committee. Jason still didn't understand why, but he was determined to find out. He was on the inside now, after all.

"It's only for you, Jaybone. I have another idea for you."

He'd stopped by the Blue Drake for lunch, and sat at the bar munching on fries and waiting for the brief moments when she had time to chat.

"Hit me with your brilliance."

"That big donation. You should purchase a boat for the fire department and name it after Tyler. It would make a great story for the tourist brochures."

"Love the boat idea. We need one. But Caldwell doesn't want any extra publicity." He dipped a fry in Alvin's homemade ketchup. "How's this? I'll run a contest for the best name."

"Now you're talking." She blessed him with one of her knee-weakening smiles. "See, you're a natural at this. I knew you'd be a great fire chief."

One of the servers called her name and she rushed away to deal with an unhappy customer. As he finished his burger, Jason watched her in action, handling the disgruntled tourist like a pro. Always decisive, always authoritative. Within moments, she had him bustling out the door, a coupon in hand.

"Nicely done," he told her when she finally made her way back to him.

"One thing about this job, I'm improving my people skills. Dominic used to handle the front-facing aspects of Explastica, but I'm getting pretty good at it."

"Front-facing? Why does that sound dirty?"

"Because you're a sex maniac."

"Only with you, superstar. And that's on you."

She smiled at him and plopped another basket of fries in front of him. "You always know how to get extra fries out of me."

"I feel like that sounds dirty too?" He squinted into the air. "But I don't really want to visualize it."

They laughed together, the way they did whenever they managed to find time to hang out together. Along with the laughter, there was lots of sex, but none of the pressure he'd felt with Gretchen. No silent pushing—what are we doing? Why aren't we planning for the future?

He knew now that Gretchen had done the right thing when she dumped him. Jason could see clearly now that they'd been each other's safety blanket. They'd kept each other from growing and expanding.

With Kendra, it wasn't like that at all. She never hid her thoughts or her opinions, and he always learned something from them. Often it was that he'd missed something, or been an idiot. But that didn't bother him. Better to know than not to know, right? He'd learned that lesson a long time ago—from his learning disability, ironically.

As the summer season got into full swing, both of them got crazy busy. At the beginning of August, Alvin's Burgers and Blues got a writeup in a national travel magazine that brought a constant flood of customers. Kendra had to add several staff members, including an assistant chef for Alvin. The challenge of finding someone Alvin could accept nearly wiped her out.

"Why is he so damn hard to please?" she moaned to Jason one evening as she quick-stripped her clothes off. They had exactly half an hour before he was due to attend his first town meeting. She had to close the restaurant that night, so they couldn't see each other later.

But quick sex was better than no sex, they figured. He was busy unbuttoning his shirt because she always found his bare chest a turn-on.

"Because he has high standards. Just like the rest of his family. I mean..." Joking, he gestured at himself as proof.

"I'm not asking him to fuck the new assistant. Just allow someone to chop a few veggies for him." Kicking off her black pants, she got one foot stuck in a leg and hopped in place.

"I love it when you say 'fuck.' It makes me so hot. Then again, so does 'veggies.'"

"Veggies make you hot?"

"No, hearing you say it does. You could say almost anything and I'd get turned on. Don't you know that by now?"

"Oh really?" She finally got her pants all the way off. Her legs were so long, her ass so firm and curvy, he loved filling his hands with those gorgeous twin cheeks. "Let me ask you something, then."

Her voice turned serious. *Shit.* He didn't want to be serious right now, not when they only had a few minutes. To fend off the change in topic, he strode toward her and crowded her against the wall. She liked it when he played the macho man, so long as he listened to her in case she changed her mind.

"Later," he growled as he dove into the crook of her neck for a nibble.

She tilted her head back to give him space, and he feasted on the sweat-salt taste of her skin. He put his hands under her ass and groaned from the pleasure of touching her again. "I missed you."

"Mmmm." She ground her sex against him, all that heat and wetness hidden behind her panties. His cock thickened inside his pants. He'd barely managed to get them unzipped before pinning her against the wall.

In a moment, they were both panting for breath. Incredible how that fire flared up between them so quickly. All he had to do was touch her, or even see her across a room, and he started craving their next time together. She reached down between them, into his unzipped pants, and stroked his penis. *Ah God.*

He swore softly as she fondled him into full arousal. His cock swelled against her hand as if it had met its true master.

Not that he would tell her that, he thought with a silent laugh. She didn't necessarily like hearing his wild compliments. He understood why. This wasn't serious. This was just fucking, and being friends, and supporting each other's dreams, and if that seemed kind of like a relationship, well, think again. *Rebound, not relationship.*

"You go somewhere?" She tilted her head back down to match his gaze. "You're supposed to be fucking me, not drifting off somewhere."

"I'm not drifting. I'm planning."

"Planning what?"

"You're about to find out."

He let her slip to the floor so he could retrieve a condom from his pocket. Once he had it in his hand, she snatched it from him and tore it open with her teeth. "You're always so slow," she said impatiently.

"They're slippery," he complained. "I'm thinking of writing a letter of complaint. It's like they make them that way on purpose so you think twice before having sex."

She shook her head at his complaining tone. "You're such a goofball, how the hell are you a functioning member of Lake Bittersweet society?"

"Am I though? I feel like I'm faking it."

She kneeled down to slide the condom onto his cock, but before she did so, she put her own mouth on it first. Her lips closed over the tip. He ate up the sight of her working his cock into her mouth. Sweet Jesus, the way she suckled him made him feel like a god.

When he knew he couldn't handle any more, he pulled away

so she could roll on the condom. He wanted to get back to that same position, the one that had gotten them so hot and bothered a minute ago, but somehow this time they ended up on the floor. Which would never do, so he picked her up and tossed her onto his loveseat. Face down, over the arm. Legs spread, her wet sex beckoning, the most sexy and erotic sight he'd ever seen.

"Jason," she moaned when he slid inside her, not bothering to take it gentle, because he knew just how turned on she was. So juicy, so hot, her flesh trembling with each deep thrust of his hips.

He reached around to her front, found her slick nub plump and swelling, and fingered her in a fast rhythm guaranteed to drive her over the edge. As soon as she tipped over, crying out in her throaty voice, he let himself loose. He nearly blacked out from the pleasure as he exploded deep inside her channel. When his vision cleared, he was still inside, pulsing with the after-shocks, one hand still clamped on her pussy.

He pulled her to her feet, worried that maybe he'd gone too far. "Was that okay? Tell me that was okay. Or tell me it wasn't."

"Jason." She turned to face him, and all his fears evaporated. The satisfaction written in the relaxed lines of her face and the softness in her eyes told him she'd had just as much fun as he had. "Do I ever hold back if I need to say something?"

"Not that I know of." She'd flat-ironed her hair, which she did occasionally for a change, and styled it in pretty waves that framed her face. He tucked a strand behind her ears, but she shook him off.

"Please no messing with my hair when I have to get to work."

He snatched his hand away. "Sorry."

"See? Didn't I just prove my point? If I don't like something, you will know about it." She scanned him with a sassy up-and-down. "Are you telling me you never even took your pants off?"

"More efficient." He peeled off the condom and hauled his

pants up with his other hand. "It's sexy, right?" He pumped his hips in a strip-tease kind of grind, waving the condom in the air. Dancing like a cross between a cowboy and Magic Mike, he made his way to the nearest waste basket to toss the condom.

His act had her laughing so hard she had to rest her hands on her knees. She waved air toward her face to catch her breath. "Don't...don't make me get a stitch in my side. I still have to work tonight."

He grinned at her as he fastened his pants back up. "And I need to get to that meeting."

That sobered her up. A shadow crossed her face and she knelt down to gather up her clothes. Her body radiated a bronze glow in the lamplight of his bedroom. She was so beautifully formed, then wrapped in that gorgeous skin. How had he gotten so lucky to end up as her rebound?

But he shouldn't have mentioned that meeting. By rights, she should be there too, delivering a report on the town manager's activities. The position had finally been filled by someone from out of town, a highly experienced woman whose name Jason kept forgetting out of sheer peevishness.

"Before you go, remember how I said I wanted to ask you something?" She fastened the button of her pants. "It's been on my mind for a while."

He groaned silently. Kendra was impossible to fool because she remembered everything. That business brain of hers never turned off all the way.

"You sound serious. I thought we weren't doing serious."

"Of course we aren't. This isn't that kind of serious."

He turned away to hide his disappointment. Absurd to feel disappointed when he knew perfectly well they weren't serious. It was a mutual choice and it made complete sense. Neither of them were ready for a new relationship. He was still recovering from...for a moment he blanked on her name.

Gretchen.

Good God. Had he just forgotten Gretchen's name? Maybe rebounds really did work.

The next thing she said had him spinning around in shock.

"Back in high school, why didn't you tell me you had a learning disability?"

sixteen

When she saw Jason's expression, Kendra wished she could take back the question. He looked stricken, embarrassed, even ashamed.

He turned away to finish buttoning the crisp cotton shirt she'd recommended he wear to his first big town meeting. "How do you know? Did something give it away?"

"No. Jason, you don't have to hide it. It's nothing to be ashamed about."

"Easy for you to say," he murmured.

"Okay, that's fair. But I was your tutor. It might have helped if I'd known."

He buttoned his cuffs. Tucked the shirt into his pants. Fastened his dark leather belt. He looked hot in a suit—except for that somber expression on his face.

"Why does it matter now if I told you or not?"

"Because..." The truth was, she didn't entirely know. It had been nagging at her ever since Holly had told her. But why? This was just a rebound. They didn't have to get that deep.

Jason shot her a teasing look from those deep blue eyes. "I see what's going on here. You're curious because you care."

"Of course I care."

"I mean, it's more than sex. You're falling for me. You want to know all about me. My hopes and dreams. My issues. My feelings."

"I'm going to hit you with a damn pool cue if you don't stop."

He burst out laughing, and after a wary moment, she joined in. "Had you going, didn't I?"

"You're a freaking idiot."

Now they were both laughing...back to normal, in other words. As if they'd danced close to the edge of intimacy, then waltzed away. She realized her pulse was fluttering.

When their amusement died down, he said, "When I was growing up, I didn't know I had an actual problem. All I knew was that some things were more difficult for me. I assumed I was...not smart."

"That's bullshit. You knew you were smart."

"No. I knew I wasn't stupid. I knew I was smart about some things. I could read people, I was good with my hands, I was good at math. I was good in a crisis. I had a good memory because it took me so long to read things. But when it came to school, well, you know how it was. I never got diagnosed, but I dated an occupational therapist who confirmed it, unofficially."

"Are you dyslexic?"

"Something like that."

"You don't want to find out for sure?"

"Hardly matters now. I'm a freaking fire chief!" He crossed to his closet and grabbed a blazer. Shrugging it on, he posed for her. "How's this?"

She had to hand it to him, he looked fantastic. That summer weight, light gray, well cut jacket set off his dark hair and the deep blue of his eyes. He ran a hand through his thick dark waves and tried to bring some order to them. It didn't quite work, but then again, it never did. Jason would never be a "paint within the lines" kind of guy.

"Good," she told him. "That blazer sets off your 'just had hot sex on a couch' look."

He winked at her. "Just what I was going for."

She followed him toward the bedroom door. "Even if you didn't have a diagnosis, you could have told me you had trouble with reading. I wouldn't have judged you, you know."

He looked down at her as he opened the door. "Yes, you would."

"You don't know that."

"I do. You're judging me now." Always the gentleman, he gestured for her to precede him out the door. "You're judging me for not telling you."

"Damn it. You're right." How did Jason always do that? He was perceptive in a way that always caught her by surprise. "But I could have been a better tutor if I'd known."

They started down the staircase, lost in their conversation. "You were a great tutor. But mostly you were a hot girl helping me out of the kindness of her heart. I probably would have stuck needles under my fingernails rather than tell you I had a problem."

"Well, you're talking about it now. Sounds like emotional growth."

"Emotional..." He stopped halfway down the stairs. "It was Holly, wasn't it? That damn kid." He scrubbed a hand through his hair, shaking his head, his expression so exasperated that she had to laugh.

"She had a whole theory about you."

They hurried the rest of the way down the stairs. "I'm sure she does. *Do not* tell me what it is."

"Oh hell no. That's Holly's thing."

"What's Holly's thing?" The girl herself popped her head over the railing as they reached the turn in the stairway. Her cheeks were pink with sunburn, her hair windblown. She must have just gotten off her bike. She'd signed up for an inordinate number of summer courses, which Jason said was unusual.

"Jesus," Jason said. "I thought you were at debate class."

"I demolished the competition in record time. There's just no good argument for continuing the patriarchy."

Kendra searched for an excuse for being upstairs with Jason. "Hi Holly. I was helping Jason pick out a suit for tonight's town meeting. What do you think?"

"I think it's a pretty good story to come up with off the top of your head." Holly grinned mischievously at them and took a bite from a green apple. "But it doesn't explain why your hair is messed up."

"It's not messed up. This is a style. A Black girl style, so don't be casting doubt."

"Are you seriously pulling the Black hair card on me? You must really not want me to know that you guys are hooking up. Too bad. I already know." She took another bite, then stepped aside to let Jason pass by. He tweaked her ponytail on the way past.

Kendra followed, wrapping her dignity around her like a cloak. Holly was going to find out sooner or later, even though they'd tried to keep it quiet.

"For the record, I'm not mad about it," Holly called as she followed them.

"For the record, no one cares." Jason ushered Kendra to the front door.

"Then why are you being so secretive? Chloe said she saw you making out in the alley behind the SweetBitter. She was feeding a stray cat, not spying, by the way. I had to pretend like I knew all about it, and do you know how humiliating that was for me? I'm the one who's supposed to know things!"

"Well, maybe you should step down as queen gossip bee. You might let something slip that's supposed to be private."

Jason was already out the door, but Kendra hung back. She'd caught an expression on Holly's face that alarmed her.

"Have a good meeting, Jason," she called after him, sounding about as casual as a person could when they'd just been caught coming out of someone's bedroom. "Work that suit, baby."

She closed the door and faced Holly, who munched her apple as she returned Kendra's gaze. She was wearing ripped jeans that were mostly threads held together by patches of fabric, and an off-the-shoulder top. The girl's usual bubbly manner was nowhere to be seen.

"Let slip something private...is he talking about you-know-what?"

"I'm sorry I ratted you out. I didn't mean to."

The girl gave a gloomy shrug. "Whatever."

"Are you all right?"

"I don't want to talk about it. Let's talk about you and Jason. What's up with that?"

Kendra didn't answer the question directly. Sometimes it felt more real than her past relationships, but they still agreed that it wasn't "serious." "We're having fun."

Holly let out a sigh and stared at her apple. "Oh well. It'd be nice to have more feminine energy around."

"I'm here now. Why don't you tell me what's wrong? I feel like I wasn't that much help last time, and I want to do better."

"So it's all about you, then?"

Kendra sighed and spread open her hands. "Take it or leave it, kid. Do you want a friendly grownup to vent to, or don't you? I have about ten minutes before I have to get back to the Blue Drake."

Holly tossed her apple core into the nearest waste basket, then crouched down next to Rusty, who affectionately pushed his snout into her hand. She snuggled with him for a moment, causing the dog's back leg to thump happily on the floor, as it always did. "It's...well, it's a situation that I don't know how to handle. And that really never happens, so it's confusing."

"Can you tell me more?" Kendra kneeled on the floor next to Holly and Rusty. " I'm not good with comforting, but I'm a badass when it comes to handling things."

Holly shook her head, pulling her lower lip between her teeth. "I can't. No."

"Is it more social media drama?"

"Not exactly."

The fact that Holly wasn't spilling all the tea was unusual. "Can you talk to Jason about it?"

"*No*. He might freak out for no reason. *Don't* say anything to him."

"Like what? You haven't told me anything."

"It's a first, right? Well, I've been accused by certain friends of being unable to keep my mouth shut. So I'm trying. But it's hard." Holly rubbed her cheek into Rusty's ruff of fur.

"You're doing great."

The girl spoke in a rush of words. "You don't understand how hard it is. It's on my mind all the time, I can't think about anything else."

"Aw honey." She was very curious now, but didn't think she could press any further. Her best guess was that Holly was suffering from an unrequited crush. Those were the absolute worst. She patted Holly's upper back. "You have to distract yourself."

"Why do you think I'm taking all these summer courses?" Holly groaned. "It's not helping."

"That's a good start, though. How about a new sport? Want

to start jogging around the lake in the mornings? How about yoga? There's a new class starting up that I wanted to try. You could come with me. You could start thinking about college too. One more year and you'll be on your own. You're going to meet so many people, and you might fall in love."

"Love sucks."

Ah-ha! Maybe she'd guessed right about the crush. "Ain't that the truth."

Holly lifted her head, showing the first real signs of interest. "That sounds juicy. Is it the rich guy who dumped you?"

"The memory on you. Wow."

Holly sat on her heels, curious gaze fixed on Kendra. At least she'd dragged her out of her despair. "What happened?"

"Bottom line, he screwed me over. We were business partners, but he abandoned all our plans and dumped me and took off for London."

"Why don't you get a new partner?"

She decided to keep her answer simple. "Because we have a contract. My options are limited."

Holly put her hands on her hips and fixed Kendra with her shining blue eyes, so like Jason's, but lighter and fiercer, somehow. "Why are you just giving up?"

"Excuse me?"

"You know what I mean. Are you just going to sit back and let him ruin all your hard work? That doesn't sound like Kendra to me."

"Girl, you don't even know me."

"I'm good at reading people. That's my thing." Holly was getting her mojo back now. "Anyway, I do know you. You stand up for yourself, and other people. I've seen you kick people out of Alvin's just for being rude to your waitstaff."

"Yeah, I don't put up with that shit."

"Of course you don't! You're Kendra Carter. Are you really going to let that dickwad win?"

Dominic the Dickwad. It had a ring to it. "Look, I appreciate the pep talk, but there's a lot you don't understand about the situation."

"You can treat me like a child if you want, but you know I'm right. You need to get your fighting spirit back. That's my official Holly Mosedale diagnosis. Hey!" A surprised smile lit up her face. "You were totally right. Getting distracted helps so much! I just had a full minute of not feeling like dog shit."

They high-fived each other. "Living the dream, girl. Living the dream."

seventeen

J ason's first official town meeting passed in a surreal blur. He talked about the plans for the fire boat acquisition, the new volunteer recruitment sessions, and the new budget request he'd submitted for the next year.

"It's a modest increase that will allow us to expand our outreach, especially to young people."

"Outreach," grumbled the oldest member of the board of aldermen, Scot Jenkins. "Sounds like one of those words that don't mean shit unless you're under forty."

"Well, I am under forty, you old goat. And I'm telling you this'll be good for the town." Jason grinned at him, knowing he was probably the only one who could get away with calling Jenkins an old goat. He'd set his own tractor on fire once during target practice; Jason had managed to salvage it from total destruction.

Fact was, he knew this town. He was going to rock this fire chief job. Kendra was going to be so impressed that she'd start taking him seriously. Like, really seriously, not just "in bed" seriously. She wouldn't scoff when he said things like "you're falling for me."

That still hurt, he could admit it.

"Nice job, Jason. Big hand for the newest member of the council, speaking as the second newest." Earl Granger stood up and clapped, and since people tended to follow Granger's lead, everyone else applauded too. Damn, it was good to have an ally in the mix.

Granger had taken on the job of public safety officer only a couple weeks ago, just after learning that he and Bliss were having twins. Their story had to be one of the most romantic Jason had ever heard, starting with Granger posing as the gorgeous Bliss's bodyguard. Now they were madly in love and Bliss was on bedrest for the last weeks of her pregnancy.

If anyone could handle two newborns, it would probably be the big, stern former FBI agent. Or he'd be completely over-whelmed. Either way, Jason looked forward to teasing him relentlessly, since that was their vibe.

"Thank you, it's great to be here." Jason bowed to acknowl-edge the warm welcome, but he was more than ready to be done with this meeting. He was already sweating through his jacket in the stuffy meeting room at city hall.

After the meeting adjourned, Jason caught up with Granger in the hallway and muttered, "Thinking about a petition to ban suit jackets during meetings. You in?"

"But you look so dapper," Granger said dryly. Typical Granger, pulling a word like that out of his ass. "You can always go back to the old uniform. Having second thoughts?"

"Never. I'm finally being recognized for more than my charming smile." He smiled charmingly at Granger, who drew back with an affronted scowl.

"What is that?" He circled a finger in the direction of Jason's face.

"See? You wouldn't know a charming smile if one knocked you over."

"You know I'm marrying a model, right?"

"She's a lot more than a model," Jason said severely. "You should be ashamed of yourself."

As they reached the sunny outdoors and joined the melee of pedestrians strolling down Main Street, Granger threw up his hands. "You win."

"Does that mean I can ask you a discreet question?"

"If you must know, the condom failed."

Jason snorted. "Uh...good to know, but this has nothing to do with your sex life. I was wondering if you had any intel on why they didn't give the town manager job to Kendra. Everyone knows how smart she is. She's local, unlike the person they hired. What happened?"

"Is this you asking or Kendra?"

"She doesn't know I'm asking. She's moved on."

That wasn't completely true. He knew it still bothered Kendra. She didn't radiate that same sassy confidence she used to. It broke his heart that Lake Bittersweet had inflicted one more blow on her, after what had happened in Minneapolis. She was too proud to dig deeper, so he was doing it for her.

"Okay. I do know something." Granger glanced around to make sure no one was listening. "A call came in from someone who said he was Kendra's business partner. He said she was still committed to this other business and wouldn't be able to give her full attention to the job."

Jason's stomach gave a sickening lurch. "You've got to be kidding me." He'd expected a different sort of answer, something in the realm of "pushing people off piers is wrong." He hadn't imagined anything like sabotage from her ex-boyfriend.

"He sent a copy of the contract. It seemed pretty clear that it was still in effect. But that was just the last straw. That thing on the dock, that hurt her. The dude threatened to file suit."

Now *that* didn't surprise Jason. He'd looked like that kind of guy.

"Thanks, Granger. Just so you know, I'm going to tell Kendra. She deserves to know that she got sabotaged."

"Fair enough."

"One more thing. With the twins, I want to be the first call you guys make in any kind of emergency, especially if Bliss is going into labor. I've personally delivered two babies and wouldn't mind doubling that total."

"Thanks, man." Granger clapped him on the shoulder. "We'll try to remember that when the panic hits."

Talk about panic...try figuring out how to tell someone you cared about that her ex was going out of his way to sabotage your job hunt.

Jason put it off for a couple of days, wondering if he should let it go. She'd already been turned down for the job. Would it change anything to know what happened? Would it make things even worse to know that Dominic had a vengeful streak?

In the end, he couldn't keep the truth from her.

Sundays were the one day they both had off from work. They slept late, then went for a mountain bike ride to the old quarry. In high school, they used to dive off a craggy rock into deep green water so still it was easy to confuse the reflected rock faces with the real thing.

It hadn't changed a bit. The cliffs, with their gashes and scars left from the quarry days, still surrounded the quiet water like timeless sentinels. No one else was there, making them wonder if the current high school generation had forgotten this spot.

They dove into the cold water to rinse off the dust and sweat from the bike trail. As she hit the water, Kendra's shriek echoed off the cliffs. They splashed around like kids, then climbed the rocks back up to the top.

Since they were still alone, they made love on a blanket Jason had packed into his saddlebag. The mid-August sunshine poured down on them. The chipper sounds of chickadees echoed through the tall pines. A junco hopped nearby, cocking a curious eye their way. It was such a perfect summer moment, Jason wished he could preserve it forever, just like that.

Instead, he had to shatter it.

"There's something I have to tell you," he said gravely, after pulling his swim shorts back on. Kendra lay stretched on the blanket, one arm protecting her eyes from the sun.

"You sound so serious. Are you about to confess that you're in love with me?" She scrambled into a sitting position and grabbed for her sunglasses. With her aviator shades perched on her face and her tiny thong bikini, she looked like she belonged by a Hollywood hotel pool. "Gretchen's getting divorced and wants you back? You're leaving town to follow your dream of running a hot air balloon?"

Jason blinked at that rapid-fire list. "I never told anyone about my hot air balloon dream, damnit."

Kendra laughed, which reminded him this was serious. She really never did take him seriously, did she?

"It's not about me. It's about you. I found out why you didn't get the town manager job."

"Oh." Everything about her seemed to deflate, all her shine and laughter evaporating. "I don't give a shit anymore. It's better this way. I can help my dad get through the summer season, then figure out my next move."

Which would be leaving town, no doubt. But he didn't want to think about that.

"Kendra, listen. It wasn't you. You were kneecapped. By Dominic."

He braced himself for her reaction, which he figured would be somewhere between a lightning storm and a hurricane.

Instead, she went still. "Okay, what now? What are you talking about?"

With that blank expression, he couldn't tell what she was thinking. But she was definitely thinking something. The wheels were turning back there behind those aviator shades.

"Dominic called someone on the board and told them you were still locked into your contract."

"No no no. What did he say *exactly*? I need it word for word. Verbatim."

"Damn, Kendra. I don't know. Something about not being able to give the job your full attention. This is third-hand information."

"From who?"

"I can't reveal my source. But it's real."

She took off her sunglasses and frowned down at the blanket. "He really called the board?"

Why didn't she sound more upset? She ought to be furious, but instead she came across as...impressed, maybe? "Aren't you angry that he cost you that job?"

"Yes, but..." Her eyebrows drew together and she gazed across the lake at the rock walls. "See, with Dominic, there's always an agenda. He doesn't do things unless it benefits him in some way. So how does it benefit him to job-block me?"

"Maybe he's a vindictive ass and wants to hurt you?"

She cast him a look that managed to be both pitying and patronizing. "It's a good thing you don't know people like Dominic."

Was she implying that he couldn't handle someone like Dominic? Or understand him? "Go ahead, tell me what I'm not getting."

"He wouldn't bother to be vindictive if he didn't have a purpose for it."

"You did push his brother-in-law off the dock," he pointed out.

"He doesn't care about Bob. No. To call the board takes some effort, and Dominic doesn't waste his time. So he must have considered it time well spent. The question is, why?"

Jason got a sinking feeling that he was in over his head. Kendra ought to be angry about Dominic's games. Did she actually like that kind of thing? Because he, Jason, was never going to be that guy.

"He sounds pretty calculating."

"Yeah, that's a good word for it. Everything's a chess match to him and he doesn't like to lose."

"Most people don't like to lose."

"Then they shouldn't go up against Dom."

He caught the hint of respect in her voice, and damn, it hurt. He lay back on the blanket and let the light breeze grace him with the scent of pine needles. *This is real*, he told himself. *Pine trees and wind and rocks and grass.* That shit, Dominic's shit, that was from another world.

"It's funny," he said slowly, "that you would go from Dominic to me. We're nothing alike."

"That's a rebound for you. I guess I rebounded about as far as I could."

"Looks like. I wonder where that ball's going to bounce next?"

She glanced at him, but he could tell she didn't really see him. Her phone was out, and she was checking for cell service. She'd forgotten there was no service out here.

"Look, I need to get a hold of this situation. Do you mind if we cut our picnic short?"

"No problem." Why bother to have a picnic with someone whose thoughts were somewhere else entirely?

They packed up quickly. That knot in his stomach kept on

growing. When everything was tucked back into the panniers, he paused for a moment. Surrounded by the quiet tall pines and the majesty of the scarred rocks, he put his hands on Kendra's shoulders. Her skin was warmed by the sun, and a flush of extra color glowed in her cheeks. But when her gaze met his, he could tell her busy mind was far away.

"Just want to make sure you're okay," he murmured. That wasn't exactly what he meant; he wanted to make sure *they* were okay. But were they even a *they?*

"Oh, I'm more than okay. This changes everything, Jason. Thank you for telling me, thanks for digging up that intel. I wonder if he knew I'd find out, or if he thought I wouldn't? That's the thing about Dominic, he thinks so many moves ahead, you never know."

Jason had to hand it to the man. It was truly amazing that Dominic had managed to take over Kendra's thoughts so quickly, and from so far away. That could mean only one thing, in his opinion.

Kendra wasn't over Dominic, not even a little bit.

"Happy to help," he murmured.

She stood on tiptoe and wrapped her arms around his neck. With her lips pressed to his, her breasts warm against his chest, her hips cupping his bulge, that full-body embrace sent a flood of heat through him.

He returned her kiss, because what else could he do? This was Kendra, and he wanted her. No matter how many questions were running through his mind, his body wanted her. *He* wanted her.

"See you later?" she whispered against his lips.

Relief flooded through him. They weren't done. Not yet, anyway. "Absolutely. Text me when you're heading over."

They hopped on their bikes and rode into the woods, with her leading the way. He breathed in the piney air, watched her brown legs work the pedals, and tried to reassure himself that everything would be okay.

eighteen

As soon as Kendra got back to town, she stashed her bike in the garage and hurried inside her parents' house. *Her* house, she corrected herself. She'd been living here since she left the Twin Cities, and hadn't made any moves towards finding her own place. Maybe if she'd gotten the town manager position, she would have moved out and reclaimed her independence. But why bother to do that, when she might end up leaving Lake Bittersweet again?

If she'd gotten the position.

Make that—if Dominic hadn't interfered and cost her the position.

She ought to be furious. Maybe in some pocket of her heart, she was. But mostly, she wanted to know what he was up to. Dominic trying to sabotage her was a whole different story than Dominic forgetting all about her. She wasn't sure which was worse.

That fucker always got her twisted up.

"I'm home!" she called into the spacious sunken living room

where her father spent most of his time. Her mother was back in Arkansas again with Grandma. She'd come home for a whirlwind three weeks, cleaned the house, done all the laundry, and lectured Kendra about please, please, *please* making sure Alvin took his blood pressure meds.

She also texted every other day as a reminder.

Kendra sighed and checked her father's pill tray. On track.

"In here!" her father called. "Mind helping me with something?"

Damn, she really wanted to call Dominic, and with the time difference, her window was closing. She hurried into the living room and saw that her father had gotten one leg of his favorite old track suit stuck in the workings of his recliner.

"Lordy, Pop. The trouble you get into when I'm not around."

She remembered another time, just recently, when he'd tried to move the refrigerator in the restaurant kitchen and gotten stuck behind that. And a few weeks ago, he'd worn his house slippers to the restaurant. After an hour of shuffling around and tripping over himself, he'd sent her home to fetch his shoes.

What was going on with her dad? She loved and adored her father more than any other human being in the world, even her mother. She and her mom had never been close the way she and Alvin were. Everyone in the family called her a Daddy's girl, and she never objected. After the Dominic disaster, all she'd wanted was to run home to her daddy. So it fit.

"That's me, Mr. Trouble." Her father hummed one of his old songs, "Trouble on my Mind."

She felt his deep voice in her bones as she worked on freeing his pants leg. That voice had sung her to sleep when she was little, serenaded her and her friends during slumber parties, soothed her lonely moments in Minneapolis when she played her "Redfish" channel on Spotify. For her, there was no voice in the world like his.

"I might have to rip this old thing," she told him, tugging on his pants leg. "You okay with that?"

"We could call someone to help. Where's Jason at?"

"It's Jason's day off. Besides, the fire department has better things to do than rescue a twenty-year-old track suit from getting torn."

"It's at least thirty. Picked it up in Kansas City before a show, there was an old thrift shop right down the street from the theater. They called it Threads Be Bared, I'll never forget that."

And just like that, Kendra relaxed. Her father remembered an amazing amount of detail from his days on the road. He was just fine. He wasn't showing signs of decline, she was just being hypersensitive because he was so important to her.

She pulled the velour fabric away from the metal, limiting the rip as much as she could. "You're free. There's a grease stain, but nothing Mom can't handle when she gets back."

Her mother always insisted on doing the laundry, claiming no one else could do it right, and neither of them put up a fuss about that.

"Thanks, princess. I was just going to get myself a ginger ale."

"I'll get it. You relax."

In the kitchen, she poured him a glass of his favorite raspberry-flavored ginger ale and gazed around the expansive kitchen that her mother had left in its usual immaculate state.

Dominic had never been here. She'd wanted him to spend Christmas with her family, but he'd gone back to his own family in Toronto instead.

How had he known she was going for the town manager job?

Mark must have told him. Maybe her little dunking prank had backfired on her in yet another way. What had she been thinking?

She hadn't been *thinking*, per se. She'd been remembering

the carefree days of that summer with her friends. The rush of giddy fun, the high of being young, with your whole future ahead. That old fearlessness...she'd wanted that back.

Jason brought that feeling back. That was why she'd momentarily lost her mind on that pier.

She padded across the soft taupe carpet into the living room, only to discover that her father had fallen asleep. A light snore filled the room, and his head was tilted back, mouth slightly open. Asleep, he looked...older. His cheeks sagged without his usual smile. She could hardly bear it. *Wake up, scold me for not using Mom's coaster, then wink at me.*

Gently. she set down the glass—on a coaster, of course—on the side table next to the recliner. She picked up the remote and turned down the music he'd been listening to—old-school Bootsy Collins.

Then she tiptoed from the living room and went to her own room to call Dominic. Her mother had left everything just as it was, so she'd have a place to stay during visits.

But when she'd returned from Minneapolis, she'd boxed up most of her old high school stuff—achievement certificates, photos of her with her friends, flyers for various bands who'd played at the Blue Drake—so her surroundings wouldn't seem so childish. But she hadn't put up anything in their place, so the walls were mostly bare, other than an inspirational Maya Angelou poster on one wall—"Do the best you can until you know better, then when you know better, do better"—and an Eartha Kitt quote on the other. "My recipe for life is not being afraid of myself, afraid of what I think or of my opinions." Those were worth keeping around.

She drew in a deep breath and pressed Dominic's number, which she'd never deleted from her contacts. They were still business partners, after all, in a cursed kind of way.

"Do you know what time it is?" Dominic grumbled through a yawn. His familiar voice sent a shockwave through her—it felt almost surreal to hear him on the phone.

"You didn't have to pick up. "

"I thought it was an emergency. You called twice." That was the only way to get through the "do not disturb" setting on his phone.

"It *is* an emergency." *You sabotaged my job, you devious fuck.* "Wait, are you speaking with a British accent now?"

"I'm a chameleon, Kendra. It's part of what makes me so effective. I know how to adapt to my surroundings, and then, of course, dominate them."

Was his vibrant baritone even sexier with a British accent? Why yes. Yes it was. Damnit.

She lay back on her bed and stared up at the ceiling, which she'd once covered with glow-in-the-dark stars. Most of them had fallen off over the years, and if that wasn't a commentary on her hopes and dreams, she didn't know what was.

"Why did you call the board of aldermen and lie about me?" Maybe he was so groggy that he'd answer a straight question.

"Lie? I bloody well didn't lie, Kendra."

Bloody? Jesus, he really was going all the way with this Brit thing.

"I said that our contract is still in force and it would be hard for you to give another job your full attention."

The *hypocrisy*...

"You took another job!"

"And look how difficult it is to give any time to Explastica. I do try."

"No, you don't."

"I try a little." She could picture his smirk. "Every other Friday for about an hour."

"So you can claim you're still in it?"

His tone turned virtuous. "Just because I'm trying to bring in some income until Explastica gets off the ground doesn't mean I'm giving up on it. I'm over here rooting for you to line up the funding for the next phase."

The unfairness made her want to scream. "I need to earn a living too."

"You are. Working at your dad's restaurant, I hear. Mark Jordan told me all about the Blue Balls." His mocking tone, with that extra British flair, made her face flush with heat. "That's fine, I don't want you to starve, darling. I just don't want you to put all your talent and energy anywhere important. Glorified waitress is acceptable. Running an entire town isn't."

Glorified waitress? Oooo, that fucker, what a low-blow.

Don't react. Pick your battles.

"Well, what can I say, Dom? You won. I didn't get the job. Unfortunately, I haven't had much luck with the funding. Very slow progress on that front. And all the others, come to think of it. The company's going nowhere."

"I have faith, darling."

She gritted her teeth together. "You can't do this forever."

"Can't I? Did you ever think that maybe it was all part of a bigger plan?"

"What are you talking about? What bigger plan?"

"I've learned a lot since I've been here. Working for a large corporation like Global Solutions is eye-opening. It could benefit both of us down the line."

Both of them? What was Dominic playing at? Did he not want to abandon Explastica after all? Or was he just covering his bases? Knowing him, that was probably it. Dominic would always have a plan B and beyond, all the way up to Z.

"Here's the thing, Dominic. I don't believe anything you say anymore. You can keep messing with my job opportunities until you get tired of it, but I'm not going to ever trust you again. I'll buy you out eventually. I'm patient."

"No, you're not."

"I can be. It's better than letting you fuck me over again."

"You don't want to admit it, but I did you a bloody favor by making sure you didn't get that job. You're so talented. You'd be wasted in that little dot on the map."

"You mean, my hometown," she said hotly. "The place I love, the one you could never be bothered to visit, not even once."

"Is that still bothering you? After all this time? It almost sounds like you're not over me."

And he was gone.

She slowly let the phone drop onto the bed next to her. She realized her eyes were dry from staring at the scattered stars on her ceiling for so long. Allowing her eyelids to fall shut, she let her mind go empty. This was too confusing. What did Dominic want? More than a buyout, no doubt. Maybe he just enjoyed tormenting her?

She could call her mother, who'd blasted Dom with all kinds of names after the breakup. But she knew exactly what she'd hear from Mama. *He'd better not mess with me and mine.*

Besides, Mama had enough on her hands since today was a chemo day for Granny.

What if he was telling the truth about his reasons for leaving? *He's not. He's a liar.*

What if he was right that she wasn't over him?

No. He's wrong. I don't want him anymore.

Then why was she still buzzing with the adrenaline of that conversation? *Because he's no good.*

Images drifted through her mind. The quarry lake, shining like a green mirror. Jason diving off the cliff, his body tracing a perfect arc through the air. Their laughter echoing off the rock walls.

Jason. The thought of him steadied her. Suddenly she was able to breathe again. She picked up her phone and sent him a text. *Tonight?*

nineteen

For the next couple of weeks, Jason held his breath, as if waiting for the other shoe to drop. Would Kendra decide she'd had enough of this rebound experiment? Would Dominic rule her thoughts while she tried to figure out his chess moves?

But none of that happened. She came over almost every night, and in between, they texted, FaceTimed, went to the movies, had pizza with friends, and generally acted like any other couple.

When he asked her if she'd talked to Dominic, she told him it hadn't gone well. "I don't want to think about him. That's just falling into his trap."

After enough time had passed, he let out a sigh of relief. They'd dodged the Dominic bullet. When word spread that Gretchen was pregnant, the path forward looked even more hopeful. No one was lurking out there ready to torpedo their relationship. Was it actually possible that they had a future together, him and Kendra?

He'd never felt so solid, so sure about himself. He was the

damn fire chief, and he knew how to make Kendra happy. Those two things transformed him from the inside out. He loved being with Kendra, loved the way they laughed together, made love together, the way they could talk about anything and everything. Good God, it might be even more than that. Could it be...love?

Whatever it was, he didn't want it to end.

He wanted this summer to last forever, too, but it was drawing to a close. Labor Day came, and Holly went back to school. The town began to empty out as the tourists went back to their regular lives. The days were still hot, but they didn't last as long, and the nights were chilling down. At least, they were outside. Inside, with him and Kendra, they kept getting hotter.

One day in mid-September, Colleen poked her head into Jason's office at the firehouse. "Got a minute?"

Damn it. He'd been in the middle of a hot text to Kendra. He raised a finger, telling her to wait a minute, then quickly finished his thought.

Want to make out in the fire truck later? I'll show you how my fire hose works.

Kendra always cracked up over his ridiculous firefighting double-entendres.

As long as it gets me wet, I don't need the details, she answered.

Okay then. Game on. He clicked his phone off and beckoned for Colleen to come in. She plopped down onto the chair facing the desk and crossed one ankle over her knee. Her silver-sprinkled dark hair hung in a braid down her back. She was in her late thirties, and one of the best volunteers on the crew. "I have a problem."

"Okay." All of his crew members seemed to have problems, and they all wanted to dump them on his shoulders. He couldn't remember ever going to Thomas Cooper about his problems, so either he was doing something wrong or they had very different leadership styles. "How can I help?"

"I'm getting married."

He squinted at her, puzzled. "Congratulations? That's great news. Why is that a problem?"

"That's not the problem. The crew is the problem. I'm getting married to a woman. I'm bisexual, as you probably know."

"Didn't know, don't need to know."

She shot him a skeptical look, then continued. "I've dated men and women, but then I fell in love and now I'm getting married." Her chin was raised, as if she expected him to argue with her.

"Still not seeing the problem, or at least a problem *I* can solve. I'm happy for you."

"Right, because some people won't accept me and Lisa, and you can't do anything about that." She lifted her eyebrows at him. When he stared back blankly, she said, "You're the fire chief now. You set the tone. You lead the way."

"Right. Of course. I'll make sure no one pulls any crap. If you have trouble with anyone, you tell me."

"No, Jason. I need more than that." She shifted her position and propped her elbows on her knees. "I wouldn't ask this of any other boss, but I trust you. Lisa agrees. We want you to perform the ceremony."

"*Me?*" He goggled at her. "I'm a fire chief, not a—"

"Can't fire chiefs marry people? Just like ship captains and anyone who gets a license on the internet. If you marry us, the rest of the crew will fall in line."

"Have you met our crew?" The volunteer firefighters were a motley and diverse bunch who loved nothing more than to tease each other mercilessly. As one of the few women, Colleen had dealt with everything from secret love letters to a midnight ukulele serenade. Some of the single guys were going to be crushed to learn she was off the market.

"A little teasing is one thing. I can handle that. You know I can. I can't handle..." She paused, twisting her mouth to one side. "Outright rejection would hurt, that's all. The crew is like another family, and my own family..."

She broke off again, swallowing hard. He wondered if he should go around his desk and give her a hug. But Colleen was a tough, capable firefighter who probably wouldn't want to be babied.

"We're not going to reject you, Colleen. You're one of us. I'll make sure everyone in this firehouse behaves professionally. And yes, I'll marry you."

"Whaaaat?" A shocked voice sounded from the direction of his office door. Brent was hovering just outside. "Jason's getting married to Colleen!" he yelled toward the common room where the firefighters gathered.

Within seconds, his office was filled with what felt like half the department.

"Congratulations, man!" Erwin Brown crowed. "But damn, I owe Gavin some cash."

"Right?" said Donnie O'Neill. "I had it all wrong. Fuck me. Happy for you both, but I'm gonna need a second job to pay up."

Poor Colleen slumped in her chair. Every time she tried to open her mouth, someone else talked over her.

"When's the wedding?" ... "Where are we gonna do it?" ... "My wife makes upcycled wedding dresses, I'll give her your number..." Until finally Jason planted both of his hands on his desk and rose to his feet.

"Enough. Colleen and I are not getting married."

Quiet fell over the group, but only for a moment. Then cacophony broke out again. Erwin Brown had the most powerful voice, so his won out over the others. "Then who lost the bet? I knew it wasn't Jason. My money was on Lisa."

"I said Lisa too," said Donnie. "Put a hundred dollars on it."

"A hundred? How do you have a hundred extra dollars, don't you have like, ten kids?"

"Four, but I get your point. That's why I cut myself off at a hundred. But I knew it was a sure bet, the way those two look at each other. I could have won even bigger."

Jason met Colleen's gaze, and watched her eyes slowly fill with tears. The other firefighters weren't rejecting her; they were betting on her love life in typical firehouse style.

Donnie's hand settled onto her shoulder. He was a former truck driver who'd quit his job to stay home with his kids and help his wife sell candles on Etsy. He'd joined the volunteer fire department to get out of the house more.

"Well, what do you say, Colleen-girl? Did I lose my shirt again?"

Colleen tilted her head to look back at him. Then she bolted to her feet and threw her arms around the pot-bellied older man. "You didn't. You're right. Me and Lisa are getting married."

Donnie patted her back and let out a long whoop. "Three-to-one odds, bay-beee!"

Colleen pulled away, rapidly blinking back those tears. "You guys were betting on me this whole time?"

"You know how we roll," said Erwin. "Anything worthy of a bet, gets a bet. You're going to have some pissed-off firefighters around here, I'll tell you what."

"Not because you're getting married," said Donnie quickly. "Congratulations on that. Some people had Annie Ryan on their bingo card."

"Annie Ryan? We never even dated."

"I know, but you know how some guys are. She's hot, and so are you, and that's about where it ended. Lisa's hot too," Erwin added. "Don't get me wrong."

"Wait wait wait." Colleen waved her hands in the air. "Are you guys telling me no one put a man on their bingo card?"

Donnie frowned. "Dick Spoon might have, just because no one was taking those odds. Everyone else kind of saw it coming. Seemed like you were done with men."

"So done," Colleen agreed. "Except for all of you here. You're the best." She blew kisses to every man in the room. "And you're all invited to the wedding, which will be conducted by our very own fire chief, Jason Mosedale."

Jason sketched a bow as the crew broke out into applause. Then he motioned for everyone to pipe down. "I know it's a big day, but is there any chance we could try to get some work done? Maybe restock the paramedic van? Polish up the ladder truck? Clean the kitchen? Who's up on that chore list? Wait, where's everyone going?"

They were all backing out of his office, bumping into each other, clearly trying to avoid getting their name called. "I guess I know how to clear my office," he called after them. "Donnie, don't act like I don't know you're on kitchen duty!"

Then he sank back down into his chair and picked up his phone.

Kendra had texted him. *Just heard some hot gossip at the bar. Hint: wedding bells.*

Way ahead of you, he texted back. *Hint: how can I acquire an online minister's license?*

A moment later, a link popped onto his phone.

He skipped past it. He'd deal with that later.

Kendra texted, *I still can't believe the firehouse gets more gossip than the bar. That's all kinds of messed up.*

*Life event, not gossip. *Scoldy-face emoji**

Are you making up emojis now?

He chuckled at that one, then sent the fireman emoji, along with a flexed bicep and a flame. Then he drew in a steady breath, and texted, *Wanna be my date for the wedding? Give the town something to talk about?*

They'd given up keeping their relationship to themselves. Between the firehouse and the Blue Drake bar, that would be impossible. But hanging out at Mariano's was one thing; going to a wedding together would mark them as a real couple.

You mean, besides the town's first same-sex firehouse wedding?

Plz, not even shocking anymore.

But an interracial rebound is?

Doubt it. But Kendra and Jason might be.

You seriously want to go pubic?

He burst out laughing, and was still chuckling when she sent the followup, *PUBLIC!!! Geez.*

I always want to go pubic with you, baby.

Shut up. Can't stop laughing. Gotta go.

He did too; the tone was sounding—a call was coming in. Structure fire at 2400 Bailey Drive. Three-alarm fire.

Shit. He knew that address. The Lake Bittersweet Home for Seniors was located there. A fire at a nursing home could be a disaster. He snatched up his pager, with which he could contact all members of the volunteer department, even those not currently on duty.

All-crew alert: we can use all the hands we can get at 2400 Bailey. 3 alarm fire.

Adrenaline surging through his veins, he ran to the apparatus bay and donned his turnout gear. The familiar process helped calm his nerves. This was the biggest fire event that had happened under his watch. He had to get it right.

He swung into the ladder truck along with Colleen, Erwin, and Donnie. The rest of the crew loaded into the paramedic van, which was the only other official rig. Sirens sounding, they hurtled down Main Street. A blur of faces in the streets watched them career past.

They reached the senior home in just a few minutes. Heavy dark smoke rose from the rear of the structure. Soaring flames licked at the roof, aiming for the sky. Jason saw that ten or so volunteers had already assembled and were busy donning helmets and fireproof pants. Everyone kept a set of turnouts with them at all times, just in case they couldn't make it to the firehouse to gear up.

Jason climbed out of the vehicle, already assessing the situation. He'd spent many hours at the nursing home, doing everything from locating missing residents to running fire drills with the staff. He'd even taught dance classes here. He knew the layout inside and out. The flames were coming from the kitchen area on the bravo side. The kitchen occupied an L that had been added on in recent years, which meant that if they could get the fire out quickly, the rest of the structure could be saved.

He quickly took command of the scene. He directed Colleen, the engineer, and Donnie, the best aerial operator, to position the truck around the back. From there, they could extend the ladder and attack the flames from above.

In the meantime, the most important thing was to clear the building. The staff members had already started the process, and a steady stream of wheelchairs and gurneys and oxygen tanks trickled from the building. Jason knew that eight of the residents used oxygen tanks, and when he head-counted those eight, he nodded in relief.

A number of residents were mobile enough to walk themselves outside, but now they were milling around, confused, not sure what to do.

"Set up a triage area," Jason ordered the volunteers. "Set up barricades and get the residents to stay behind them. Paramedics, where are you?"

Someone gestured behind them, and he saw Brent hurrying forward with the emergency kit.

"Find out if anyone needs medical help," Jason told him.

One of the elderly people in a wheelchair raised his hand and shouted. "I left my teeth behind. Can't talk without my teeth."

"I understand you just fine without your teeth," Jason reassured him. "We'll look for them as soon as we can. First we have to get all the people out."

"But someone might steal 'em, they're real good ones."

Don't laugh, Jason lectured himself as he focused on managing the scene. Serious situation here.

But fortunately, not life-threatening. Over the next hour, Jason, his crew and the staff members managed to get the forty or so residents out of the building and into the triage area. From there, everyone watched Donnie send a heavy stream of water onto the roof, while a two-person crew operated another fire hose from the ground.

The most dramatic moment came when the roof of the L collapsed, sending gasps and sobs through the crowd of elderly onlookers.

"It's okay, everyone," he called. "They're getting it under control. It's all good as long as we can save the music room, right? We'll be putting on another dance class before you know it."

He got a few laughs out of the seniors, which made him think of his father's comment. *Some of us just try to bring a little fun into the world.* That was good too, along with carrying people out of burning buildings.

Gradually, the flames died back, shrinking away from the constant flow of water like a demon going back into its cave. When he saw only black smoke and no show of flame, he knew they'd gotten the upper hand.

He refastened his facepiece—he'd lifted it to talk to the elders —and beckoned Erwin to follow him inside. The two of them did a thorough search of the entire premises to make sure that no one had been left behind, and to assess the damage. All the residents' rooms were intact, but the entire place reeked of smoke. It wouldn't be safe for them to stay there tonight.

Now they had another problem on their hands. What to do with forty seniors with various degrees of disability?

Back out front, he searched out the director, Alicia Moore, a forty-ish woman who wore her hair in a coronet of graying braids. He suspected she wore that style to connect with her more elderly charges.

"We have to find another place for everyone tonight. It's very smoky in there, and you'll need to set up a temporary kitchen."

She twisted her hands together. "C'mon Jason. I mean Chief Mosedale. Where am I supposed to find space for forty seniors with a combined total of a hundred and thirty medical conditions?"

"That's not our responsibility," Erwin grumbled. "We just put out the fires."

Jason shook his head at him. "We can help. We're the Lake Bittersweet Fire Department, we can handle anything, right?" *Set the tone. Lead the way.*

Erwin nodded grudgingly. "Of course we can."

"Let's break it down into groups, from those with the most medical needs to those who can handle crashing on someone's couch. Not literally," he added quickly. "We'll make sure it isn't a couch."

Alicia Moore laughed a little, visibly relaxing. "Good idea. Thanks, Jason. Chief Mosedale. I'm a little rattled, to be honest."

"You're doing great. No injuries, that's the important thing. Everything else can be fixed."

After consulting with her assistant, Alicia came back with a list divided into the groups Jason had suggested. He called the hospital in Braddock on behalf of the top tier of patients. It took some strong-arming, but they agreed to step up and fit them in somehow.

A call to the next closest independent living home took care of the middle-tier group, those who didn't need oxygen tanks or more consistent monitoring. As he was hanging up with the last call, a text from Kendra came in.

Just heard about the nursing home fire. How can we help? I'm here with Carly. We can feed people, we can open up some cabins. Whatever's needed.

He caught Alicia Moore's eye. "The Blue Drake is offering to help."

"We'll take it. Is that Kendra?"

"Yes. I'll get her on speaker."

As soon as her voice came on the line, a sense of relief filled him. She was so smart and coolheaded. He quickly explained the situation. "We still have about fifteen people who need a place to stay."

"No problem, so long as they don't mind doubling up in a cabin. Everyone will get their own bed."

Alicia nodded. "I'm sure that will be fine. Would it be okay if some staffers stayed over as well? Some familiar faces would probably help."

"Absolutely. We'll make it work. And Alicia—my dad and I are going to close the restaurant for the night and serve only residents. It'll be like a night out for them."

"Oh Kendra. That's above and beyond."

"This is an emergency. Lake Bittersweet always comes together in an emergency, right? Consider it done, no arguing. What are you going to need down the line?"

"Well..." Alicia seemed so overwhelmed that Jason took over.

"The kitchen is a smoldering pile of debris, so they'll either need a camp kitchen or a whole lot of pizza delivery."

"I'll organize a kitchen setup. I did that here when we renovated. I'm happy to take that off your shoulders, Alicia, if that's a help."

"You're an angel, Kendra."

Jason's heart swelled with pride and a feeling of...was it destiny? He and Kendra were an amazing team. He'd just handled his first big crisis without a hitch. And Kendra was stepping up to handle the aftermath. Between the two of them, they could do anything. The thought was intoxicating.

The call ended, and a moment later, a text came in for him.

For your eyes only. Your nephew live-streamed from the scene of the fire. You're about to be famous again. So freaking hot! I mean you, not the fire.

His head jerked up and he scanned his surroundings. There he was, the little punk. His fourteen-year-old nephew stood off to one side, his iPhone held up to catch all the drama. At least he wasn't doing stupid graffiti dares like he had been recently.

"Bobby!" he called. "What the hell are you doing?"

Bobby snatched his phone against his chest, but lifted his chin defiantly. "I'm reporting the news."

Jason strode over to him and planted his fists on his hips. "You're fourteen."

They locked gazes. Jason's older sister had been tearing her hair out over Bobby and his rambunctious nature, but Jason remembered all too well what it felt like to be a bored teenage boy.

"Is there anything you want to say to the audience?" Bobby waved the phone at him. "You're on live."

"Yes." He leaned toward the phone's camera, and squeezed Bobby's shoulder as he did so. "If you live anywhere near Lake Bittersweet and want to help, contact me at the firehouse, or send a message to my nephew Bobby here. We can use your help."

Jason knew he'd never forget the way his nephew's face lit up. *That's what it's all about, inspiring the kids*, he thought as he hurried back toward the others. The next step was to figure out how to transport everyone to their night's lodgings. Logistical nightmare, coming up. His brain was already working on that problem when it took a sharp left turn. *Why not kids of his own?*

Why not? Seriously? What had stopped him all these years when Gretchen kept bringing it up?

The time hadn't been right. He hadn't felt solid enough in either their relationship, or in himself.

But now...everything felt different. He was a fire chief. He'd survived his first crisis. And then there was Kendra.

twenty

This was Lake Bittersweet at its very best—everyone pulling together in a crisis—and Kendra loved every second. After she'd offered to take the logistics off Alicia's hands, she somehow ended up being the point person for all aspects of Operation Respected Elders, as she insisted on calling it.

After all, her father wasn't much younger than some of the seniors who'd just gone through the trauma of a fire.

Phase one was a repeat of her long-ago days as a chambermaid at the Blue Drake. She and Gina and Carly did a speed-clean of each empty cabin, sweeping out the dust, making up beds, turning up the heat. Luckily, with the season nearly over, only two cabins were booked. The rest could go to the seniors.

"Oh my god, these dusters are just as awkward as I remember," she told the others as they wiped down the Venetian blinds in the Wood Duck Cabin. "I always swore I'd never do this job again, and now look at me."

"It's not a job," Carly pointed out cheerfully, "since you're not getting paid this time." Baby Teddy snuggled happily in a sling on her chest. He didn't seem to mind the cleanup, though Carly covered his face every time there was dust involved.

"Oooh, good point. I'm a volunteer fuckup now."

"You are not now and never have been a fuckup." Gina dumped a full dustpan into the garbage bag they were carrying from one cabin to the next. "Besides, I bet I know why you signed us up for this."

"I'm not the only one who volunteered."

"Right, but you're the only one that Jason Mosedale has on speed dial." Gina made a sassy face at her. "Don't even try the fake innocent face. I know you too well, especially after all the shit we pulled that summer."

"What shit? I was always the good one," Kendra said virtuously. "I even saved up bail money for you guys just in case it was ever needed."

They all burst into laughter, then moved into the bedroom to quickly make up the beds. "So how is everything in Rebound City?" Gina asked as she plumped the pillows.

"The traffic is crazy." Kendra tried to keep a straight face, but couldn't when Carly snorted out loud.

"Now that's what I like to hear. Not the details," Carly added quickly, "since Jason's kind of like a brother to Thomas, and therefore to me."

Kendra's phone buzzed. "It's Jason, hang on."

"We got this, you go do your thing." Gina waved her away. "For which you should be getting credit for as town manager, by the way. Still trying not to be bitter about that."

Kendra tuned them out so she could listen to Jason. Her friends didn't know the full story of the town manager job. What would they think if they knew her ex had cost her the job? She hadn't told them because it would require explaining about Dominic, which she still hadn't done. He'd called her three times since that first conversation, but she hadn't answered the phone.

Jason, on the other hand...she always answered when he called. Just seeing his name on her screen made her smile. " How's it going over there, babe?" he asked, his intimate tone sending a flush through her.

"The cabins are just about ready. I called in a few favors from some vendors, so now we have access to two delivery vans and three pickup trucks."

"Sounds like a convoy. I've had a bunch of people call in offering blankets and casseroles and other stuff like that. Can I forward all that to you?"

"Absolutely. We'll set out the casseroles in the restaurant." Or maybe freeze them for use in the temporary kitchen, once that was set up. "I've lined up some appliances for the camp kitchen. When do you think my guys can get in there to start setting that up?"

"Your guys?"

"I have guys." She found herself grinning, despite the circumstances. "And they're ready to do my bidding."

The "guys" in question were mostly people who owed Alvin favors. He had a way of helping people when they most needed it —like when they first got out of rehab, or even prison, in one case. Those people never forgot his nonjudgmental kindness, and jumped at the chance to repay the Carter family.

"Of course they are, who wouldn't be? I'll do your bidding anytime, night or day, but especially night, of course."

A shiver passed through her as she pictured the last night they'd spent together. She'd woken him in the middle of the night, wild with desire. They'd made love in the sweet, sweaty darkness and she'd felt so close to him, tears had come to her eyes.

She shook off the memory and took a lighter tone. "You're not calling just to flirt, are you? Because about twenty texts just came in." Her phone had been dinging up a storm for the past two minutes.

His tone shifted to professional. "Yeah, that was me forwarding offers of help. We're about to do another damage assessment, so I'll have an answer about the kitchen in half an hour or so."

"Sounds good. And Jason, be careful in there."

"Are you worried about me?" The flirty tone was back.

"The fire looked bad in that live stream."

"The fire's out. I'm considering doing the walk-through without a shirt on, though, just in case someone else has a camera rolling."

"Oooh, I dare you." She let out a gleeful laugh. "Seriously, I'll make it worth your trouble if you go in there all man-sexy and bare-chested. I'm talking sexual favors. Only if it's safe for you," she added quickly.

"It's against protocol. And I am the fire chief, so I'll have to earn sexual favors some other way."

"I'll think of something."

"Tonight?"

"Tonight." When she ended the call, she turned to find her two friends—and a baby—staring at her.

"You are freaking glowing." Gina pointed at her face.

"I'm sweating."

Carly joined in as she kissed her baby's curly head. "You're happy."

"Yes, because it's so nice to be back with my two besties doing what we do best."

"Cleaning cabins?" Carly screwed up her face.

"Giving each other shit."

They all laughed at the accuracy. Then Gina shook her curly head. "I don't believe you. It's because of Jason."

"Rebounds rock. Just like you said."

"No. I mean, yes. But the way you look right now, we're not dealing with a rebound anymore. Back me up, Carly."

Carly was swaying from side to side to soothe Teddy. She cocked her head as she aimed a smile at Kendra. "Kendra can handle her own business."

"That's right, Moretti." Kendra tossed Gina a sassy flip of her hair. "Back off."

"Fine, but you're going to need to handle it pretty soon. Sooner or later, all relationships reach that point where you either go forward or you stall out. At least back me up on that, Carly."

Carly made an apologetic face at Kendra. "She's right about that one."

"Whatever. We're having fun and it's working and I really need to make some calls right now." She checked her phone, which showed a new string of texts. "This is like an airlift operation, except with pickup trucks and a FedEx van."

"We'll finish up here. Just let us know if there's anything else we can do."

"Thank you, that'd be great." Kendra gave them each a quick hug, and stroked Teddy's silky hair. "Catch y'all later."

"Tick-tock," Gina called after her as she hurried away.

Operation Respected Elders took up the rest of Kendra's day and most of the night. She rallied all the servers and kitchen workers to make food not just for the displaced seniors, but for everyone who was pitching in to help. She coordinated vehicles to shuttle back and forth from the nursing home to the residents' various destinations.

As soon as Jason gave the all-clear, she called in the work crew she'd lined up to construct a temporary kitchen in the undamaged dining room of the nursing home. She coordinated the delivery of the appliances she'd retrieved from storage, where they'd been living since the latest renovation of the Blue

Drake's kitchen. Before close of business, she contacted the local health department and explained the situation with enough urgency that they scheduled an emergency inspection of the temporary kitchen for the next afternoon.

She left the insurance issue to Alicia Moore. The director would be responsible for getting them to sign off on allowing the residents back on the property.

When all the appliances had been delivered, she gathered together her crew of workers. They had long hours of plumbing in appliances and roughing in countertops ahead of them. She needed to give them some extra motivation.

"When I first came back to Lake Bittersweet, all I could think about was when I was going to leave again. But today, I remembered what's so great about this place. We take care of each other here. We might disagree, even fight—but in the end, we're there for our neighbors. Right? Just imagine, we can personally keep forty elderly people from being homeless. I thank you, my dad thanks you, and you'll all eat for a month for free at Alvin's Burgers and Blues. Are you with me?"

The cheers and applause made her heart swell; there really should have been a soundtrack. Chariots of Fire, perhaps.

Besides, it was true. She hadn't thought about leaving Lake Bittersweet since she and Jason had gotten together—well, maybe briefly, when Dominic had suggested London. But only briefly.

Throughout the day, she served as everyone's main point of contact. If anyone had a question about where to go next, who to pick up, where to drop the blankets, what freezer to put a casserole into, they called or texted Kendra.

The biggest glitch came when her phone died and she had to dash into the SweetBitter Cafe to recharge it, since her car charger was too slow.

While her phone was plugged in, Rick plied her with quad-shot espressos and homemade donut holes. A small group gathered around her to get updates. Everyone seemed to have watched the live stream of Jason and the rest of the crew battling the fire.

"Check out this part," Rick told her. He flashed his phone at her, and showed her a shot of Jason emerging from the glass double doors of the nursing home, a frail elderly woman in a housedress in his arms. She was gazing up at him with a look of pure adoration. "*Ai muchacho bellino curado.*" Rick had a quirk of making up Spanish curse words. "Now that's a hero. I think we need that on a fireman recruitment poster."

The crowd chimed in.

"I saw that clip on Instagram."

"It was on the news too."

Kendra couldn't wait to tease Jason with the fact that he was about to be in the news all over again. This time, he'd have to handle his own press, but she knew he'd have no problem now. He'd really come into his own since he'd become fire chief. So confident, so commanding—but still funny and sweet.

She couldn't wait to see him tonight.

Rick filled her Hydro Flask with espresso to go, then gave her a big sloppy kiss on the cheek. Then an extra one.

"That was for Jason," he said with a wink. "Don't go skimping, either. Make it a good one."

Rick would have been proud of how she delivered that kiss, once she and Jason were alone together at the end of that exhausting day. Since Holly sometimes volunteered at the nursing home, she'd offered to spend the night at the Blue Drake in case any of the seniors needed anything. That meant she and Jason had the entire house to themselves.

They fell into each other's arms like two storm survivors. She wrapped her arms around his neck and kissed him long and deep and slow. It wasn't a kiss meant to arouse, since they were both worn out. It was more about coming together, connecting, appreciating. Cherishing. He'd been a hero for a lot of people today, and she wanted to make sure he knew it.

"Wow," he said when they finally separated. She ran her tongue over her tingling lips. "That kiss just set a new world standard."

"Black excellence." She winked, and he laughed, then shook his head wearily.

"I could use a shower. There was a line for the shower at the firehouse."

"Let's do it." She took his hand and led him upstairs to the en suite bathroom that he used. There was just enough room in the shower stall for both of them.

As the hot water cascaded over them, Jason kneaded her sore shoulders. She moaned, her forehead resting against the tiled wall of the shower stall. "I can't believe how good that feels. I didn't know I was so tense."

"I knew as soon as I saw you. Your shoulders were up around your ears."

"What about you? You must be sore too."

"Nah, I got off easy. Donnie did the hard work up on the aerial. And I didn't have a phone clamped to my ear all day."

"I couldn't find my earbuds." She tilted her head so he could massage her neck with one strong hand. He knew just where to press to release the knots of tension. "You know where I eventually found them? In the freezer at the Blue Drake."

She felt the satisfying vibration of his laughter against her back.

"Frozen earbuds aside, you did great today. The whole town is talking about it."

"No, they're talking about you," she corrected. "I caught the headline in tomorrow's Clarion." Now that it was summer, the town's newsletter had started publishing again, although nowadays it was digital only. "It says, *Fire Chief Mosedale Faces and Aces First Big Test.* They're using that photo of you that everyone loves."

"The one with Mrs. McMurray?"

"Yes, the one people are turning into a caption contest, making up things that she was saying to you."

"All she said was 'didn't I give you a C in my English class?'" His lips against her ear made her shiver.

"Really? Because if you go online, you'll find out that she said, 'Are you single? My sixth husband just died.'"

He groaned and nibbled her ear lobe. "That's dark."

"Yeah, best to stay off the internet for a while. You're a hot topic." She felt his hand curve around one of her ass cheeks. She adored the way he cupped her back there, the way he openly appreciated every curve. When his hand dipped around front and stroked her wet folds, she shuddered into an immediate but gentle orgasm, like sliding down a mossy slope.

Afterwards, she leaned back against his chest and let the water sluice over her body. Every part of her hummed with contentment. If she could stay awake long enough, she was going to thank him for that sweet release in the best possible way.

"Did you decide about the wedding?" he murmured against her hair.

She had no idea what he was talking about. "Wedding?"

"Colleen and Lisa. I'm officiating. I asked if you'd be my date. You never exactly answered."

"Oh. Well, I don't even know when it is. They haven't invited me. I don't know either of them very well. Isn't Colleen a few years older than us? And I've only chatted with Lisa a couple times at Alvin's. She doesn't drink, you know. She says no one wants their elementary school principal to be partying on the weekends. That is one dedicated lady. I'd think a school principal would need twice the alcohol."

Her nervous babble didn't do anything to distract Jason.

"You'd be my plus one."

A plus one. That was serious, more serious than anything they'd done so far. It felt like a big step. Or was she overthinking it?

"Jason." She turned within the circle of his arms. "Do we have to talk about this now?"

"Why not? Is it so hard to talk about?" His full lips set in stubborn lines, while the rest of his face just looked exhausted. Bloodshot eyes, deep grooves on either side of his mouth. They should be in bed, not arguing in the shower.

"Yes, it's hard, because you're changing the game on me."

She stepped out from under the stream of water and pushed aside the shower curtain. Grabbing a towel, she gently pressed the water from her hair, then grabbed the body lotion that she'd stashed in his cabinet.

"I'm sorry," she called to him. "All I'm saying is, let's talk about it another time. I have other plans for tonight. See you in bed?"

She took his mumble as a 'yes,' and headed to the bedroom with her lotion. Before she got down to moisturizing, she checked her phone. A text from Dominic flashed on the screen.

"Lake Bittersweet in the news again? What are the odds? Looking good, K. Better than ever."

Adrenaline shot through her. Damn that Dominic. What was he up to?

twenty-one

J ason took a long time finishing his shower. He struggled to collect himself. Pushing Kendra wasn't going to work. He knew that about her. This wasn't the right time anyway. They were both spent from the long day. Honestly, that conversation with Colleen felt like an eon ago. He didn't know why the wedding question had popped back into his mind.

But it had, and he'd been too relaxed to stop it.

That doesn't mean you have to go there. You know where the lines are. Don't fucking cross them and things'll be fine.

Would they, though? As he toweled off his hair, he knew that depended on what "fine" meant. If he wanted things to continue just as they were, things would be fine. If he wanted any kind of change, maybe not.

It's hard because you're changing the game on me.

Message received, Kendra. Loud and clear.

He ambled into the bedroom, towel around his hips. Kendra was in the midst of powering down her phone.

"Are you sure you want to do that? You might get some emergency calls tonight."

"You know I'm *not* the town manager, right? Everyone's where they're supposed to be for the night. If there's an emergency, that's what nine-one-one is for."

"Right." He groaned and checked his own phone, then the pager from the fire department. "There's a good chance I'll get some kind of call tonight."

She set her phone face down on the nightstand, then stretched out one long leg for the always sensual moisturizing process. Ordinarily he loved watching her smooth lotion into her skin. He'd even helped her with it a few times.

But right now, he wasn't in the mood. Something was off. *He* was off. He wished he'd never brought up the "plus-one" invitation. He'd bumped against one of her walls and it didn't feel good.

He went to the window to close the blinds, and noticed that Holly's bike was gone. Right—she was spending the night at the Blue Drake with the seniors. "I didn't see Holly once today."

"Doesn't she have that Indigenous Arts class on Tuesdays?"

"Right. Is it Tuesday? Jesus, I lost track. Have you noticed anything off with Holly? I think something's bothering her and she won't talk about it. You know how much she loves to vent. Has she said anything to you?"

With one knee bent so she could reach her calf, Kendra shot him a cautious glance. "Why would she say anything to me?"

So she had. And Kendra didn't want to betray her confidence.

That was good news. At least Holly was talking to someone responsible, someone other than her fellow teenagers.

"Why not? She likes you."

Kendra shrugged one slim brown shoulder. "I think that's thanks to my free burger for every 'A' policy at Alvin's."

He stretched out next to her, his towel still firmly wrapped around his hips. He didn't want to get distracted by lust right now. Something had shifted between them since the shower. He thought about how she'd been powering down her phone when he walked in.

Had someone reached out to her that she didn't want to talk to? Someone from London, perhaps?

Keeping his tone as casual as possible, he said, "Have you heard anything more from Dominic? Any more moves on the chessboard?"

The pink tip of her tongue peeked from between her lips as she focused on the sleek brown length of her shin. "I don't really know what he's up to."

Which didn't exactly answer the question.

"So you talked to him?"

Her sharp glance made it clear she wanted him to back off. "I had one phone conversation with him, but he made no sense, and I haven't answered his texts since then."

His stomach dropped. So Dominic was texting her. That was the kind of thing that happened during "rebounds," right? The former partner sometimes reappeared. Sometimes they wanted to get back together. Sometimes they actually *did* get back together.

And sometimes, like with Gretchen, the ex-partner married someone else, got pregnant, and lived happily ever after.

He really needed to know what was going on here. He wanted to know where he stood, but he couldn't push her right now. She'd made that clear.

She put the cap back on her body lotion and tossed it onto the nightstand. In a quick move, she climbed on top of him, her thighs straddling his hips. "I can think of about eighty-five things I'd rather talk about than Dominic."

"That's a very specific number."

"Well, forty of them are those respected elders you rescued today."

He shaped his hands around the taut curves of her waist. "That was a community effort. I can't take credit."

A flash of annoyance crossed her face. "Don't you ever take credit for anything? You don't always have to be humble, you know."

"I'm not being humble. The whole town pulled together, you know that. Fuck, I wasn't even the one on the aerial putting out the flames." He frowned at her, which was the last thing he wanted to do to the goddess perched on his thighs. "I take credit all the time."

"Okay, let's hear it. Take credit for something."

He slid his hand between her legs, into the soft nest of her sex. "I made you come in the shower just now."

She spread her thighs just a little farther apart. He'd take that as a "continue, please."

"I put you in charge of Operation Respected Elders. I'll take credit for that."

"Um, thanks, but I kind of stepped into that myself." Her hands went to his towel and worked at the knot until it eased open. His cock was already half-hard just from the sight of her naked, still-damp body over his.

"So that wasn't me, sending everyone to you with their questions? And letting the board members know that you were handling logistics?"

"Fine. But it's kind of funny to take credit for delegating."

"Why? Isn't that part of being a leader? You have to know who's the right person to handle what task, assign it to them, and inspire them to do a good job at it."

Her eyes swept up to meet his. The soft light of the bedside lamp made them shine. The lines of her face relaxed, all irritation gone. "That's a really good point, Jaybone. You're an excellent leader."

"Why do you sound so surprised? You're the one who told me I should go for the job."

"Yes, because...because you're trustworthy and hardworking and smart and I thought you deserved a promotion. I didn't think about you being a good leader because you're not a hard-ass. But you are a good leader."

She ran her hands down his chest, her fingertips lightly stroking wherever they found a ridge of muscle. If she was trying to distract him from her compli-sult...well, it was working.

"Feels like there's a lack of compliment in that compliment," he murmured.

She traced a path to his lower belly, where skin untouched by sun reacted with a shiver. His cock was already rising to meet her hand.

"That was *not* a compli-sult. You know I'm your biggest fan." With perfect timing, she curved her hand around his erection. It responded with instant, full-throttle arousal.

"Talk about someone's biggest fan..."

She giggled as she stroked him lightly, keeping a loose grip around his still-hardening member.

He arched his hips up and yanked the towel out from under his ass. He didn't want anything getting in their way.

Even as hot desire flooded through his system, something kept bugging him.

Kendra still underestimated him. Just because he didn't play the blowhard didn't mean he wasn't a good leader. In fact, from his perspective, it made him a better leader. He tried to lift up everyone who worked for him. He wasn't a bully and he always tried to be fair.

Why didn't Kendra see all that?

But when Kendra lifted herself onto her knees and brought his hand to her sex, everything else fled from his mind. At least she didn't underestimate him in bed. She knew how quickly he

217

could get her revved up. That orgasm in the shower had been just a little teaser.

He stroked through her tender folds, focusing on the little nub begging for his attention. God, he loved getting her turned on. He loved watching her eyes glow and her chest rise and fall as her breathing sped up. He loved watching her nipples harden. *Feeling* them harden was even better, so he lifted the hand that wasn't buried between her legs to her breasts.

As soon he squeezed one dark nipple, she moaned and pressed his hand harder against her breast. Her free hand covered her other breast, fondling her own flesh in a way that sent new heat directly to his cock.

"Jesus, Kendra, you're so fucking hot," he groaned. "I need to be inside you. Lift up."

She obeyed, her body trembling as she tightened her thighs. He fisted his hand around his erection and adjusted her position so she was directly over him. As he flexed upward, she lowered herself down, and somehow the mechanics worked perfectly. She slid onto him, her breath catching in a deep moan somewhere inside her chest.

He clamped his hands onto the flesh of her hips and worked her onto his cock, up and down, deep and deeper, so deep. She rode him like that, grinding into him, seeking her own pleasure on his thick cock.

He gritted his teeth and slitted his eyes so he wasn't bombarded with the erotic images right before his eyes. Keeping himself in check was frickin' heroic under the circumstances, but he didn't want to cheat her out of the electric orgasm they were generating together.

It wasn't until she reared back, her body arcing with joy, her fingers squeezing her nipples, that he allowed his own orgasm to burst out the gate like a racehorse. He pulsed into her in deep spasms, each one an eternity in itself. Each one an experience written on his soul.

Damn, why did he always get poetic like that after making love to Kendra? Images would sneak into his dazed brain, little snips of poetry or magical thinking.

Did that happen to her too? Or was he the only sentimental one in this relationship?

She still sat astride him, chest heaving, sweat dampening the pretty area above her breasts. With one finger, he blotted a droplet sliding along her collarbone.

After a moment, he realized she wasn't really moving. "Are you asleep?" he whispered. How could she sleep on top of him like that?

"Mmm. No. Just mellow."

He drew her down next to him and settled her under the covers. They'd recently gone through the birth control drill, determined they were both free from STDs and she was on the Pill. He didn't have to interrupt the afterglow by peeling off a sticky condom anymore.

That was an important milestone in their relationship.

Relationship being the key word. That was what it felt like to him. They'd blown way past rebound and were in new territory now, whether she knew it or not.

"Kendra," he whispered.

Her eyelids fluttered, as if she was trying to lift them, but couldn't because they were just too heavy. She was either asleep or nearly so.

"Would it be so bad to change the game?"

twenty-two

When Jason opened his eyes the next morning, Kendra was gone.

Damn it. Had he scared her off? He never should have mentioned anything about changing the game. This wasn't a game. Not for him. Not anymore.

Then he realized that a banging sound from downstairs had woken him up. Maybe Kendra was in the kitchen doing something loud...like...renovating? Clog-dancing?

Shaking himself awake, he rolled out of bed and pulled on a pair of shorts before jogging down the stairs. The banging turned out to be someone knocking on the front door.

Galen Cooper, of course, because who else would treat knocking on a door like a wilderness survival event?

His bushy-bearded friend burst through the door. As always, he brought the smell of the forest with him.

"I'm surprised you didn't just cut it open with a chainsaw," Jason grumbled at him as he barreled past him.

"My chainsaw's in the shop."

Jason followed him into the kitchen, where Galen hoisted himself onto a stool and looked around expectantly.

"You know this is my house, not a coffee shop?"

"You always have coffee ready."

"Ready?" Jason slapped a hand to his forehead. "Damn. I forgot we're supposed to go fishing today."

"*Supposed* to? What is wrong with you?" Galen peered at him with an expression of utter betrayal.

"It was a busy night. You heard about the fire at the nursing home, right? Or were you out in the wild with no service?"

"I heard. Good work." He slid off the stool and went to make the coffee himself. "'Fire Chief Faces and Aces First Big Test.' Not bad, bro. Still no excuse for forgetting a fishing trip."

Jason poured himself a glass of orange juice, downed it, then grabbed another glass and filled it for Galen.

"Something bothering you, Galen?" His old friend didn't seem like himself. He and Galen had been buddies since they'd both played on the hockey team in high school. Galen had filled the position of goalie with a mad rabid intensity that made opposing players afraid to approach the goal.

"Nah." He swallowed down some juice in his typical beast-like manner. Galen had the sweetest heart in the world, but on the outside he came off as entirely uncivilized. "Okay, yes. You're the fire chief now."

"Yup." Jason grabbed a stool and straddled it. A glance at the coffee maker told him it was still early. Barely six. What time had Kendra left? Before dawn?

"Thomas is married."

"That's the usual outcome of wedding vows," Jason said drily.

"*And* they have a kid. Billy has his two boys. I'm the only Cooper brother without offspring."

"Offspring, huh? I've never heard you talk about wanting offspring before."

"Are you kidding? Kids love me. They think I'm some kind of cartoon character. Like a troll," he added gloomily.

"No way, you're too tall to be a troll. You'd have to be an ogre."

"An ogre." Galen buried his head in his hands. "I'm fucked, aren't I?"

Jason poured the freshly dripped coffee into a Thermos and screwed on the cap. "How about we go catch some trout and finish this convo over breakfast?"

Jason's house was just a short walk away from a launch spot where he kept a couple of kayaks and a collection of fishing rods stashed under a tarp. Within ten minutes, they were gliding across the lake, its surface flat as a mirror, reflecting pink and pearl morning light. This time of year, with the water temperatures dropping again, some spectacular bass could be found.

A sense of peace came over him as he dipped the paddle into the water. Kendra had probably left this morning because she had work to do. Operation Respected Elders, day two. Maybe she wasn't fleeing from him and his threat to "change the game."

But back to Galen's problem. He dug in the paddle so he came up alongside his friend. "Remember how we used to talk about being the favorite uncle, the one who gets to go home at the end of the day and sleep in peace?"

"Yeah, but that's not me anymore. I got to tell you, Jason, I don't think it ever was me."

"You always wanted a family?"

Galen shook his head, squinting away from the rays of the sun just beginning to pierce through the tops of the trees. "I didn't even know what family was. To me, family was my brothers. We always stuck together. Thomas brought us here after that summer camp for poor kids, and we all decided to stay. Mom didn't care, so long as she didn't have to send too much money. First time I went into the woods to camp, I didn't want to leave. *That* was home. The forest. The wilderness. My brothers. I didn't need anything else."

"Gee, thanks."

"Buddies were cool too," Galen added with a roll of his eyes. "Girls, yeah, I liked them too. But I didn't *need* them. I thought Billy was crazy when he got married at twenty-one."

"You might have been right about that one." Billy and Jenna had gotten divorced a few years and two kids later.

"I was right. But I was also wrong. Because now Billy has a family and I have a bunch of trees."

Jason couldn't help laughing at that. "So what's stopping you from branching out?"

"Is that supposed to be funny?" Galen's bristly indignation made Jason laugh even harder.

"No man, I didn't even realize. I swear."

Galen relaxed, then slapped a mosquito that had landed on his neck. "I'm just ready, man. I saw a therapist. He helped me think about how I grew up and why that made me reject the whole family scene." He back-paddled to bring his kayak to a standstill, then dropped a line into the water. "This is good. Walleye love this spot."

Jason was still too stunned to grab his own fishing rod. "Hang on. You saw a therapist?"

"Yeppers."

"Why? When?"

Galen flicked the fishing rod through the still water. "It was my hair."

"Your *what?*" Jason wondered if he was actually still asleep, and none of this was really happening. Maybe he was snuggled in bed with Kendra, having a really weird dream. "Did you say your hair?"

224

"Yeah. I couldn't cut it. I tried. I've made sixty-three appointments at every barber shop, hair salon, spa, what have you, within a hundred-mile radius. I show up, too. But I can't go through with it. I pay the barber and move on. Sometimes they say, let me at least trim your beard, but I can't do that either." He pointed at his head, where black hair flowed to his shoulders in wild, untidy waves. "This is the most expensive fucking haircut in goddamn Minnesota. And it's never been cut."

Jason was laughing so hard he nearly fell out of his kayak. Only Galen would make and break sixty-three hair appointments and pay up anyway. Sure, his hair and beard were a mess—you could even say unkempt—but that was Galen, and his friends loved him anyway. "So you got therapy for a haircut?"

Galen looked affronted. "I figured maybe the problem was inside my head instead of on it. You should think about it. I learned a lot."

"Me? I'm fine. I get a trim every six weeks from Nate Baker. He does an excellent job."

"I mean for the inside."

"Something wrong with my inside?"

"You're single too. And you're a natural-born family man. Raising Holly doesn't count because she mostly raises herself. But that was probably good training." A fish tugged his line, and he reeled it in with practiced skill. As he flipped it onto the kayak, the trout traced a silver arc through the air.

Hadn't he been thinking something similar himself when he'd caught Bobby live-streaming the fire yesterday? But in the busy-ness of the day, he'd forgotten about it.

"If I'd wanted a family, I would have gotten married to Gretchen. She kept talking about our biological clocks."

"You never would have been happy with Gretchen. She's too..." Galen dropped the fish into the cooler of ice they'd brought. "She's too much like you. You need someone who challenges you, who gets your blood moving, who—"

"Okay, okay," Jason interrupted before he got too graphic. "Didn't know you were such a matchmaker."

"I don't have to be. You already found someone good."

Yeah, someone who didn't want to "change the game."

"We're not talking about me. Let's get back to you and your problems. You still haven't cut your hair, have you?"

"Baby steps," growled Galen.

Jason snorted so loudly he nearly capsized his kayak. Galen leaned over and steadied it for him.

"Are you going to look me in the eye and tell me you want to be single forever?"

He glanced away from Galen and stared into the deep water of Lake Bittersweet. Prisms of reflected light danced around him like morning fairies. He had lots of family already. He had two sisters, his nephews, his parents, his friends, his firehouse crew. The entire town of Lake Bittersweet sometimes felt like family. Maybe that was enough. Maybe it wasn't.

The only thing he knew for sure was that he wanted Kendra. He loved her.

He had to tell her how he felt. He didn't need to push her. But he had to be honest.

When he finally met Galen's eyes, his friend peered at him across the two kayaks and shook his bushy head. "Uh oh. I know that look. Need the number of my therapist?"

twenty-three

Day two of Operation Respected Elders was nearly as chaotic as day one. Kendra spent most of the day at the nursing home saying things like, "we can't hook up the gas until the fire department has signed off on it," and "no, we don't really have space for a pizza oven, but I'll put it in the suggestion box for the permanent kitchen," and "if they say they need five blenders to puree the meals, then that's what they're getting."

Keeping busy was good; it kept her from dwelling on what Jason had whispered last night. *Would it be so bad to change the game?*

Then there was Gina's comment. *Sooner or later, all relationships reach that point where you either go forward or you stall out.*

She remembered the moment when she and Dominic had reached that point in their relationship. They'd gone out to dinner after a meeting with the lawyer helping them with the contract.

They'd gone to an upscale Asian-fusion place, the kind that left her longing for her father's jambalaya.

Dominic was fired up about everything—the business, the lawyers, the contract-in-progress. And them. "How many people in this restaurant would love to be us right now? We're young, we're hot, we're going places. It's all right there ahead of us, all we have to do is reach out and grab it."

"Grab what? Maybe more of these teeny tiny mini spring rolls pretending to be an appetizer."

He barely laughed at her joke, which happened a lot. He was always looking ahead to the next point he wanted to make instead of listening to her quips. "Success. Life. Money. Everything. We can do this, Kendra. We can be those people. The It couple."

His enthusiasm swept her right along with him.

"I always wanted to be the 'It Girl.' When I was younger, I wanted to be the Beyoncé of business. But now Beyoncé's a business queen herself, so..." She shrugged and looked around for the waitress, who was barely bigger than one of those spring rolls.

"I'm serious, Kendra. You and me. Think of the possibilities." He swept a hand through the air. "Billionaire. CEO. Power couple extraordinaire."

A shiver went through her. It sounded like he was talking about marriage. "Are you...is this a proposal?"

"Sure, maybe. Eventually." He leaned forward, eyes ablaze with promise. "Would that be so strange? An expat Canadian and a princess from Minnesota?"

"Princess? My dad's the only one who ever called me a princess, and he's biased. I'm about as practical as it gets."

"And that's why I love you. Smart, practical, beautiful, you're the complete package."

Her heart melted under his intense gaze. "Did you just say you love me? You've never said that before."

"And now I have. Do you love me?"

Somehow she'd imagined something more romantic for a declaration of love. You're practical, she reminded herself. You're not a romantic. "Maybe?"

Dominic put a hand to his heart, as if she'd aimed a bullet there. "Don't break my heart, princess."

"It's all good, Dom. We're perfect together." That must mean love, right? "I do love you. You're the most exciting man I've ever known. And all of those things you said before, the power couple, the It couple, I want that. I want to show the world what I can do."

"What we can do. Together."

She nodded as he clasped his hands around hers. Everything would be so much easier if she was doing it with Dominic. She could take on the world as part of a couple instead of as one single Black woman.

If a small part of her mourned the disappearance of her own personal dream, the one in which she strode up on that awards stage alone, she didn't dwell on it. She was practical that way.

And Dominic...

Maybe she hadn't been in love at the beginning, but he'd become the center of everything. Her dreams, her life, her heart. Getting dumped by him had devastated her. Could she ever trust a man with her heart again? Did she *want* to? What was the point? If anyone had ever been perfect for her, it was Dominic. They had the same goals, the same dreams. Since that relationship had imploded, what hope could any other relationship have?

Which brought her back to Jason. Changing the game...was she ready for that? Would it mess everything up?

So she didn't answer the phone when he called. She sent him a quick text saying that she was very busy with the kitchen construction all day.

All night too?

Need to catch up on sleep, you sex maniac.

Immediately, she wished she could take back that text. Mentioning sex just brought back all the delicious memories of the past few weeks. Sex with Jason gave her so much—adventure, escape, comfort, release.

Was it distracting her from more important things, like her future? Since she'd lost the town manager job, she hadn't done one thing to look for something else. She was just...here. Running her father's restaurant. Going nowhere.

"Kendra." Someone was snapping their fingers to get her attention. She looked up from her phone to find Brenda, a teacher at the middle school, standing before her. All she knew about Brenda was that Galen Cooper had a massive and supposedly secret crush on her. Understandable, with her flowing auburn hair and her sunny optimistic smile. "Sorry to disturb you, you must have a lot on your mind."

"I was thinking about sex."

Brenda's sea-green eyes went wide. "Then I'm *really* sorry to interrupt."

Kendra had to give her credit for rolling with it. "If you had to explain why sex with a rebound is better than sex with an ex, what would you say?"

"I'd say it depends on the person."

"Right. Of course. But in general, maybe it's because a rebound isn't as serious, so you can just have fun and not put so much pressure on it, or—"

"Kendra." Brenda waved a hand in front of her face. "As much as I'd love to talk about sex for the rest of the day, I'm actually here to get my grandmother's things. Do you know if it's okay to go into the rooms yet?"

"Oh. I'm so sorry." She blinked herself back to a semi-rational state. "I didn't get a lot of sleep last night. Not because of sex.

Well, somewhat. Anyway, yes, you can go ahead. Just step carefully. How is your grandmother doing?"

"She's a little shell-shocked. She's never been on the news before."

"Oh wow, is she the one Jason carried out of the building? Mrs. McMurray, who reminded him she gave him a C while he was rescuing her?"

Brenda laughed. "Yes, that's my granny. She gets feisty around handsome men." Brenda adjusted her grip on the cardboard box she was carrying. "Anyway, she's going to stay with me for a while, until I'm sure it's safe for her to come back here. I always wanted her to live with me anyway, but she wanted to be around people her own age. Her words, not mine. The real reason is that she thought I'd have an easier time dating if I didn't have a live-in chaperone. She called that one wrong. God, listen to me blab on about grandmothers, when we could be talking about sex."

Kendra laughed as Brenda headed for the wing where the rooms were located. She made a mental note to get to know Brenda better. The redhead had a better sense of humor than Kendra had realized. Did she have any idea that Galen Cooper had such a crush on her? Probably not, because everyone in town had a soft spot for Galen and no one would want to betray his secret.

"Kendra."

That deep voice sent an automatic thrill through her. She turned to see Jason, wearing his official fire chief uniform. She saluted, a completely involuntary gesture solely attributable to her lack of sleep. "Chief Mosedale."

His eyebrows lifted. "Are you okay?"

"Tired. I didn't get enough sleep last night."

He lowered his voice to bedroom level. "When did you leave this morning?"

"Oh...early." She wasn't exactly sure of the time, but it had still been dark. Back at home in her own bed, she'd tossed and turned the rest of the night. "Are you here to sign off on the gas line?"

"Yeah, I got a guy checking it out. Thought I'd come see how it's going with the new kitchen." He gazed around at the construction mess. "Work in progress?"

"We're getting there." She gestured at the workers mounting the triple sink into the countertop, which was currently balanced on two sawhorses. "We still need the water and gas hooked up. The fridge and chest freezer were easy. They'll have to do without a garbage disposal for the time being. The head cook came by and said everything looked functional enough. How are things on your end?"

"After the inspection, our part's done, unless someone here manages to set something on fire." The joke didn't quite land right. She could see a seriousness in his eyes that wasn't normally there. Her heart sank.

They were going to do this. Did they have to do this?

"Can we talk somewhere more private?"

Crap. "Jason, I am not in peak conversation condition. I only got a couple hours of sleep and my all-nighter days are long gone. All-nighter days? Does that even make sense?" She shook her head, trying to focus. "See? This just isn't a good moment. I need to save my brain cells for things like gas line clearances."

He looked down at the floor for a moment, as if debating with himself. Then back up, his blue eyes more clear than she'd ever seen them. "Be honest with me, Kendra. Do you really think anything would be different if you'd gotten more sleep?"

She let out a sigh. Her heart fluttered like a trapped hummingbird. "I don't even know what you're going to say."

"Yes, you do."

She should have known he wouldn't fall for the clueless act. *Woman up. He's asking for honesty. That's fair.*

She glanced around the construction area and realized that everyone was either watching them or pretending not to watch them. If they were going to do this, they needed privacy.

"Let me show you how they plan to handle meal deliveries," she said in a louder voice, then beckoned for him to follow her. They walked down the hallway, which was wide enough for wheeled racks of meals and wheelchairs going both directions, until she found a large room set aside for group activities. Easels filled one corner, a crate of bongo drums and a grand piano another. The room still smelled faintly of smoke.

"I used to teach dance classes in here," Jason murmured. "I learned a few things, too. Some of the folks really know their Lindy hops."

She closed the door behind them and turned to face Jason. Best to face this head on.

"I do know what you want to talk about. I heard what you said about changing the game."

She couldn't quite look him in the eye. So strange, since she usually had no trouble confronting people. But Jason...and those deep blue eyes...those dimples...she couldn't.

"Why do you want to change something that's working? Don't they say if it's not broke, don't fix it?"

"What if it could be better? Maybe the saying has it wrong. A lot of things could be better."

"So what are you saying? You and me, we could be better?"

"We could be a 'we,'" he said simply. "Let's start there."

His cheek twitched, as if he wanted to smile. Of course he did; he was Jason, and his first instinct would always be a fun-loving one. But he was obviously trying to be serious.

"What kind of 'we'?" She folded her arms across her chest. It was a self-shielding gesture, but also a way to keep herself from reaching out to touch him. With so little sleep, her defenses were down and she could feel her body yearning for him.

But that was just physical. Physical wasn't everything. She and Jason weren't suited to each other, were they?

"Whatever kind we decide. Sky's the limit." He glanced away, then back again. "I want a family, Kendra. I've been thinking about what was stopping me before, when I was with Gretchen. Part of it was Holly. I wanted to give her everything she needed. But she's going to fly the nest soon."

Kendra knew she should say something, anything, but her mind was a blank. A *family*? They'd never talked about that kind of thing before. Even she and Dominic hadn't. They'd been so focused on putting the business together that everything else took a back seat.

"Also, I think I had a mental hurdle. It was probably left over from childhood, from not feeling good enough. I don't feel that way anymore. I think I'd be a great husband and father, with the right woman."

This was too weird, too disorienting. Too similar to that dinner with Dominic. She put a hand on the nearest wall to steady herself. "Is...is this a proposal?"

What woman wanted a proposal in a smoked-out nursing home on two hours of sleep?

"What? No. It's not a proposal. Shit, did I screw this up?" He looked appalled as he scrubbed a hand through his hair. "I'm talking about the future. Down the line. Right now, I just think we should take things more seriously."

Her shoulders slumped in relief. "Good, because there would be so many things we'd have to figure out. Like, we'd be an inter-racial couple. Our kids would be biracial. My in-laws would be white people who run a dance studio." She pressed the heel of her hand into her forehead. "Sorry. No sleep."

"No, it's okay. I want to have these conversations. That's

what I'm saying. All those awkward, difficult topics like in-laws and kids, bring them on. I'm here for it. Because I'm here for you. I—"

"Wait. Don't—" She flung up a hand to stop him. But it was too late.

"I love you." Then he realized what she'd just said. "Shit. You don't want me to say that."

"I'm just...not ready." She laced her hands on top of her head and paced around in a little circle. At least that way she didn't have to look at him. "I might not ever be ready. It might not even be you. I trusted Dominic and he threw my trust back in my face like dirt. I don't know if I can do that again. I don't want to hurt you, Jason. I care about you."

"It's okay, Kendra. It's all right if I get hurt. It's worth it as long as you know how I feel. I love you. You don't have to say anything back. I just want to be honest with you."

Finally she forced herself to meet his eyes. She saw so much in those dark blue depths that her heart stuttered. Caring, concern, compassion, and...love. So, so much love.

She didn't know what to do with it. Overwhelmed, she turned away. "Okay."

"Okay?"

"You were honest. That's...that's good. I...I need to think. I can't deal with this right now." She backed away from him and bumped into the door. With a quiet flash of amusement, he reached behind her to turn the knob.

"Just breathe," he told her gently. "It'll be okay. No matter what, it'll be okay."

Breathe? *Breathe?* He made it sound so simple, when she was actually having a hard time getting her lungs to work. He really was good in a crisis, reassuring *her* when he'd just bared his soul.

Without looking at him again, she fled down the empty, echoing hallway of the nursing home. Why was she freaking out like this? It wasn't the first time a guy had told her he loved her.

So had Dominic.

Images of Dominic flooded her brain, an unstoppable flow of taunts from the past. The text he'd sent her. *Let's put this on pause.* The way he picked at the chili she made, or the jambalaya, or the collard greens with smoked pork, or the cornbread, or any recipe she'd gotten from her father. It wasn't "upscale" enough for him, which meant she hadn't been either. The expression on his face when she put on the little black dress he'd bought her for a gala fundraiser. Privately, she hated it. She liked dresses that flaunted her curves, while he wanted her to disguise them.

The way he'd never ever, not once, come to Lake Bittersweet to meet her family. She'd never understood it, because her father was famous, in certain circles. He was a blues legend. But to Dominic, he hadn't been worth meeting. Too Southern? Too uneducated? Too country?

The truth was, maybe Dominic had never seen her as good enough for him. Maybe for a time she'd been promising raw material for his ambitions. But deep inside, she'd probably never measured up to his vision. And all those little judgments, those micro-moments, had settled into her soul like lake sediment.

She'd failed at love. Failed to keep Dominic's attention. Failed to live up to his expectations.

Before she rounded the corner into the dining area turned construction zone, she stopped and rested her hands on her knees, desperately trying to catch her breath. Was this some kind of panic attack? A type of PTSD incident? Had Dominic wounded her so deeply that love from another man triggered an emotional meltdown?

Get a hold of yourself. This wasn't her, this shaky emotional wreck.

Or maybe it was, and she'd never given herself permission to feel all the devastation Dominic had inflicted on her heart.

Fucking Dominic. Why couldn't she just banish him from her mind for good? Why did he keep lurking inside there like a freaking jack-in-the-box?

She must be starting to hallucinate, because she could swear she heard his voice. One of the delivery guys must have a similar fake-British accent. And a very similar baritone. Even the slightly superior tone he used reminded her of Dominic. Who in this town would sound remotely like a sophisticated boarding school business whiz from Toronto?

Curious now, she stepped into the dining room, then stopped dead. In the middle of the sawdust and power tools and workers and recycled appliances stood the one and only Dominic Robb.

twenty-four

Jason took a few beats before he left the music room. Kendra hadn't exactly rejected him. She hadn't been coherent enough to reject him, which on the one hand was weird, because she was Kendra, but on the other hand gave him room for hope.

He knew that Kendra had a habit of digging in on her ideas about things. It could be hard for her to change course. She thought of their relationship as temporary, nothing more than a casual in-between sort of thing. A fun diversion until the next important relationship came along. Getting her to change her mind might be a challenge.

He'd give her plenty of time to think, plenty of time to wrap her head around the fact that his feelings had changed. Then he'd try again. And again, unless he got a flat-out "no, get out of my face."

But if she could just see what he saw, that they filled in missing pieces for each other, that he loved her, that he believed in her, that he saw her completely, flaws included, and loved everything about her. And that he believed in himself now. He knew he could give her what she needed, now and forever, if only she could accept his love.

She didn't reject you, he repeated to himself as he strode back toward the makeshift kitchen. *That's something. For now.*

But as soon as he walked into construction zone, all his optimism shattered like a third-grader's piñata.

Kendra was standing with a man who could have stepped out of an article on "30 hotshots under 30." The way he held himself made the entire construction zone look like a backdrop —the daring developer posing with the worker bees. His crisp white shirt set off his stunning good looks, accentuating his dark brandy skin and amber eyes. He wore a jaunty smile that seemed to say, "come away with me, I'll give you the adventure of a lifetime."

It had to be Dominic.

Had Kendra mentioned that Dominic was biracial? Jason couldn't remember. Somehow that fact made him feel even more unsettled. He could understand a lot about Kendra, but he could never know what it was like to be Black. Dominic could.

And he was here. Why?

Kendra seemed to be in some sort of trance state, staring at her ex as if she wasn't sure he was real. And as if she couldn't think of what to say. Very unlike Kendra. He remembered her strange reaction to the news that Dominic had sabotaged her. She'd buried all her anger and tried to outguess him.

What exactly did this man do to her?

Everyone else had stopped what they were doing, as if a show was about to start up and they didn't want to miss anything. That was another anomaly. Under normal circumstances, Kendra would never let all work come to a stop under her watch. Maybe she needed an assist.

He strode to join the two of them. "Can I help you? This is a construction zone, it's not safe for visitors."

Dominic flicked him a glance, then turned back to Kendra, as if Jason was barely worth his time. "No worries, old chap, I found what I'm looking for."

Kendra finally startled out of her trance. Without looking at Jason, she addressed her ex. "What in the world are you doing here, Dom?"

"I went to the Blue Drake first. They told me you were here." He slid another look at Jason, who folded his arms across his chest. He wasn't going anywhere until Kendra told him to. "I'm sorry, who are you?"

"Lake Bittersweet Fire Chief Mosedale." It felt good to say his full title out loud to this business-hipster-model.

"Well, Chief Mosedale, nothing's on fire at the moment, but we'll let you know if that changes. Or come to think of it, maybe we won't." He winked in a way that was both charming and smug. And was that a British accent?

Jason wasn't a violent person, but he wanted to smash the guy's face in. He'd never wanted to punch a guy the way he did right now. His body trembled with the effort of holding himself back. Volcanic, that was how he felt. Like he could erupt in boiling molten rage if that guy fucking winked again.

"It's okay, Jason." Kendra put her hand on his forearm. Maybe she sensed the fury coursing through him. "I got this."

Her touch burned into his arm. Scalded him with longing. But her gaze was firmly fixed on Dominic. And the man knew it, judging by the smirk tugging at his lips.

Jason didn't say another word. He turned on his heel and went in search of his crew. Do the job, get the hell out. He couldn't be in the same space as that prick for one more second.

He was barely aware of signing the certificate of inspection. Didn't recall getting into his truck and driving back to the firehouse. Whatever he put in the report he filed, who knew?

Everyone kept a wide berth from him. He was grateful for that. Ordinary conversation seemed utterly impossible.

He shouldn't have told Kendra how he felt. Especially right before her ex showed up. Talk about bad timing. It was like fate was laughing in his face. *Oh, you think you have a chance with her? Dream on, lowly human.*

Oddly, it wasn't his conversation with Kendra that kept running through his mind. No, it was long-ago comments from his parents that were doing that. *Not everyone can be a superstar. Don't set your sights too high. Be realistic. Do you really think you can handle that class? Or that after-school job? Or band practice?*

Or woman? Maybe he really was stupid after all. Stupid enough to aim for the stars and land flat on his face.

Kendra wasn't quite sure how it happened, but a short time later, she found herself driving Dominic into Lake Bittersweet. His aftershave filled her Lexus with the scent of Armani and crushed dreams.

An Uber had dropped him off at the nursing home. An Uber from *Minneapolis.* She didn't even want to know how much that must have cost. He'd booked himself a suite at the Bittersweet Inn. When she'd asked him for how long, he'd refused to say. That made her nervous. His very presence made her sick to her stomach. Her head was still in a fog and she desperately needed some sleep.

"Let's make a stop at the Blue Drake," said Dominic. "I want to meet your father. Besides, that place is beyond even what you described. I need photos of that gigantic duck up on the stage." Dominic kept behaving as if everything was normal, and his magnetism made it hard to resist. But she had to draw the line somewhere.

"Absolutely not. My mother's in Arkansas and you can't meet my father."

"Why not? He always sounded like a real character."

"He's a real *person*," she corrected. "Also, we broke up and now you're dead to him. He won't want to see you. I don't even know why you're here."

He gave one of his familiar jaunty shrugs. "We're still business partners."

"Sorry, but there's no way I'm letting the man who ditched me on his way to London meet my father. Call me a coward if you want."

"You are many things, Kendra, but one thing you absolutely are not, is a coward."

"That sounds like a compli-sult."

"A what?"

Right, that was one of her and Jason's running jokes. Of course Dominic wouldn't get it. Did she and Dominic ever have inside jokes? They hadn't had that sort of easy relationship. They'd talked a lot of business, so much business. And dreams. Goals, plans. What else?

"Let it go. I'm not going to put on some farce in front of my father."

"That's a shame, I love a good farce."

He sounded so British that she had to ask, "Do you fool the people in England? Do they think you're one of them?"

"No, but they appreciate the effort," he said lightly. "They adore me there. I'm like a unicorn, a witty, sexy, diabolically clever Canadian."

"Then what are you doing here? Why fly all the way from London where they all kiss your feet?"

"Are you saying you won't—" At her look, he dropped that line of thought. "I have a reason. A few reasons. The first one is so I can apologize in person."

She waited, but apparently he considered *that* the apology. "Is that it?"

"Oh, the apology? No, of course not." He covered quickly, she gave him that. "I want to take you out to dinner and do it properly. You pick the place."

She didn't want to go to dinner with Dominic. But she wouldn't mind an apology. Some groveling would be super. Besides, she was curious about the other reasons too. Dominic always had many reasons for everything he did.

"How does the most expensive restaurant in Lake Bittersweet sound?"

"Perfect. Is it also the best in Lake Bittersweet?"

"No, that would be Alvin's Burgers and Blues. But we're not going there."

"Overpriced and second-best it is, then."

As they drove past the firehouse, she saw that Jason's truck wasn't parked in the fire chief's designated spot. Had she even said goodbye to him at the nursing home? She couldn't remember, she'd been in such a fog. But she'd never forget the look on his face when Dominic had made that crack about things being on fire. She might have feared for Dominic's safety if she hadn't known that Jason wasn't the type to go feral on someone.

Dominic caught the direction of her glance. "So, that fire chief. You're fucking him, aren't you? Is it serious?"

She hated hearing him refer to Jason like that. It was more than "fucking," even if she didn't know exactly *what* it was. Jason had just told her that he loved her. She hadn't even had a chance to let that soak in before Dominic showed up.

After pulling into a parking spot in front of the Bittersweet Inn, she turned to him. "He's an old friend. I've known him forever. Leave him alone."

"So the fire chief needs someone to stand up for him. It's a bloody good thing he has a warrior like you in his corner."

Dominic got out of the car, while Kendra sat fuming in the driver's seat. He'd put his finger on something; he had a knack for that. His instincts about people were uncanny. In such a short time, he'd figured out that she felt protective toward Jason.

Which meant she worried that he wasn't strong enough.

Dominic is a manipulator, she reminded herself. She couldn't trust him to do anything but look out for himself. The question was, what did he want from her that he hadn't already taken?

"Coming in?" he asked lightly, suggestively. "I hear the rooms are top-flight."

"No, thank you. I'll wait here while you check in."

"I need to change, too."

"You're already overdressed for Lake Bittersweet."

"Good God, are you serious?" He looked around as if he'd suddenly landed on a movie set. "Then I'll find some ripped jeans."

She laughed at that. "Don't bother. Just be yourself, that's what everyone does here."

She watched him walk into the inn, gathering attention from passersby like honey. He was the kind of man who got people looking. It was his striking looks, the way he carried himself, his charm. That was why she'd wanted to partner with him. He could win over investors in his sleep.

Tilting her seat back to be more comfortable while she waited, she scanned her text messages. She answered everything having to do with the nursing home kitchen and ignored all the curious questions from people who had heard that a gorgeous man had arrived in town looking for her.

Jason hadn't texted anything. She should reach out to him. Tell him...what? That she had no idea why Dominic was here? That she was going out to dinner to find out? That he had nothing to worry about when it came to Dom? That she was still reeling from what he'd said, but had no answer yet?

Just say anything, she told herself. It didn't have to be deep. Just something to let him know she hadn't been whisked off her feet by Tornado Dominic.

As she stared at her phone, the empty text box blurred. Her eyelids drooped. Her phone slid onto her lap. Exhaustion wrestled her into sleep and she couldn't fight it. Just a quick nap until Dominic came out. Some quick zzz's and she'd be more prepared for whatever he flung at her.

twenty-five

J ason was in the worst mood of his life when he got home that evening. He found Holly curled on the couch with Rusty's head in her lap. He gritted his teeth. Rusty wasn't supposed to get on the couch. Holly knew that, Rusty knew that. Didn't anyone bother with house rules anymore?

Earbuds in place, Holly tapped away on an iPad balanced on the arm of the couch. For a fleeting second, he wondered why she was home instead of out with her friends on this glorious September night. But she took one look at him and ripped out the earbuds. "What happened to you?"

"I don't want to talk about it. Get off the couch, Rusty." The dog scrambled onto the floor and trotted over for a pat on the head. Jason obliged, since he loved his dog no matter what, but Rusty must have picked up on his mood. After a brief moment, he loped over to his fleecy bed and curled up there instead.

Jason headed for the kitchen, where there had to be a cold beer that could help this situation.

But the fridge held none of his favorite Red Stripes. It occurred to him that he hadn't actually had a beer in a while.

That was weird. His life had changed without him even realizing it. Being fire chief and being with Kendra had transformed him.

Holly had followed him into the kitchen. She came toward him and gently closed the door of the refrigerator. "You're letting all the cold out. You're the one always lecturing me about looking for imaginary snacks. Why don't you just tell me what's wrong?"

He looked down at the floor and saw that she was barefoot, and that her toenails were painted like a rainbow, each nail a different color. She must have done that to support her friend.

"How's Chloe?" he asked abruptly.

"Desperate attempt to change the subject, noted." She guided him to the kitchen island and pulled out a stool for him. Then she grabbed a red plastic bowl and filled it with his favorite salt-and-vinegar chips. "Eat. You look shell-shocked. Your blood sugar is probably low."

"I'm fine." He shoved aside the bowl of chips. The last thing he wanted was something crunchy in his mouth. It would taste like ground glass.

"Is this about the hunkalicious ex-boyfriend who barged back into Kendra's life today?"

He swiveled to look at her. "You met him?"

"No, but people are talking. I went to Alvin's Burgers to interview for a part-time after-school job and all the servers were buzzing. Alvin had to scold them to stop gossiping."

"You want to work at Alvin's? What about the job at the counseling center you applied to?"

"They said I need a high school degree, but to try again next year after I graduate. But they also said that I should keep doing what I'm doing. You know, advising my friends. With one little tweak. They said I should listen more and say less." She made a little face. "It was like they could see into my soul. And here I am blabbing on while you stare into space. Jason, I'm here. You can talk to me. If it helps, look at it as helping *me* in my listening journey."

Although it was sweet of her to care, Holly was still a kid. How could she possibly understand what he was feeling? He didn't really understand it himself.

"I want to rip his fucking face off and grind it under my boot." Shocked at his vicious tone, he propelled himself off the stool and took a few steps away. "Sorry."

Holly's eyes were about as round as the hoop earrings she wore. "Jeezo. It sounds like you're jealous."

"Jealous? Of what? His thousand-dollar blazer? Million-dollar smile? Multi-million-dollar bank account?" He scrubbed his hand through his hair.

"Wait a minute. You probably have just as much money as he has."

He'd finally told Holly his secret. She hadn't even believed him until he showed her the account balance. God, he hated thinking about that money. The thought that it might make a difference to Kendra...no, he refused to think that.

"No, I don't. I told you all that money is in a trust for you and Donna's kids. And my kids, if I ever have any."

"If you ever have any?" She spun a full circle on her stool. "That's the first time I've ever heard you mention even the possibility of having kids."

"People change," he said tersely. "But it doesn't matter now."

"Why not? This is a major breakthrough for you. I thought you'd keep pretending that you wouldn't be an amazing father for at least a decade more."

Her therapy-speak, which he usually tolerated with good humor, grated on his nerves. "It's not a breakthrough. It's just a thought. And it's over." He turned his back on his sister and opened the fridge again. "Why don't we have any beer?"

"Don't look at me, I'm not even old enough to work at a counseling center."

"I bet you could," he said absently. "Front desk, answering the phone, whatever. You'd probably like that better than working at Alvin's. Weren't you thinking about going vegetarian?"

"Thinking about is not the same as actually doing. I love those Blue Balls burgers. And there you go, changing the subject again. But maybe you aren't. Hang on, a stroke of brilliance is coming your way."

He groaned out loud. "Holly, can you just give it a rest? You can't fix my life. You can't fix anyone's life. Haven't you learned that yet?"

She recoiled, making him realize that he'd snapped at her more sharply than he'd intended. Maybe more than he ever had before.

"Sorry," he muttered.

"It's okay. I guess you're really hurting. Hurt people hurt people."

He gritted his teeth to hold back the profanity that wanted to spurt out of him. The last thing he needed right now was some cliché, even if it was true.

Undaunted, Holly continued. "You're telling me I shouldn't give up. Well, you should take your own advice. Don't give up on Kendra just because her ex came back. Fight for her. You're better than him."

But that was the thing. He wasn't at all sure he was better than Dominic. "Have you seen him?"

"I don't have to. Because I know you and there's no way he's better. I mean, he might be better for Kendra..."

He slammed the refrigerator door closed. "Is that supposed to make me feel better?"

"Sort of?" She made a face. "I don't know. That's the thing

about rebounds. Sometimes people go back to where they started."

"Good God, Holly."

"Sorry." His expression made her wince. "Can I start over?"

"Yes. Go back to the couch and meddle in someone else's life. I don't need your insipid teenage advice."

She crossed her arms over her chest. "That's a little harsh."

"Sorry," he said curtly. He didn't want to talk to his sister. He wanted to go find a beer.

For the first time since he'd gotten home, he gave her a closer look. Her face was puffier than usual, her lashes clumped together as if she'd been crying. "What are you doing home?"

"Getting insulted by my brother."

"I said I was sorry. Seriously, what's up?"

"Nothing." She tucked a wisp of hair behind her ears.

He frowned down at her. It wasn't like Holly to keep secrets. "You're really not going to tell me?"

"No." A flat no, just a single solitary word. Wow. Very unlike Holly, who usually had a thousand words to say when one would do. "Just some insipid teenage stuff," she muttered finally.

"Oh for fuck's sake. How many times do I have to apologize?"

"Doesn't matter how many if you don't mean it."

"Good one, did you hear that on a podcast or on TikTok?"

She flounced away from him, shooting him the finger as she went.

Fuck.

She hadn't deserved that. He wasn't fit company for anyone right now.

He gave up on his kitchen and decided to find a beer somewhere else. Anywhere but the Blue Drake. If there was one thing he really couldn't handle right now, it would be the sight of Kendra with Dominic.

twenty-six

When Kendra woke up, she was wrapped in warm male arms. Where had Jason come from? A moment later she sniffed and then jerked upright. Armani aftershave. *Dominic.*

He grinned at her from the passenger seat. She'd fallen asleep in her damn car and he'd slid inside and repositioned her against his chest.

She shoved away from him. "Goddamn, Dom. Get off me. What the hell?"

"I thought you needed the sleep," he said innocently.

"Don't ever do that again."

"Sorry." He lifted his hands in a surrender gesture. "I didn't mean anything by it."

She looked out the window of her car. It was almost dark outside, and the flow of tourists had ebbed. "What time is it?"

"Dinnertime. Are you hungry?"

Hell yes, she was starving. Her stomach actually growled. "We probably missed our chance to get a table at the Loon Feather. It's busy this time of year."

"You leave that to me."

She took a long drink of water from a bottle she'd left in her cupholder. Feeling more awake, she started her car and headed toward the eastern shore of the lake, where the Loon Feather was located.

While she drove, Dominic called the restaurant.

A few murmured words later, he hung up and said, "We're good."

"Excuse me? Just like that?"

"It's my superpower, babe. I can talk anyone into anything."

Outside the car, the buildings of town gave way to tall pines. "Are you sure it wasn't the British accent?"

"Pure magic, darling. You should try it."

Yeah, that would go over well at the Blue Drake. She could just imagine her staff laughing their asses off at her first "bloody hell."

"Well, you can drop the act when no one's listening. It's not going to work on me."

"Are you deliberately trying to make that sound like a challenge? You know challenges turn me on."

"*Dom.* Shut up, okay? At least until I get some food in me. Low blood sugar."

Ten minutes later, Kendra steered into the parking lot of the Loon Feather Bistro. It was located on a wooded rise overlooking the lake, with a wide view of the lake and the sparkling lights of the town. It was too pricey for most locals, so the clientele tended to be tourists. Perfect for Dominic. Expensive restaurants were his natural habitat.

As soon as she parked, Dominic swung out of the car. He had a thing about opening car doors for his dates. She remembered how impressed she'd been the first time he'd done it. *The perfect guy*, she'd thought. How wrong she'd been.

She hated being wrong. It almost never happened. Was she wrong to be having dinner with him now? Was he going to manipulate her into something? Was she going to fall for it?

Ugh, she hated self-doubt. She didn't like losing her confidence, but Dominic had a way of making that happen.

A sudden, fierce need to talk to her father came over her. She locked the door before Dominic could open it, and pressed Alvin's number on her speed dial. Dominic tapped on the driver's side door, but she held up a finger to hold him off.

As soon as her father answered, she realized that this was his jam session night. She heard laughing voices and guitar riffs in the background. Was Jason there? She listened for the deep brass tones of a trombone warming up, but didn't hear anything like that.

"Hello? Kendra, is that you?"

The sound of his beloved voice grounded her. "Hey Pop. Sorry, I forgot it was your jazz night."

"Are you okay, sweetheart?"

"Yeah, I just wanted to hear your voice."

"Did that fire out there shake you up? I don't want you to worry. I made sure we have the right fire insurance for Alvin's. The first time Gault set his purple hat on fire in the kitchen, I doubled our coverage. You know what I told him? I said, it ain't a *literal* stovepipe hat. I also told him to smoke longer cigars if he was going to light them on my burners."

She smiled, even though she'd heard that anecdote a hundred times. "He was lucky to have you."

"And he knew it. If he didn't, I wouldn't have stayed around. You know what I always say. Stick with the people who know your worth."

She nodded along to that last piece of wisdom, which was another thing he'd repeated a thousand times. He believed that repetition was important. *Your life isn't about the big things, it's all the little things added up,* he'd say. Over and over.

"I love you, Pop," she whispered.

The sounds behind him coalesced into an actual rhythm with a chord progression. The musicians were done warming up and ready to start jamming.

"I love you, too, sweet pea."

"Wait, before you go, I have to tell you something."

The sound in the background was drowning out their conversation. It was pointless to talk anymore, but she had to get all of this out, even if he couldn't hear it.

"Remember I said that me and Dominic's business didn't work out? It was worse than that. He's had me in limbo since we broke up. I thought he wanted me to buy him out, but now I don't know what his game is."

"What's that, honey?"

The fact that her father couldn't hear her over the music set her free to spill even more.

"Dominic just showed up and he wants something from me, and I don't trust myself to do the right thing. Not about anything. Even Jason. I'm worried that Dominic messed me up so much that I can't love anyone ever again."

On the other end of the phone, the music swelled even louder.

"I can't hear you, princess. I gotta go, they can't play 'Lakeside Blues' without me."

"I love you!" she said, squeezing it in before the call ended.

Her heart ached. She tucked her phone into her pocket and wiped off her sweaty hands.

Even a daddy's girl reached a point where she had to figure out her own life.

Dominic was waiting for her outside, scrolling on his phone.

Be practical, she told herself. At the least, she should find out what he wanted, what had inspired him to journey across an ocean and half a continent to see her. That was the logical thing to do.

Feeling more like herself, she touched up her lipstick—her favorite shade of red—and got out of the car.

"I wanted to open the door for you." Dominic practically pouted that she'd done it herself.

"Of course, because that's the kind of chivalrous thing men do after they've destroyed your business and sabotaged your next job."

"You got your sass back. I guess you're wide awake now."

Behind him, light spilled from the Loon Feather Bistro's windows. It occurred to her that the parking lot was emptier than usual. Looking around, she said, "Where is everyone?"

"There's only one way to find out." His smug expression told her he had something up his sleeve.

Sure enough, as soon as she stepped inside, she knew what he'd done. All the other guests had been seated in one section of the restaurant, leaving the best corner unoccupied, waiting for them. "You booked that entire section?"

"I set it up while you were napping."

"And the phone call to book a table?"

"Fake. I wanted it to be a surprise. It's a dramatic apology gesture."

Manipulation. But a sweet one? She couldn't decide. Damn it. She hated feeling indecisive.

"Come on." He put a hand on her lower back, but she shook him off.

"I'll listen to your apology, but don't touch me."

With a shrug, he led her to the only table set for dinner in the private corner section. A crystal vase held a bouquet of her favorite yellow roses. Tall taper candles softly flickered, illuminating the rose petals scattered across the tablecloth. The soft jazz playing in the background made her think of her father and his rowdy group of improvisers.

It all looked so romantic. Too romantic.

He caught her expression. "Don't worry, I'm not about to propose. This is an apology dinner."

Making a gallant gesture out of it, he pulled out her chair for her. She sat down, feeling more like a sack of potatoes than a lady at a dinner table. She should have changed into a better outfit. Then again, why did it matter when hardly anyone was here to see them?

After he'd settled into the chair across from her, he pulled out his phone and turned in his chair to take a selfie. "Love the lipstick," he said as he snapped the photo—him in the foreground, her in the background.

He hadn't asked her permission before taking that shot. Why did he need a photo and where did he plan to post it?

She reached across the table, grabbed his phone, deleted the photo, then handed it back with her best killer smile. "Dominic, I'm going to need you to cut the crap and tell me what you're scheming."

"I told you, this is my apology. We need drinks." He gestured to a server behind the bar, who immediately hurried over with a tray that held two drinks. A martini for him, a vodka-tonic with lime for her. Dominic still remembered her favorite drink.

As soon as the server was gone, she firmly pushed her drink away. "I'm not taking a sip until you answer some questions."

Dominic put his own frosty martini glass to his lips. "Too bad for you, this is top-tier liquor. I'm impressed so far."

"Why did you *really* call the board?"

"You didn't really want that job, did you? You're an

entrepreneur at heart. Working for a town government? You'd be miserable."

He might be right about that.

"That was my choice. Why did you care what I did?"

"I've always cared about you." Innocent amber eyes shimmered at her over the rim of his glass. While she'd been asleep in the car, he'd changed into a black cashmere shirt that probably cost more than her Lexus.

She clenched her jaw so tight she felt a muscle spasm. "The job, Dom. Why didn't you want me to get that job?"

"It would have been a waste of your abilities." She narrowed her eyes, refusing to back off. He set down his glass. "Fine. I should have known I couldn't play games with you. The company I'm working for wants to acquire Explastica. I'm here with an offer. A substantial one. And tickets to London so we can close the deal in person. They want you to stay on in some capacity. That's all negotiable."

Kendra put a hand to her head. "Tickets to London? When?"

"Tonight. Well, tomorrow, strictly speaking. The flight leaves at three in the morning from Minneapolis. We can finish dinner and then catch an Uber. Sleep in our first-class seats and wake up in rainy London. They'll put you up at the Dorchester. It's one of the best hotels in London."

"And...us...all this...you're not..."

"Look, Kendra. I know I did you dirty. Maybe I can win back your trust, over time. But that's not what this is about."

"So it's not an apology dinner. That was a lie."

"Why are you so stuck on that apology? This is better than that. It's an opportunity. You should at least come to London and talk with my superiors. I've been raving about you. It'll be bloody brilliant, Kendra. Your chance to see the world. If you don't want to accept the offer after you meet them, you can always fly back home to this..." he waved a hand at the picture window, through which she could see the moon rising over the lake, "Beautiful little dot on the map. Come on, Kendra. When's the last time you had a vacation?"

Her last vacation, she and Dominic had spent a weekend at an AirBnb on the Mississippi River. But instead of canoeing or swimming or fishing, they'd spent the entire time brainstorming ways to recruit investors. Did that even qualify as a vacation?

The quarry flashed through her mind, her and Jason making love on the sunlit rocks. Stretched out on the blanket together afterwards. So relaxed, so happy.

"None of this means anything in terms of *us*, right?"

"Us as a couple? No. I'm not expecting instant forgiveness. But there's hope for us as a business partnership. We were brilliant together, and you're a practical woman. Business comes first."

The server arrived with the first course. Kendra barely listened as he described the special five-course tasting menu based on indigenous recipes from the area. Sage-stuffed mushroom caps with wild rice were the first course.

"I know you love all that Native American stuff," Dominic said proudly after the server left. "Remember when you dragged me to that new restaurant with the indigenous chef?"

"Is that supposed to make me forgive you? That you remember random details like that? And by the way, this was their home before the settlers—"

He cut her off before she could go any further. "Let's stay on topic. We have a time crunch here. I'm not asking you to forget anything that happened between us, or anything I might or might not have done to you."

Goddamn. *Might or might not?* She could fight him over those words alone, but what was the point? This wasn't about their romantic relationship.

Dominic continued. "I'm suggesting you think logically and practically, as I know you always do, about your future and what this offer could mean. You'd be hanging out with the big boys. The power is in your hands, Kendra Carter. Isn't that what you've always wanted?"

twenty-seven

Halfway to Galen's house for that beer, Jason remembered that it was jam session night out in Braddock. Luckily, his trombone case was still in his truck from the last session, taking up half the crew cab. No time to practice when he was hanging out with Kendra so much.

He could use a good jam session right now. That would be a great way to let off steam; besides, the group always had a cooler of beer on hand. He did a U-turn in the middle of an intersection and headed toward Braddock. Another advantage—he wouldn't be in the same town as Kendra and Dominic for a few blessed hours.

Maybe that would give him time to figure out how to "fight for" her, as Holly suggested. What would that look like? He'd already told her how he felt. Should he go after Dominic in a physical way? He could probably take the guy, and damn, that would feel good. He'd been fantasizing about it ever since he set eyes on him.

Would that impress Kendra? It didn't seem like the kind of thing that would, but maybe he was missing something. Maybe his willingness to sustain physical injury would prove his love in a way that baring his heart didn't.

Of course, he had a scar on his lip to prove he wasn't afraid to put his body on the line for her. He'd done it before, he could do it again. But was he really what she wanted, or did she want a hotshot business dude who looked like a model?

By the time he made it to Braddock, the jam session was well underway. He grabbed a folding chair and put together his trombone, latching the slide to the bell, then screwing in the mouthpiece. The familiar process relaxed him. He couldn't wait to lose himself in the music.

Alvin nodded at him, and gave him a signal that he wanted to talk. Jason scooted his chair over. In the group, Alvin switched between bass guitar and vocals, with an occasional stint on the drums. Tonight he was gently plucking a bass line that he could have played in his sleep.

"Got some texts from Kendra, but I can't take my hands off this guitar," he murmured to Jason. "Take a peek for me, you mind?"

Damnit, so much for losing himself in the music. "Your phone is supposed to be off."

"Ringer's off. I was about to turn it off when I saw the texts."

Jason set his trombone across his knees and picked up Alvin's phone from the extra chair where he'd set it down.

Dominic wants me to go to London with him. What should I do?

Jason's chest clenched so hard it felt like a heart attack.

Another text had come in ten minutes after that one.

U there, Pop? I really need your help. Can you call me during the break?

Then another one, about five minutes after that.

He's making really good arguments. We could sell the business to a huge firm that could really do something with it. They want me to work for them. I could write my own ticket, according to Dom. But can I trust him?

Of course not! Jason wanted to scream.

In a neutral voice, underneath the music flowing around them, he read the texts to Alvin.

"Did you say she's going to London?" Alvin hissed.

"She's trying to decide."

He scanned through more of the texts. "Jesus, he wants her to go tonight. She's thinking about doing it just so she can meet with these guys for herself. Or it could just be a vacation. But she wants to make sure you're covered at the restaurant. She wants you to call her when you're done here."

Alvin focused on the strings for a moment. Jason stared down at the phone. She hadn't sent *him* any texts. Would she really leave without saying goodbye? Without even letting him know?

Another text popped onto the screen.

Maybe I need to see for myself if there's anything for me in London. I owe it to myself. I've been in professional limbo too long. If I can kick my career back into gear, it's worth it, right?

In the next moment, his own phone dinged, drawing a glare from the keyboardist. It was a text from Kendra.

Jason, can we talk?

No. If she wanted to break the news that she was leaving for London, she'd have to wait until the damn jam session was over.

He turned off his phone and shoved it into his pocket. He wasn't even supposed to have it on right now.

Alvin hissed at him, jerking his head toward his phone. "Tell Kendra to do what's in her heart."

"You tell her," he whispered back. "That's a dad thing to say."

"From my phone. No capital letters and all that. Just the words."

Jason typed out the words and sent the message. Then he

firmly handed back the phone. "I'm done playing secretary and I need two hands for this trombone."

"London," Alvin muttered, shaking his head. "It does nothing but rain there. She ain't going to like it, I'll tell you that. They might not like her much, either. Look at that girl that married the prince."

Jason put his mouthpiece to his lips so he couldn't say what he wanted to. Which was, Kendra is going to knock them out with one smile, especially when she followed it up with her keen mind and can-do attitude. Any business anywhere would appreciate those qualities.

He waited for a good moment to join the flow of music. There it came, a shift in the chord progressions, the perfect chance to jump in. He softly blew into the trombone, adding a quiet deep brassy note to the mix. Most people thought of the trombone as a loud, almost obnoxious instrument, but not the way he played it. He liked to create a lovely sonorous understructure with his playing. He didn't blow out all the other instruments—unless the piece called for it.

He glanced down at Alvin's phone as more texts popped onto the screen, but he ignored them. It wasn't his business. Kendra was texting her father, not him. She was making her choices on her own. Doing what was best for her. He couldn't blame her for that. In fact, he wanted that for her. So where did that leave him?

Blowing on a damn trombone in a dusty rehearsal room in Braddock.

twenty-eight

Kendra stopped at home to pack an overnight bag.

"Bring enough for a week. If you decide to stay, you can buy everything you need there," Dominic told her. "You'll love the stores in London. Some of them serve tea."

"Not a tea drinker. Stay in the car, I'll be right out." She didn't want to have to introduce Dom to her dad, in case he came home early from the jam session. Her mother wasn't due back from Arkansas until next week. Most likely, Kendra would be back by then. *I'm not moving to London. I'm just possibly selling my business and checking out an opportunity.*

She filled an overnight bag with her most chic business-type attire, then grabbed her sharpest pantsuit—white with a black camisole underneath—and zipped it into a wardrobe bag. That outfit always filled her with confidence. If she had to face a hiring committee or a CEO, she wanted to be wearing that, along with her four-inch Louboutin heels that made her feel like a warrior.

She hadn't worn any of these clothes since she'd left Minneapolis. They felt like old friends she hadn't seen in a while.

A tingle of anticipation danced through her. She'd been licking her wounds for too long. There was so much more for her to accomplish in the world than running her dad's restaurant. She wanted to get out there and make something happen. She was ready.

Sleepwear. She needed something for bed, but her favorite sleep shorts were at Jason's. She was rummaging through her drawer of nightwear when she found one of Jason's t-shirts—a comfy faded oversized shirt with a cowboy-hat-wearing trout on the front. Holly had given it to him for his birthday, and he loved it for its random goofiness. He'd lent it to her after they'd gone skinny-dipping one night in the lake.

She tossed it into the bag, and immediately felt better about this trip. She'd have a piece of Jason with her.

Silly, she scolded herself. It was just a dumb t-shirt. But even in her rush to pack, she knew it was more than that. It was like a hug in the form of a t-shirt. A smile from someone who cared about her. Who always supported her, no matter what.

She scrawled a note for her father on the dry-erase board mounted on the kitchen wall. *Read your texts. They explain everything. Carly will handle things at the Blue Drake while I'm gone. I love you!*

Outside, she found an Uber already waiting. Dominic was chatting exuberantly with the driver, but he cut off his charmfest to help her load her things into the trunk of the Honda.

"Only two bags, that's my girl, always the efficient packer."

"Not your girl," she reminded him.

"Of course not. You're your own person. An independent, modern woman."

Was he mocking her now? Or did that damn British accent just make it sound like that?

Their shoulders bumped as Dominic closed the trunk of the car. He edged closer to her, but she shifted to keep enough distance between them. "Don't make me regret this," she warned him.

"You won't regret it because you're making the right choice. I knew you'd never resist an offer like this."

She hated the way that sounded, as if he knew everything about her. "I haven't decided anything yet."

The buzz of her phone made her jump. It was a local number that she didn't recognize.

"Please don't answer that." Dominic frowned at her across the seat. "We don't have time for distractions."

"I have to. Operation Respected Elders."

"What's that? Sounds dull as hell."

Ignoring him, she answered the call. It was Holly, her words tumbling over each other, audible even without the speaker. "Kendra! Where are you right now? I need your help, or someone's help, like a grownup's, and my sister's too busy and Jason was a dick to me, and his phone isn't answering anyway, so I called you. Can you come help me?"

Dominic shook his head in a firm "no." She ignored him. "How urgent is it? What's going on?"

"I...I think I need to go to the police. I didn't want to, because Chloe thinks I'm being a paranoid toxic friend, but I've been looking at the stuff her boyfriend is posting on social media and it scares me. I'm worried he's going to do something crazy."

"Where are you?"

"I'm at home. Jason has the car, and it's too late to bike around town. I was going to tell Jason before, but we had a fight, sort of, and Chloe says she'll never speak to me if I tell the police and—"

"Holly." Kendra cut her off. "What does your gut say?"

"I'm scared," she whispered. "Scared for Chloe. He said he was going to buy a gun as soon as he got old enough, and he just had a birthday."

"I'll come get you. We'll go talk to Granger. He's the new safety officer."

"Her boyfriend lives in another town, so I don't know if it should be Granger or..."

"He'll know what to do. We got this. I'll be right there." She pulled the phone away from her face and addressed Dominic. "I have to do something before we go anywhere."

"Jesus, Kendra—"

"Will you take me?" she said sharply. "Or should I drive myself?"

"I suppose we can afford a short detour."

Kendra turned back to the call. "I'm going to call Granger and give him a head's up," she told Holly. "We'll go see him together."

"Okay. Thanks, Kendra." The relief in Holly's voice made her heart twist. The poor girl. This must be what had been bothering her all this time. Wanting to respect her friend's wishes versus worried for her safety.

She and Dominic climbed into the backseat and the Honda eased out of her father's driveway. Night closed around them, enveloping the car in soft darkness.

The Honda sped toward the part of town where Holly and Jason lived. She wondered where Jason was, and why he wasn't answering Holly's calls. He hadn't answered her text either. Was he okay? A growing sense of unease filled her.

In the dark masses of trees, she saw the occasional twinkle of someone's lights. The moon was about to dip behind the tree-tops, and already the stars were brighter.

As it turned out, Earl Granger met them at Jason's house. They arrived almost at the same moment. Holly rushed out of the house and huddled close to Kendra, who kept an arm around her shoulder while she spilled all the details.

270

Dominic hovered a few yards away, constantly checking his phone and shooting impatient glances their way.

"I kept screenshots of all his posts even though Chloe got mad at me. She says he just talks shit and I'm taking it too seriously."

"You did the right thing," Granger told her. He took notes in a little book while she talked. His big frame and stern manner was wildly reassuring. "I can take it from here."

Holly burst into tears. Her body shook against Kendra's, the release of weeks of worry pouring out in the form of sobs. Kendra held her tight. "I'm so glad you called me," she whispered to her. "This is good. Hard but good."

Holly just nodded, her head buried in her hands.

"Can you keep Holly's name out of it?" Kendra asked Granger. That would probably be Jason's first question if he was here.

"For now, yes. We'll take this one step at a time."

Holly drew away, wiping her tears. She glanced at Dominic, who was slouched against the Honda. "Are you going somewhere, Kendra?"

Yes, across the ocean, to one of the most cosmopolitan cities in the world. "Nowhere important. I can stay if—"

"No no. I'm fine. Jason will be home soon. I just remembered that it's his jam session night and he probably turned off his phone. You can go."

"But I thought he was being a—"

Holly didn't let her finish that sentence. "He'll be great. He's Jason." As if that explained everything, which, in fact, it did. "Thank you, Kendra." She threw her arms around Kendra again, and they shared a long hug.

It was hard to leave her, but both Granger and Holly insisted they'd be fine. So she got back into the Uber.

"I have to stop for gas," said the driver, a young man named

Ahmad.

Why did that fill her with relief? She directed him to the nearest gas station and they sped away.

Dominic scrolled on his phone, his perfect profile illuminated by its blue glow. "I changed our tickets and gave us an extra two hours to get there. Your little detour didn't cost us too much."

Little detour. As if that was all it amounted to, rather than supporting a young woman in a moment of crisis.

The "detour" had done something else, though. Kendra no longer felt swept up in the excitement of rushing off to catch a midnight plane.

At the East Lake gas station, which doubled as a video rental and convenience store, she got out of the car and drew in a deep breath of the September air. The sight of Jason's house—the warm light spilling out the windows, the bicycles leaning under the shed, the brass flowerpot shaped like fireman's boots—had shaken her up.

How could she leave town without talking to him first? She couldn't. Why was Dominic rushing her like this?

Dominic emerged from the car, still scanning his phone.

"Is there some kind of deadline coming up?" she asked him. "Why do we have to go tonight? What if I'd needed more time to wrap things up?"

"It's always best to strike while the iron is hot." He closed his phone, putting his face into shadow. "Ancient business proverb. I don't want them to change their minds before we close."

That was true enough, she supposed. "Who am I going to be meeting with?"

"His name is Colin Atwood. I'll email you his bio so you can brief yourself beforehand. I know you like to be prepared."

That was also true. So again—why were they rushing off like this? "Why didn't you call me, or have Colin Atwood call me, before you hopped on a plane?"

"Dramatic gesture, darling. Apology dinner, remember that?"

But he never had apologized. He'd never once said the words, "I'm sorry" or "I apologize." Was booking a restaurant and whisking her off to London his version of an apology?

Kendra had fantasized about Dominic groveling many times since he'd dumped her. But in her imagination, there had been a lot more confessions of being an asshole.

"Can we circle back to the moment you picked up a phone and decided to call the Lake Bittersweet board?"

"That again?" He let out a sigh. "When Mark told me you were applying for that job, I was afraid you'd get stuck in Lake Bittersweet and that there'd be no chance for us in the future. No chance for our business partnership," he added quickly.

"Why didn't you just call *me*? Why go behind my back like a devious dickhead?"

"I'm sorry to say I *am* a bit of a devious dickhead." He gave a disarming laugh, as if everyone was supposed to know that. "It's one of my charms."

"I'm going to need more than that. Were you too afraid to face me, even by phone?"

"I'm facing you now, aren't I?"

"Why now, this particular point in time?" She snapped her fingers as the pieces fell into place. "You saw the fire livestream, and Jason. The news stories mentioned the boat rescue too, and you saw me talking to the news. You were threatened by Jason."

Anger flashed across his face.

She sucked in a breath. For one brief moment, she'd glimpsed Dominic's real feelings, and they had nothing to do with getting back together. He didn't even want to work together again, not really.

Something had happened, and he needed her. She had to figure out what and why before she committed to anything in London.

As if trying to hide that raw moment of exposure, Dominic turned away and got back into the car. Good. She needed a moment to think before Ahmad came back from using the bathroom.

She pulled out her phone and searched for the name Colin Atwood. At least that part was real. He was one of the top executives in Global Solutions. Just out of curiosity, she searched for Dominic's name and saw that his position was exactly as he'd described it.

At least he wasn't lying about the company.

But what did it mean that she even questioned if he was lying? It meant she didn't trust him and never would, and she was on her way to another country with someone with a hidden agenda.

This trip was feeling more and more like a mistake. The incident with Holly had shifted things. What was going to happen next with that situation? What if she needed more support? What if her friends abandoned her? What if Chloe's crazy boyfriend came after her?

She looked back at her phone and shot Holly a text. *How are you doing?*

Okay, came her answer. *Still with Granger. He's awesome.*

Is Jason back yet?

No.

That was strange. The jam session had to be over by now.

It occurred to her that she hadn't heard anything back from her father since she'd sent him that flurry of text messages. The last thing he'd texted was "do what's in your heart," about three hours ago. It was after midnight, and Alvin liked to get to bed by eleven, midnight at the latest on the nights he went to Braddock.

She sent him a text, but got no answer. It didn't even read as "delivered." Maybe his phone was dead. Should she call the home phone and risk waking him up? Logic told her that his phone had probably run out of battery, and he'd driven home without realizing it, then gone straight to bed.

But it bothered her that he hadn't texted again, or called. That wasn't like him. If he knew she was about to get on a plane, he'd call her and make sure he'd told her he loved her. It was a superstition he had. *Never let someone get on a plane without telling them you love them.* He applied that to all trips, in fact. Under normal circumstances, he certainly would have reached out.

So maybe she'd upset him by taking off so suddenly. No, that didn't make sense. He would have told her so. He would have said something like, "it's your choice, but princess, you're rushing this." Or, "I know you're not leaving me with an entire restaurant to run by myself." Or, "Sweet pea, let me get some rest and we'll talk this through tomorrow. What's in London that you can't get here in the U.S. of A.?"

Her stomach tightened. Something was wrong, she just knew it. This wasn't about logic, this was her spidey sense—based on a lifetime of knowing Alvin Carter.

Ahmad hurried back to the car and jumped into the driver's seat. Dominic rolled down the window and leaned his head out. "Get back in, Kendra. We have to go."

"I think I need to go back," she said in a low voice, almost to herself.

"Excuse me?" Frowning, Dominic pushed open the door and climbed out.

"I haven't heard from my dad."

"It's late. I'm sure he's asleep." He checked his phone. "We'll miss the flight if we turn back now."

"You already changed the tickets once. Why not again?" That nagging feeling was growing stronger. She didn't think of herself as someone with much intuition. She liked to base decisions on concrete evidence. Maybe she was just imagining things, but she couldn't ignore this feeling.

"Kendra, this is our chance to cash in on our hard work. Can't you have a neighbor check on him?"

"It's too late." She couldn't possibly wake up Nellie and her kids next door, or old Elmira, who loved to flirt with her dad. "I'll call one of his music buddies. They might still be awake."

She flipped through her contacts looking for names of jam session members. She could call Jason, of course. But she didn't want to do that. *Hey, I'm in a car with my ex on the way to London, would you mind hauling ass over to my dad's house to check on him?*

Obviously he would do it, but just as obviously, she couldn't ask him to.

She found the number of the keyboardist. He answered right away. Relief flooded through her.

"Hi, it's Kendra, Redfish's daughter." All his musician friends called him by his stage name. "I haven't heard from my dad. Is he okay?"

"He rocked it at the session tonight. Seemed fine."

"When did the session break up?"

"About an hour ago. We went a little later than usual."

An hour ago? And he still hadn't texted? "Did you see him leave?"

"I was one of the first out the door because I had a babysitter at home. I said goodbye, I know that. He might have been heading to the bathroom. He looked normal, maybe a little... hm...unbalanced?"

"Unbalanced?"

"Unsteady. That's a better word. Like he'd had too much to drink. But I didn't see him drink. He usually doesn't because of the drive back to Lake Bittersweet."

Unsteady. She *really* didn't like the sound of that. "Thanks, DeVaughn. Guess I'd better go check on him."

"Don't worry too much. Jason Mosedale was sitting next to him. If there was anything going on, Jason would have noticed."

Right. That actually *did* ease her mind. If anything was wrong, Jason would have handled it.

Dominic crossed to the driver's side window and said something to Ahmad. He was probably telling him to go back to her house so they could check on her father.

"He said he can break a few speed limits," Dominic said when he came back to the passenger side. He opened the door and took her arm to tug her toward it. "We can still make it."

"I can't. I need to go back. Something's wrong, I can feel it."

"You're being absurd. Call someone. Call that fire chief. That's what he gets paid for, isn't it? Say you need a wellness check."

"Don't talk about him like he's a servant," she snapped. It grated on her nerves, that condescending tone he took.

"I'm just saying—"

She cut him off. "I get it. I'm calling him now. Just...go back over there." She gestured for him to step away from her.

"Jesus," he muttered under his breath.

She dialed Jason's number but got his voice mail. Why was no one answering their phones? Should she call nine-one-one dispatch and ask whoever was on duty to do a wellness check on her father? It seemed excessive, considering that she had no evidence that her father was in any kind of trouble. Most likely things had unfolded exactly as she imagined—he'd driven home and gone straight to bed. His phone was probably plugged in and charging, set to "do not disturb."

A wellness check might scare him. She'd heard horror stories of wellness checks gone wrong. Luckily, every firefighter in Lake Bittersweet knew her father. That probably wasn't a huge concern, but there was always a risk.

Do not disturb. There was a way to get past it, she suddenly remembered. You had to call twice in a row. She called Jason again, twice. No answer. Then her father, twice. No answer. Then finally she called the home phone, just in case his cell phone was still dead. No answer.

"We've got to go back to my house, Dominic. I can't get through to Jason and my dad's not answering any of his phones."

"Absolutely not," Dominic said sharply. "Kendra, listen to yourself. You're being paranoid. We just left Lake Bittersweet an hour ago. What could possibly have happened in that amount of time?"

"I don't know. Anything. Everything."

He gazed into her eyes with that familiar intensity that used to absolutely liquefy her. "Where's my logical queen? Won't you feel like a fool when you get back and everything's fine, and we've missed our flight and I have to explain to Colin Atwood that my brilliant partner has a paranoid streak and can't be relied on and they'd better find someone else to head up Explastica?"

"I don't care about any of that!" she cried.

Their argument had drawn the attention of Ahmad, who popped his head over the top of the Honda. "Is there a problem?"

"Ahmad, I need to go back to where you picked us up. Will you take me?"

"Scratch that," said Dominic. "We're not doing that. Get in the fucking car. Ahmad, we're staying on track."

"I'm not getting in that car unless you go where I tell you." Kendra fixed Ahmad with a firm stare.

The poor driver gripped the frame of his Honda in a kind of panic. "I don't know the rules. Will I get in trouble? I don't know what to do."

"I'm the one who booked you, so you answer to me," said Dominic. "She'll be fine, she's just being hysterical."

"Dominic, I swear to fucking God, if we don't get to my father's house in the next five minutes, I will not get on that plane with you. I will never go to London. I will never sell. You can tell Colin Atwood to go fuck himself."

"We have to sell."

For a flash, she caught rage and panic on his handsome face. Then it was gone. "This is your chance, too, Kendra. You can start new with a chunk of cash. I know you, you'll love it in London. It's fast-paced, high-stress, high-stakes. It's everything you've always wanted."

The quickly suppressed desperation in his voice told her there was more he wasn't telling her. But it didn't matter anymore. Because finally, for good, she was done with Dominic Robb.

"You think you know me so well, but you don't. Because you never came to meet my father and therefore you have no idea how important he is to me. You only know one thing about me, that I want to succeed. And you use it to manipulate me."

God, it was liberating to say these things out loud. Finally, she was speaking her mind to Dominic. Being herself. Living up to her favorite Eartha Kitt quote.

Did she owe Jason for that? She couldn't think about him right now, she had to get home.

"Can you just get in the fucking car, Kendra?" Dominic yelled. "I'm done with this shit."

"Good, because I'm done too. I'm calling my own Uber." She whipped out her phone. "And shouldn't you be saying 'bloody' car, you fake-ass grifter?"

Just then her phone rang. It was Jason. Her heart racing a mile a minute, she accepted the call.

"Sorry I didn't pick up before. I'm with Alvin. We just got to the hospital. He's in the exam room right now. I don't know what's going on yet, but he seemed disoriented so I insisted that he get checked out. He didn't want me to bother you, but I knew you'd want to know."

twenty-nine

"I'll call you right back," said Kendra tensely, then ended the call.

In the waiting room at the Braddock hospital, Jason stared at his phone. Had he done the right thing?

"She's on her way to London, let her be," Alvin kept saying. "I feel fine."

But he was so confused that he hadn't remembered some of the information on the check-in form. Jason had played the fire chief card and convinced the charge nurse to overlook a few details until he could track down a family member.

After that, Jason gave Alvin a choice. He could either call his wife Ruth, who was still in Arkansas, or Kendra. Or both. But someone from his family had to be notified. As the nurse guided him toward an exam room, Alvin had given in and told Jason to call Kendra first.

It hadn't been easy to dial her number. She was in the process of ditching him, after all. But Alvin's health was more important than any relationship drama. She would be furious if something was going on with Alvin and no one told her. And if the worst happened, she'd be devastated.

So far, he hadn't gotten much information from the medical staff. But he'd seen enough medical emergencies to know that this was more than dehydration or exhaustion. Stroke? Something worse? They'd know soon.

His phone rang. Kendra.

"Are you in Braddock?" she asked tensely.

"Yeah. He's in an exam room right now. It might be nothing. Do you want me to just keep you posted?"

"No, I'm coming. I just have to wait for another Uber. Dominic left."

"I'll come get you," he said right away. He didn't like the idea of her waiting for a ride at this hour of the night. As for Dominic...he really wished he'd gotten one more chance to punch the dude out.

"No. Stay there with him. I'll be fine. And Jason...thank you for calling. You did the right thing, I don't care what my dad said. Did you call my mom?"

"No, I didn't have her number and Alvin refused to give it to me. He didn't want to worry her." He rubbed at the back of his neck, where tension had been gathering all night long.

"I'll call her. My dad can get mad at me if he wants."

"By the way, there's a good chance he'll ban me from the Blue Drake for dragging him in here."

"Fuck that, you're eating for free at the Blue Drake from now on. I knew something was wrong. I could just feel it."

He caught the sound of a car engine pulling up next to her. "Is that your Uber? Listen, Kendra. Stay on the phone with me while you get into the car. It's late and it might be sketchy."

His tone of voice left no room for discussion. She didn't argue in any case. As she spoke to the Uber driver, he paid close attention for any hint of sketchiness.

"I'm on the phone with my boyfriend," he heard her say. "He's working tonight or he'd come pick me up himself. Yeah, night shift. He's in law enforcement. Actually he just got promoted to chief of the department."

So bittersweet, being called her boyfriend as a kind of shield.

"Boyfriend, huh?" he said when she was safely settled into the Uber. "Are we in eighth grade again?"

"That would be nice. Things were simpler back then. So tell me everything that happened. From the beginning."

He started with the jam session. "He kept stopping in the middle of a riff, wiping his face, saying he didn't feel right. I made him drink some water, then I actually ran out and got some Gatorade from a vending machine. Electrolytes can make a big difference. He drank that, and it seemed like he might be doing better. Then when everyone was leaving, he went to use the bathroom and I caught him veering into a wall. He started rambling about something, but none of it made sense. I checked his vitals as best I could. Erratic pulse, no sign of a fever, elevated heart rate. Altered mental status. It all added up to a big red flag."

"My heart rate is elevated just hearing about it." The strain in her voice made his heart ache for her. He wished he was with her right now, holding her close while she traveled through the night toward the hospital. All he could do was use his voice and his love.

"He's okay, Kendra. He's in the right place, with the right people checking him out."

"Thanks to you."

He didn't answer that directly, but she was right. If he hadn't been there, who knew what would have happened? Maybe Alvin would have tried to drive himself home. Or maybe someone else would have noticed something wasn't right and stepped in. Or tried. It hadn't been easy getting him to the hospital.

"I'm glad I was there. He wanted to go home, and he got confrontational about it. He's got that Carter family fighting spirit."

"Where do you think I got it from?" Her voice sounded a little lighter this time. Her imagination had probably been going wild with potential life-threatening scenarios. "Dominic and Ahmad just got a big dose of it too."

"Ahmad?"

"The first Uber driver. I hope he doesn't testify against me if Dominic files charges."

"*What?*"

"I kicked Dominic in the balls. Well, probably more like his upper thigh because of the close quarters. It was the only way to get my point across that I wasn't going anywhere with him! He's fine," she added quickly. "I'm sure he'll be back in charming seductive mode by the time he reaches Minneapolis."

Jason didn't know whether to laugh or applaud—or fly to London and smash his face in after all. "I've been having fantasies of punching him out. I guess you took care of it yourself."

"You already got one scar while defending me."

He'd risk a million more scars for her...but he didn't say that. She already knew it.

"So you're not going to London?" he asked cautiously, almost afraid to hear the answer.

"I'm not going to London. I figured out why Dominic flew all the way here to lure me to London."

"It's...not because he wants you back?" He could barely get the words out, and every muscle in his body tensed as he waited for her answer.

"Hell no. He doesn't want me back. He claimed his firm wanted to hire me, but that's not it either. He made some bad investments and needs to sell Explastica right away. He knew I didn't have the money, so he talked his firm into purchasing it. He was in a rush to close."

The rush of relief made his head swim. He looked up to see an older man in scrubs coming toward him. "The doctor's coming out. How far away are you?"

"I can see Braddock now. Maybe ten minutes?"

"I'll put the phone on speaker."

He bolted to his feet to greet the doctor, a pleasant but tired looking man in his sixties. "How's he doing?"

"We have him on IV fluids. We're running some tests. Nothing definitive yet. Are you his family?"

"No, but his daughter is on the way. She's on the phone right now—" But his screen had gone dark. Damnit, he must have hung up when he tried to put the speaker on. "Can you wait until she gets here? Is it urgent?"

"We can wait. Tell the nurse when she's here and we'll go from there."

"I have paramedic training, so I'm familiar with signs of stroke. Did he have a stroke?"

"Let's wait for his family."

As soon as the doctor was gone, Jason texted Kendra. *Sorry, didn't mean to hang up on you. They're going to wait for family, aka you, but he's stable. IV fluids. Running tests.*

She sent a thumbs up emoji.

He paced the perimeter of the emergency room, watching the reflections in the windows and bracing himself for the sight of Kendra. He hadn't set eyes on her, even in passing, since he'd confessed his feelings to her. His stomach roiled at the thought of seeing her again, being so close, but so far.

But he had to put all that to the side right now. Her only concern should be Alvin.

A car pulled in out front and he started toward the entrance, only to see a pregnant woman emerge from the passenger side, a tote bag in hand. A nurse came out with a wheelchair and she settled into it gratefully. She seemed so calm. Maybe this wasn't her first child. Maybe she was all about that Minnesota Scandinavian stoicism.

Either way, the sight made him think of Bliss and Granger and their newborn baby twins. He'd driven the paramedic van and Kendra had ridden in the back with Bliss, while Granger rushed to meet them at the hospital. Afterwards, he'd given Kendra a ride back and they'd both been flying high from the experience. They'd parked the van somewhere private and made out like reckless teenagers.

He was ready for the next step. He'd been ready. All he'd needed was the right person to fall in love with. But there was a catch; that person had to want him too.

Another car pulled up. He spotted the Uber logo on the dashboard, and rushed toward the entrance. Kendra burst out, a whirlwind in a brown suede jacket, tight jeans and heeled boots. She flew into his arms, nearly knocking him over. He stood firm, soaking in the sensation of her aliveness, her warmth, her presence.

"You forgot your bags," called the Uber driver.

"I'll grab them," he told Kendra. "You go tell the charge nurse that you're here. I'll be right in."

"Thank you, Jason. Thank you for everything." Her voice was broken, emotional, with none of her usual sass.

"Hey hey. It's okay. It's my job."

He didn't want her to feel like she owed him anything for doing the decent human thing.

"It's not just your job, Jason. It's you." There was something in her tone, something in her eyes, but he didn't dare hope.

And then she was gone, dashing through the double glass

doors into the ER. His heart racing, he grabbed the two bags that the Uber driver had left on the sidewalk, and hurried after her.

Since a family member was now present, the medical staff allowed both of them into Alvin's exam room while the doctor explained the situation. Kendra sat next to the bed, holding her father's hand, calmly receiving the information as if she hadn't been in a panic a moment ago. She probably still was, but didn't want to add to Alvin's worry.

"We think he had a small stroke. The MRI shows some damage in the cerebral cortex, but it's minimal. He may find it hard to come up with words, but occupational therapy can go a long way. He should start that immediately. No driving for a while. He should probably take some time off from work."

Alvin muttered unhappily. His hospital gown did nothing to diminish his presence, but he looked older, more tired.

"Oh, he won't lift a finger at work," Kendra said firmly. "I'm sort of his boss, and I'll make sure of it."

"I might know someone who can help out for a while," Jason said after the doctor had left. "One of the assistant chefs at the nursing home is being put on temporary leave until the kitchen is rebuilt."

"We'll figure it out." Kendra scooted onto the hospital bed next to her father and rested her head on his shoulder. "I'm not going to London, Pop. I'm staying here."

He pulled away to look down at her, and finally spoke. "You sure?" His voice sounded rusty and hoarse, like a true bluesman's.

"I'm sure. I have other plans that don't depend on an ex and a flight to London."

She glanced at Jason, causing his heart to skip some beats. "Other...plans?" he managed.

"Later," she mouthed. Then she turned back to Alvin. "The most important thing is for you to rest and get better. Don't worry about the restaurant, don't worry about anything. I got you, Pop."

"Jason..." Alvin gestured to him.

He stepped toward the door, thinking they probably wanted a family moment. "Want me to leave?"

"No," they both said simultaneously. He froze right where he was.

"Jason helped me." Alvin formed the words carefully, one at a time.

"Yeah, and you didn't make it easy for him. It must run in the family." She sent Jason a look so loaded with intimacy that his heart nearly burst. "I didn't make it easy for him either. Thank goodness he's good at overcoming obstacles."

He couldn't speak. Couldn't say a word. What was she implying?

A nurse came back into the room and said, "That's enough for now. Time for him to sleep."

Indeed, Alvin's chin was dropping to his chest. Kendra kissed him on the cheek and got to her feet. "When can we take him home?"

"We'll monitor him for a few hours, then release him."

"I'll stick around and drive you both home," Jason said instantly. "Or I can take you to pick up his truck. Whatever works best."

Kendra's eyes filled with tears again. She stepped away from the bed while the nurse tended to Alvin. Jason's heart ached for her.

He took her hand and led her out to the corridor, then gently blotted her tears with his thumb. "He's going to be okay, sweetheart."

The word slipped out; he couldn't help it. Her gaze darted up to meet his. "You mean it?"

"You heard the doctor. It's a small stroke and therapy should—"

"No. The sweetheart part."

What he saw in her brilliant eyes made his heart turn over. He glanced up and down the corridor, then spotted a supply closet. Still holding her hand, he waited until the coast was clear, then pulled her inside it.

thirty

Among the towels and cleaning supplies, they faced each other. Kendra had been through a roller coaster over the past few hours, but now everything went still. All that mattered was Jason and his steady presence and warm hands holding hers.

"Of course I mean it." His voice was unsteady as he answered her "sweetheart" question. "Always."

Her throat worked as she struggled to get words to come out. "After I left the house with Dom, everything felt wrong. Then Holly called and I helped her out, and I didn't even want to get back into the Uber. I was so relieved when we stopped to get gas, and I knew I wasn't going anywhere. Something wasn't right. When you called about my dad, I figured that was the reason." She laid a hand on his chest, feeling his heart thump against her palm. "But it wasn't just that. When I heard your voice, I almost started crying. I love you, Jason."

He shook his head, as if he didn't believe her. "I know you're upset, Kendra, but—"

"No. It's not that. I love you."

She could still see the doubt in his expression, and couldn't blame him for that. After all, she'd been on her way to London an hour ago, with her ex. She had to make him believe, and that meant she had to be honest.

"When you told me you loved me, in the room with all the bongo drums, you know why I was so surprised? And why I didn't say anything back?"

"Because I chose a room with bongo drums?" he asked cautiously. Despite his semi-joke, she could see him bracing himself for her answer.

"No, because you seemed different. Sure of yourself. Confident. Maybe...mature? All that time, I think I was seeing you as... young. I wasn't seeing all of you. But you stood there in your uniform, all hot and hunky and loving and just, putting yourself out there, and I kind of...blanked out from surprise. I wasn't ready."

He squinted down at her. "That sounds sort of like a complisult."

She burst out laughing. Oh Jason, sweet, wonderful Jason, always able to bring lightness to every moment. She loved him so much. "Face it, Jaybone. I love you. I want to be with you. I *love* being with you. You make me smile, you make me feel grounded, safe, happy, peaceful."

"Peaceful?" He pulled her against his chest and nuzzled her neck. Warmth surround her, inside and out. She was with Jason again and everything was going to be okay.

"Here's the thing. It takes a strong man to let a woman like me be everything she can be. I didn't see it at first, but that's because I was used to something different. With Dominic, I mean. With you, I feel like myself. Do you feel that way too?"

His cheek rested against hers. "You help me be the best of myself. I didn't quite believe in that without you."

That intimate confession made her heart swell.

He cupped her face in his hands and kissed her on the lips, deep and gentle. Light filled her from her toes to her heart. It shone through her and into him and somehow managed not to set the supply closet on fire.

He paused only long enough to whisper, "You're really not leaving?"

She shook her head. Before she could explain, a janitor opened the door and they sprang apart.

"What the heck?" he exclaimed.

"Fire inspection," said Jason, fumbling over the words. "Lake Bittersweet Fire Department here. We got a report of—"

"Get the hell out of here. No smashing in my damn closet."

"It's not like that," Kendra told him sternly. "We're in love."

"Be in love somewhere else. Cafeteria's open."

They were still laughing about it when they found an empty nook under a stairwell. Kendra settled herself onto Jason's lap with a sigh. It felt so good to be with him. She could do anything in the world, go anywhere, and he'd be there for her.

She'd do the same for him.

"Have you talked to Holly yet?"

"No, haven't had a chance, but we've been texting. I know what's going on. They're interviewing Chloe's boyfriend right now, but we haven't heard any more. Holly said you really came through for her tonight. Thank you, my love."

"Just like you really came through for my dad. Isn't it kind of funny how it happened again?"

"What did?" He nestled her into a more comfortable position, her head tucked against his shoulder.

"First, you tried to help me get a job and I tried to help you get a job, all on the same night. This time, I helped Holly and you helped Alvin. All on the same night." He said the last sentence along with her. "It's just funny, that's all."

"I think it's beautiful. We put ourselves on the line for each other."

"And we're hot for each other," she added.

"So hot."

They lost themselves in more kissing at that point. Kendra couldn't imagine anywhere she'd rather be than under this hospital stairwell with Jason. Who needed the lap of luxury when you had the lap of Jason?

Although...she still intended to book a room at the Dorchester someday. On her own dime.

"So what are these other plans?" Jason asked her after some time had passed. "And what happened to London?"

"I don't want to sell my business to a big firm. The deep pockets are nice, but I like to be in charge. At least when it comes to business." She winked at him. "Besides, in the Uber—the second one—I called Colin Atwood, the exec I would have been meeting with. He was going to completely change the concept to benefit the plastics industry. He also let slip the price he was offering, and it's a lot less than what Dominic wanted me to pay. In other words, Dom's desperate and I can probably buy him out for a fraction of what Explastica's worth. I'm going to get my company back."

Jason grinned at her happily, but didn't seem to quite get it.

"It's going to be here," she explained. "Well, in Lake Bittersweet."

Finally, the wonder in his expression told her the news was sinking in. "You're going to stay?"

"It has to be headquartered somewhere, right?"

He snatched her up in a fierce hug. "God, I love you."

"I'll probably have to travel a lot." Those words were crushed against his chest.

"I can live with that." He drew back, his eyes sparkling down at her. "I'll love watching you take on the world. But won't you feel like you're missing out on something by staying here?"

"Everything's a choice. Sure, I'll probably miss out on something. But I'm choosing another path. I choose this one, here, with you. And my family," she added. "Especially now."

He tightened his arms around her. "I choose you, too, Kendra Carter. My heart chose you, and it's never wrong."

"Are you sure? I'm a pain in the ass sometimes. I'm stubborn, I like to get my own way, I don't like to watch my words, I—"

"You're perfect."

When she started to object, he put a finger to her lips. "To me, you're perfect. Argue all you want, I'm not going to change my mind. I can be stubborn too. I wasn't giving up on you, you know. Holly lectured me about that, but she didn't have to. I hoped I'd win you over eventually. It might take me a while to get where I want, but don't count me out."

Someone walked past the stairwell, heels clicking on the tile floor. She waited until they'd passed by.

"I never did. I believe in you, Jason. Ever since that pool cue, and probably before." She touched her finger to that scar on his upper lip. "And now I love you. Maybe I caught you on the rebound, but the important thing is, I caught you."

He caught her finger and kissed it. "Can we say we caught each other, or do you have to be the one? Works for me either way."

She released a sound that was part laugh, part yawn. "I'm too happy to argue about it. All I know is I want to be with you. The fire chief and the starting-from-scratch entrepreneur. Who would have thought?"

He shifted under her. "About that starting from scratch part... there's something I should probably tell you..."

thirty-one

The home office of Explastica held its grand opening a month later. It took time for Kendra to get things settled with Alvin's Burgers and Blues. And then, of course, to locate and lease the office, hire a lawyer to close the buyout, and hire a coder. And none of it would have happened without an infusion of funds from one secret millionaire—Jason Mosedale.

He finally told her the whole story when they were back in Lake Bittersweet. They were sitting on the end of the Blue Drake pier, waiting for Galen to bring in a bucket of fish for that night's special. Alvin was at home, and the temporary substitute chef had an insanely good blackened trout recipe.

"It was a fluke," Jason explained. "I won the lottery. I've always been a lucky guy, but that was just insane. I never played the lottery, like ever. But when I helped Mom and Dad move to Minneapolis, I went to pick up ice for them at the corner store. I bought a scratcher on a whim. I won two-point-three million dollars, but I didn't tell anyone. I didn't want my life to change. I stuck it in a trust to cover college expenses for Holly and my sister's kids, and mine if I ever have any. Then I basically forgot about it."

"All this time, you've been a freaking millionaire? And no one knows?"

"Nope. I only told Holly after she got upset about that donation that she thought was for us."

"You said something about it when you were sick." She shook her head, remembering. "I thought you were delirious."

"I was, or I never would have said that. I'm glad you didn't believe me. Now I know you fell in love with me, not my two-point-three million dollars. Minus taxes. So it's more like one-point-six million."

She swatted him on his hard upper arm. "You could have told me when Dominic showed up, flaunting his thousand-dollar suit and all."

"I don't do dick wars."

His dignified tone made her burst out laughing. "You should put that on a T-shirt."

He joined in, good-naturedly as always. "Seriously, I'd do anything to prove my love to you, everything except flash my portfolio."

"Portfolio? God, that sounds sexy." She fanned herself. It sounded especially sexy coming from a handsome firefighter in jeans and a t-shirt. "But don't worry, I fell in love with you way before I knew about it."

"I know." He smiled smugly. "Guess I won that dick war."

She laughed even harder, because it was true, so true.

"Anyway, I want to invest in something new. Diversify my portfolio. I'm very interested in ways to promote plastic recycling, and I really love supporting local businesses."

"You'll get your investment back, with interest."

"I know I will."

"I might out-million you."

"I bet you will."

"Are you really serious?"

"Serious as a two hundred dollar Uber ride."

She hugged him so enthusiastically that they both teetered on the edge of the pier. "I accept," she told him. "Whatever you're offering, I accept."

"Please don't put that on a T-shirt."

Now, a month later, she had a surprise for him. The Explastica office, located in a newly built office complex with a view of the lake, was filled with family and friends and acquaintances from all over Lake Bittersweet. Many of the firefighters were there, as well as most of the waitstaff from the Blue Drake.

Bliss and Earl Granger brought their newborns, each nestled in a cloth sling against a parent's chest. They'd finally named them, going with neither the "hippie" theme nor the "royal" theme that had inspired their own names.

"Meet Austin and Ariel," Bliss told them. Kendra wiggled one twin's bootie-covered foot and Jason let one twin wrap a tiny hand around his finger. "These two owe a lot to both of you."

Kendra shared a glance with Jason. She loved being part of this community, loved letting everyone know that they were together.

"We would have named them after you guys, but that might be weird, considering Lake Bittersweet already has a Kendra and Jason. Who are epic, by the way."

"We are pretty epic, aren't we?" Jason laughed down at her, then jumped as someone tapped on his shoulder. Kendra didn't recognize the stranger. Odd, since she'd only invited friends and family.

Jason turned around, then staggered backwards as he stared at the dark-haired man before him. "No fucking way."

"Yup. I finally did it."

"Did what? Who is this?" Kendra looked from one to the other of them, utterly confused. The stranger was exceptionally good-looking, with striking dark eyes and classic bone structure. Come to think of it, he looked vaguely familiar... "*Galen?*"

"Yup. Do you think she'll like it? Is she here? Is she coming?"

"She's not here yet." Jason squeezed his shoulders. "Stay frosty."

"I might throw up." Galen clutched at his stomach and wandered away.

As soon as he was gone, Jason explained. "When we got together, he decided it was time to go for it with Brenda."

"Good luck to him. Brenda's a peach."

She caught sight of Holly and waved at her. Thanks to Holly, a mentally unbalanced young man was now getting treatment, and no one was in danger from the stash of weapons he'd been accumulating. If Holly hadn't reported Chloe's boyfriend, a disaster might have happened. Even Chloe recognized it. They were friends again, and Holly was supporting her through the aftermath, as only Holly could.

A bass line strummed, grabbing everyone's attention. Kendra clutched Jason's hand in excitement. "Ready for your surprise?"

He twisted his face in doubt. "Hmmm..."

"Stop. You're going to love it. Stay right here."

After motioning to the other key players in her surprise, she joined the group of musicians at the back of the office, where a big Explastica banner hung.

"Welcome, everyone, to the grand opening of Explastica. Thank you so much for being here. This is a dream come true for me and I have so many people to thank. Starting with my father, Alvin Redfish Carter, who's back on bass tonight."

Alvin tipped his cap and grinned at her. The fact that he could play again made the world shine even brighter. Now that Mama was back, she was taking charge of his recovery. They worked on his therapy exercises every day, but he still had trouble with certain words.

"We've had a lot of changes in this town lately, including a new fire chief. You know Fire Chief Mosedale doesn't like to hog the spotlight, but this place wouldn't exist without him. That's true of a lot of things around here. As a show of our love and appreciation, please enjoy this throwback to one long-ago summer, with a little help from the fire department. Carly and Gina, come on up here."

She took off her wrap dress, revealing one of her white chambermaid's outfits from the summer she worked at the Blue Drake with her four best friends. Carly and Gina, also wearing white, joined her. They all clustered around the microphone.

"Jason, this is for you."

Alvin's band launched into "Summer Loving" from Grease.

Like out-of-practice backup singers, the three of them danced and sang, pointing to Jason every time the line "met a boy cute as can be" came up—changing it to "met a fireman."

Jason slowly turned red as a fire truck.

Then came the best part. From stage right, a conga line of volunteer firemen and women strutted toward the microphone. Kendra held it out for them so they could sing too. They preened, they grooved, they ground their hips, and every time that line came along, everyone gestured at Jason. The last fireman was Brent, dancing with that same plastic damn blowup doll she'd first met at that infamous training exercise.

Everyone was laughing by now, hearty belly laughs, the kind

that you only heard around people who knew each other really well.

She beckoned to Jason to join them. Being the ultimate good sport, he did. He could really move, her Jason. She couldn't take her eyes off him as he grooved to the funky beat. Someone from the band passed up a trombone. Without missing a beat, he raised it to his lips and blew.

Kendra looked around at her new office space, filled with old friends and new love. A year and a half ago she'd been at her lowest. But boy, had she rebounded.

Jason handed the trombone back to the band and stepped to Kendra's side. He swept her off her feet into a smooth, professional dip. One of his wicked twinkles lit up his eyes. "You're going to pay for this," he growled.

"Ohh, is that a promise?"

"It's a vow."

The look in his eyes told her exactly what he was vowing. To be hers, now and forever. She knew he'd keep that vow. Because, just like her, he knew how blessed they were to find each other. To love each other. To *see* each other.

"I always knew I was a lucky guy," he murmured. "I didn't know how lucky."

She smiled up at him. "Do we have to have an argument about how you make your own luck?"

"Sure. Just one question." The groove in his cheek deepened as he spun them into another dip. Jason never stayed serious for too long, and she loved that about him. "Can we do it in bed?"

Thank you so much for reading! Galen Cooper's story, THE CRUSH, is next in the Lake Bittersweet series. You can find all the Lake Bittersweet novels here.

For more contemporary romance set in far-flung locations, explore the completed Lost Harbor, Alaska series here.

For all up-to-date news about new releases, sales, deals, and life in Alaska, sign up for Jennifer's newsletter. You'll receive a free full-length novel as a welcome gift.

about the author

Jennifer Bernard is a *USA Today* bestselling author of contemporary romance. Her books have been called "an irresistible reading experience" full of "quick wit and sizzling love scenes." A graduate of Harvard and former news promo producer, she left big city life in Los Angeles for true love in Alaska, where she now lives with her husband and stepdaughters. She still hasn't adjusted to the cold, so most often she can be found cuddling with her laptop and a cup of tea. No stranger to book success, she also writes erotic novellas under a naughty secret name that she's happy to share with the curious. You can learn more about Jennifer and her books at JenniferBernard.net. Make sure to sign up for her newsletter for new releases, fresh exclusive content, sales alerts and giveaways.

Connect with Jennifer online:
JenniferBernard.net
Jen@JenniferBernard.net

also by jennifer bernard

Lake Bittersweet

The First Love ~ Book 1

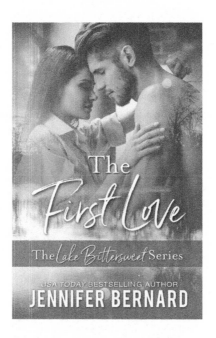

The Fling ~ Book 2

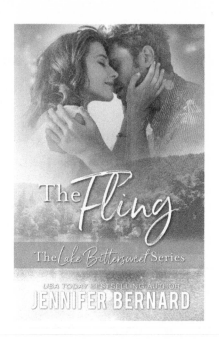

The Setup ~ Book 3

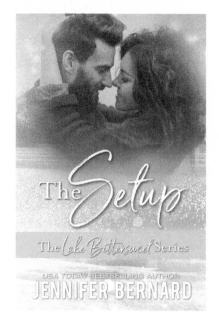

The Seduction ~ Book 4

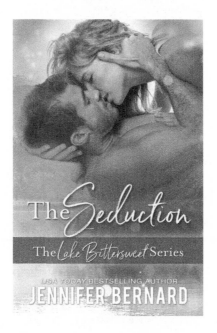

Lost Harbor, Alaska

Mine Until Moonrise ~ Book 1

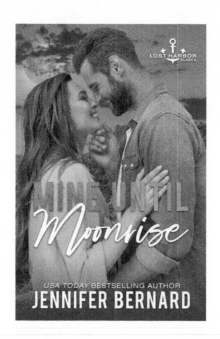

Yours Since Yesterday ~ Book 2

Seduced by Snowfall ~ Book 3

Wicked in Winter ~ Book 4

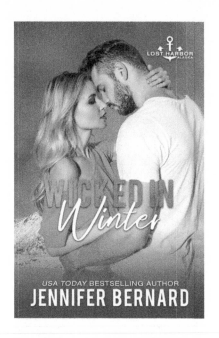

Naughty All Night ~ Book 5

Love at First Light ~ Book 6

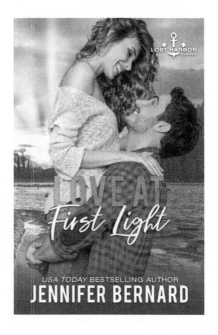

Head over Heels for the Holidays ~ Book 7

Flirting with Forever ~ Book 8

Mischief after Midnight ~ Book 9

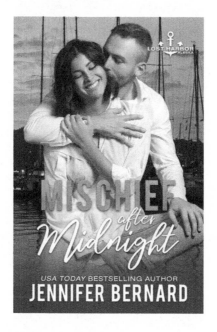

Slow Burn by Starlight ~ Book 10

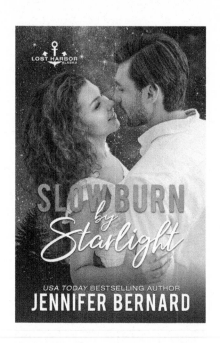

First Kiss before Frost ~ Book 11

The Rockwell Legacy

The Rebel ~ Book 1

The Rogue ~ Book 2

The Renegade ~ Book 3

The Runaway ~ Book 4

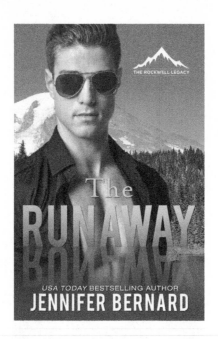

The Rock ~ Book 5

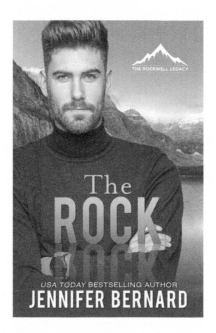

Jupiter Point ~ The Hotshots

Set the Night on Fire ~ Book 1

Burn So Bright ~ Book 2

Into the Flames ~ Book 3

Setting Off Sparks ~ Book 4

Jupiter Point ~ The Knight Brothers

Hot Pursuit ~ Book 5

Coming In Hot ~ Book 6

Hot and Bothered ~ Book 7

Too Hot to Handle ~ Book 8

One Hot Night ~ Book 9

Seeing Stars ~ Series Prequel

The Bachelor Firemen of San Gabriel Series

Love Between the Bases Series

Made in the USA
Las Vegas, NV
27 June 2023